CW00547097

THE HIDDEN GRAVES OF ST IVES

SALLY RIGBY

Storm

PUBLISHING

To request permissions, contact the publisher at rights@stormpublishing.co

Ebook ISBN: 978-1-80508-303-0
Paperback ISBN: 978-1-80508-305-4

Cover design: Lisa Horton
Cover images: Trevillion, Shutterstock

Published by Storm Publishing.
For further information, visit:
www.stormpublishing.co

ALSO BY SALLY RIGBY

A Cornwall Murder Mystery

The Lost Girls of Penzance

The Hidden Graves of St Ives

Murder at Land's End

Cavendish & Walker Series

Deadly Games

Fatal Justice

Death Track

Lethal Secret

Last Breath

Final Verdict

Ritual Demise

Mortal Remains

Silent Graves

Kill Shot

Dark Secrets

Broken Screams

Death's Shadow

Buried Fear

Detective Sebastian Clifford Series

Web of Lies

Speak No Evil

Never Too Late
Hidden From Sight
Fear the Truth
Wake The Past

PROLOGUE

'If you can keep your head when all about you are losing theirs and blaming it on you...'

The opening words to Rudyard Kipling's poem 'If', like an earworm, go round and round my head.

The irony isn't lost on me.

The fear radiating from the bound woman is suffocating and intense. Her head hangs limp, her eyes pleading.

But I ignored her pleas.

Gripping her hair in my fist, I raise her head until all she can see is my face, mere inches from hers.

My eyes bore into hers as I speak. 'I once believed in love. The sacred bond between two people. In having a soul mate. But now...' My voice hardens like the tentacles of frost that have encased my heart. 'It's all meaningless. Nothing but lies and deception.'

Her body shivers and tears stream down her cheeks. She opens her mouth but emits a whimper instead of words.

I'm past caring. She's like the rest of them. Not worthy of life.

Her breaths come in short, ragged gasps, as panic shines from her eyes. I see it clearly... the regret... the guilt.

It's too late for remorse. Too late for redemption.

'Every lie you've told. Every deceit. Every broken promise. You, and everyone like you, deserves to be punished.'

Her sobs fill the silence. But I feel nothing.

No pleasure.

No satisfaction.

Only duty.

'You're a reminder,' I say, my voice steady. 'A reminder of the agony of betrayal. You don't deserve to live.'

Stepping back, I cross to the other side of the room and begin my preparations for what must be done.

'If you can keep your head...' I think to myself as her screams subside into nothingness.

Justice will be served... my purpose revealed.

ONE

TUESDAY, 5 MARCH

Detective Inspector Lauren Pengelly carefully ran her hand over Tia's sleek black and white fur, her heart aching while her usually energetic Border Collie lay motionless on the sterile table. The fluorescent light in the treatment room cast a harsh, unflattering glow over her precious dog, who could barely open her eyes.

'We need to run a few tests, Lauren,' Elliot, the tall, imposing vet, said. 'I'd like you to leave Tia with us for the day while I give her a thorough examination.'

Lauren knew it was for the best, but what about Ben, Tia's brother? They hadn't been apart since Lauren had rescued them from the animal sanctuary when they were only a few months old. They'd been found in a dreadful state, abandoned in a derelict house. Initially, Lauren had only wanted the one dog, but as soon as she saw them both she knew they couldn't be separated.

How was Ben coping? She could only imagine his confusion at being home alone with his sister suddenly gone. He'd assumed he'd be going with them and hadn't been pleased when Lauren had left him behind. His whines had echoed in the hall when she'd closed the front door behind him. And she couldn't go back to be with him. She had to go to work after the vet's appointment.

'Okay.' She nodded. 'Do you have any idea what's wrong?'

'I don't wish to speculate until we've checked everything, but I promise we'll take good care of her.' He gave a reassuring smile.

But Lauren was far from reassured, especially considering the worry lines etched across Elliot's forehead. For a few days now Tia hadn't been herself and her usually sparkling eyes had lost their gleam. It wasn't until this morning when her dog hadn't touched her breakfast and had refused a walk that alarm bells rang in Lauren's head. It was then that she'd phoned the vet clinic and they suggested she should bring Tia in to see them immediately. When they'd arrived, they were rushed through to the treatment room, despite the waiting room being full of people with their pets.

Lauren glanced at her watch, realising that she was due at the station for the team's regular morning briefing. But part of her wanted to stay with Tia. She couldn't bear to leave her like this.

'Don't worry, we'll look after Tia,' said Cali, the vet nurse, a petite woman with a warm smile and comforting manner. 'We'll get in touch as soon as we know what's wrong. You were right to bring her in. She's in the best place.'

Tears welled in Lauren's eyes and she quickly blinked them away. She couldn't break down. Not now.

'I know. Thank you.'

With a final pat and whispering a promise in Tia's ear that she'd be back soon, Lauren left the treatment room, her heart heavy. What if this was it, and Tia had something incurable?

Tia and Ben were her family. Tia had to survive. She just had to.

Lauren hurried out of the building, the spring sunshine

seeming unusually harsh. She squinted against it and upon reaching her car she got in and started the engine, worry gnawing at her insides.

She pulled out of the car park and glanced in the rear-view mirror, the clinic shrinking in the distance. 'Please let everything be okay,' she murmured.

At least once she reached the station she could immerse herself in her work, although being a detective inspector in such a small place wasn't exactly stretching. That wasn't to say they didn't get some interesting cases, because they did. And she did have her team to oversee.

She'd been a detective inspector for a little under two years and this was her first posting at that rank. Her aim was to be promoted to detective chief inspector before she got to forty, and to transfer to a larger force where the work would be more challenging.

The drive to the station didn't take Lauren long, but even so her mind kept drifting back to the treatment room. To Tia's trusting eyes as she'd left her, and to the empty space at home where two border collies should be playing.

Lauren went straight into her office when she arrived, using the door off the main corridor, not stopping to speak to anyone. The morning briefing wasn't due to start for another ten minutes, but she could see through the glass of her office door that her officers had already arrived and were at their desks.

She scanned the room, assessing the mixed bunch. Billy and Tamsin – both detective constables in their twenties – were chatting, as usual. They were the younger members of the team and Billy in particular needed firm handling or he was likely to do his own thing and go off the rails. Tamsin was a hard worker and the best at research. But she, too, could be immature.

Jenna and Clem, again detective constables, were older and more sensible. Clem had been given the nickname Clemipedia by Billy, who said he said he was like a walking Wikipedia.

Although Lauren had never admitted it to her team, it was actually a very good description of the older officer. Jenna was a solid member of the team and worked hard. The DCs all got on well together and liked to socialise. Though less so when Lauren was with them. Then, they seemed to clam up. Behind her back, they'd nicknamed her The Ice Queen, but she could live with that. Her main concern was for the team to run efficiently and effectively.

Her relationship with the team had, however, changed a little since the arrival of her sergeant, Matt Price, who was seated at his desk, staring at the computer screen. What was he doing there? Didn't he have a court appearance first thing? Unless the date had changed. She'd have to ask him. He'd been with the team a little under six months and although she'd been reticent about his employment, initially, her worries had been unfounded. Even more so, when considering that he was only recently widowed and his young daughter had been kidnapped during his first week at Penzance CID.

Matt had proven to be a calming influence on the rest of team. She liked him. Not in *that* way. She certainly didn't approve of officers fraternising with one another. She wasn't usually one for socialising with her colleagues, but thought it would be nice if they could be friends, except being his boss made it difficult.

Lauren's computer pinged, indicating an email had arrived, and she was about to answer it when she noticed Jenna leave her desk and head towards her.

The officer knocked on the door and Lauren beckoned for her to come in.

'Morning, ma'am,' Jenna said in her usual easy-going manner. 'I've just heard from Anthony Kempston, one of my neighbours, about his wife, Freya. She went out shopping yesterday to the mall at St Austell and didn't return home. Tony called the police and was informed they can't do anything until she's been missing for over twenty-four hours because she's not considered a vulnerable person. So he phoned me. He's beside himself with worry.'

'How well do you know these people?'

'Not very well, ma'am, because we've only lived in St Ives for twelve months. He knows what I do and we always say hello to each other. They live on the opposite side of the road to us. I've got nothing pressing today and wondered if I could look into it. I could go over to St Austell and speak to the centre management. I'll ask to look at their CCTV footage to see if there's anything weird on there.' Jenna leant against the door, her arms folded across her slender frame.

'If you're convinced we should look into it, then go. I'll come with you.'

Jenna's face froze. Clearly she hadn't expected Lauren to go with her. And rightly so, because it wasn't something that she'd normally do. But today wasn't a normal day. She wanted something to take her mind off Tia, and this would do.

'Okay. Yes, ma'am. But it might not amount to anything. Freya could turn up at any minute.' Jenna shrugged, her lips turning up into a small smile.

'Yes, and she might not. We'll go together.'

'I'll fetch my coat.'

Jenna left the office and Lauren watched her head straight over to Clem's desk and speak to him. They both turned and looked in her direction, so she hurriedly ducked out of sight. She didn't want them to know that she'd observed their conversation.

Her mobile rang and she picked it up from the desk. 'Pengelly.'

'Hello, it's Elliot, the vet.'

Lauren's stomach dropped. 'You have news already?'

'I've done a thorough examination of Tia, including an ultrasound. As I suspected, she has GDV. Gastric Dilatation

Volvulus. Her stomach has filled with gas and twisted on itself, cutting off the vital blood supply to her internal organs. An operation is necessary straight away if there's to be any chance of saving her.'

Elliot's words filled the air like a thick fog.

'Y-yes. Of course. Do whatever it takes.'

'It's not a cheap operation. It could come to—'

'Do it. Money's no object. Please, do everything you can to save her life.'

Elliot hesitated before continuing: 'We can only give her a fifty-fifty chance of survival. If you hadn't brought her in this morning it may have been too late. Would you like to come back to see Tia before we start, just in case...?' His voice trailed off, leaving an ominous silence.

Tears filled Lauren's eyes again and she willed herself to stay strong as she imagined what would happen if the operation was unsuccessful.

'I'm not far away. Please wait for me to get there before you start operating.'

For a few seconds there was silence and all she could hear was his breathing on the other end of the line. 'Of course. We'll see you soon. Please be quick,' he finally said.

Lauren ended the call and, bracing herself, walked over to the door and opened it. 'Matt. My office, now.'

The officer left his desk and limped hurriedly towards her. His old shotgun wound was more pronounced in the morning and seemed to get better as his leg became less stiff during the day.

'What is it, ma'am?' he asked anxiously.

'Close the door please,' she replied quietly, taking a deep breath before continuing. 'Tia's at the vet's and she's about to undergo an operation that may save her... or take her away from me forever. I have to see her, in case...' She drew in a shaky breath, trying to keep her emotions under control. 'But I've just arranged to accompany Jenna to the shopping mall in St Austell. A woman she knows has gone missing and was last seen there. Someone else needs to go instead.'

Lauren choked back a sob. It was getting harder by the second not to break down. She knew that Matt would understand, but she couldn't allow it to happen. She never showed her vulnerable side to anyone, and she couldn't start now. It would be a slippery slope.

'I'm so sorry, ma'am. I hope Tia will be okay,' Matt said softly, compassion shining in his brown eyes. 'Leave everything to me. I'll go with Jenna to the shopping centre and look for this woman.'

Lauren nodded. 'Thank you. Please keep this to yourself, I don't want the rest of the team knowing about Tia.'

He stared at her, then shook his head. She knew what he was thinking, but she still didn't want it to be public knowledge. She didn't mix her personal and work life. And that wasn't going to change.

'I'm sure they'd all understand...'

She sighed. 'Maybe, but this is how I want it. Please don't mention anything to Dani either, if that's okay? I don't want her to be upset unnecessarily. If Tia... if she... well, we'll deal with that then.'

Lauren was referring to Matt's two-year-old daughter who she'd met a couple of times and really liked. She'd introduced Tia and Ben to her and there had been an instant connection between the three of them.

'No, you're right – telling Dani would only upset her. If anything does happen, then that's different. But I'm sure Tia's in good hands and I'll have my fingers crossed for a successful outcome. When are you leaving?'

'As soon as I've made a call. I'm due at a health and safety briefing later and I've no idea whether I'll be able to make it. Officers from several local stations will be there, so they probably won't even notice my absence. But I'll let them know, just in case. I thought you were supposed to be at court today.'

'Yes, but the case was bumped for some reason. Fortunately, as it's turned out. Take as long as you need and I'll make sure everything round here runs smoothly. I know it's hard, and my words probably won't make much difference, but try not to worry. Tia's in the best possible hands.'

TWO

TUESDAY, 5 MARCH

Matt glanced over his shoulder at Lauren as he headed back into the office. Her usual tall, almost intimidating stature was much less pronounced. Even her dark hair, which was cut in a short bob and always so neat, was a little messy, as if she'd been relentlessly running her fingers through it. He'd never seen her so distraught before. Despite trying to remain in control, the hurt and concern had shone from her eyes. If Tia didn't come through... Well, he didn't know how she'd cope. She had this tough exterior, but when she was with her dogs she was a completely different person. They were like her own children and he could totally relate to that.

He headed over to Jenna, who was standing beside her desk pulling on her coat.

'There's been a change of plan. I'm going with you to St Austell, and not the DI.'

The officer gave a visible sigh of relief, but Matt refrained from commenting. It was no secret that there was tension between Lauren and the rest of the team, although he'd witnessed a marked improvement since he first arrived. He believed that in part this was due to when Dani had been kidnapped and the team had come together in a way they hadn't in the past. Even though they'd gradually slipped back into some of their old ways of doing things, there was still a notice-able difference. Long may it continue.

'That's great, Sarge. I thought it was odd that she was going to come with me to something so routine. I wondered whether it was some sort of undercover appraisal thing,' Jenna said, her brows knitting together.

'No. That wouldn't be ethical. She's had a personal matter come up,' he said in a tone intended to indicate that it was not up for further discussion.

'That sounds interesting,' Billy piped up.

Damn. Why hadn't he said that it was a work meeting? He'd forgotten that Billy was sitting nearby and would always stick his nose in when he could. Matt liked the officer and, when kept under control, he contributed well to the team. But he enjoyed causing ripples when he could.

'No, Billy. It's definitely not interesting *and* nothing to do with us,' Matt said, giving him a dry smile.

Matt already considered himself well integrated into the team and he often did let his guard down when he was with them. Apart from when it came to them being critical of Lauren. That, he wouldn't tolerate. And rightly so. There was a reason he was their superior officer and encouraging them to sound off about their boss wasn't appropriate.

'That means it is,' Billy said, smirking.

Nothing got past the guy. For all his couldn't care less and *look at me* attitude, he was as smart as they came. Matt always needed to be on his guard around Billy in case he let anything slip.

'Discussion over, Billy. Haven't you got something to work on?'

'Yes, Sarge. I'm heading out to the train station because there's been more graffiti. It never stops. As soon as they clean it off, more appears. Well, if they think I'll be scrubbing it off the walls, they've got another think coming. Especially not in these clothes. I've only just bought them.' He gestured to his sage green polo shirt and navy chinos.

'Not *more* new clothes, Billy,' Clem said. 'You should save your money and put it towards a deposit for a house or something.'

'And be boring like you? No thanks, mate. You're just jealous because I'm single and can afford to dress like this.' Billy smirked.

Clem held up his hands in mock surrender. 'Okay, okay. But I'd rather be spending my money on the wife and kids.'

'You *would* say that,' Billy said.

'Focus, please,' Matt said, smiling. 'Billy, the council is hardly going to ask you to clean the graffiti. No need to worry about that. I want you to remember to check the cameras; you might be able to spot the culprits on the footage.'

'Nah, I doubt it. Whoever does this knows exactly where the cameras are placed. I've checked in the past and come up with zilch. I reckon it's just local teens, but catching them is another matter. Unless we do an all-night surveillance on the place. But how likely is that? No way would the bosses authorise overtime for that.'

'True,' Matt admitted. 'But we still must investigate it. Off you go.'

'I could do with something a bit juicier to work on,' Billy grumbled, taking his dark blue bomber jacket from the back of the chair and slipping it on.

'Be careful what you wish for,' Jenna warned, her tone serious for a moment before she chuckled.

'Yeah, right,' Billy said, rolling his eyes. 'This is Penzance... hardly the crime hub of the southwest. More's the pity.'

The officer was right, and Matt was glad of it. He loved the slower pace of Cornwall, because it meant he wasn't always at work to the detriment of time with Dani and his parents. Apart from what had happened to Dani, his move here had been a total success.

'I agree with you, Billy. But just because you think it's boring doesn't mean we don't do our job. So, you get going and Jenna and I will do the same.'

Lauren sat in her car, staring at the exterior of the vet clinic. It seemed absurd, irrational even, that her nerves were in such a state. If she didn't hurry, she wouldn't see Tia before her operation. It seemed crazy that it was affecting her so much. But Tia was family. Ben, too. Their love for one another was unconditional. They never let her down.

Unlike people.

She'd decided long ago that she much preferred animals to humans. But that hadn't stopped her from getting hurt.

A past relationship flashed in front of her eyes like a grainy montage. It was from when she was at university. One day she'd returned to her flat from one of her lectures to find her boyfriend in bed with her friend. Publicly, she'd laughed it off. Said she didn't care. But it had hurt. It had hurt a lot. Not because she loved the guy. Because she didn't. It was more the betrayal by her friend that had got to her. That she couldn't get over.

Soon after, Lauren had found somewhere else to live. She knew the boyfriend had continued going out with the friend, but Lauren had no idea what had happened to them after they lost touch. And she didn't want to know.

Pulling in a deep breath, she pushed aside the memories and opened the door.

Marching quickly into the clinic, she approached the desk. 'I'm Lauren Pengelly. I've come to see my dog, Tia, before she has her operation.' She was pleased that her voice sounded in control.

The assistant stood up, offering a sympathetic smile that Lauren wished she didn't need. 'Yes, of course. Come with me.'

Lauren was guided to the back of the clinic and into one of the treatment rooms. Cali, the nurse who'd met Lauren earlier, was stroking Tia's head and comforting her.

A sigh of relief escaped Lauren's lips. 'Thank goodness I made it,' she said, her voice breathless, as she moved to Tia's side.

Cali headed towards the door. 'I'll leave you on your own with Tia for five minutes. Then we'll have to give her the anaesthetic.'

As the nurse excused herself, Lauren's hand instinctively moved to stroke Tia's head. Her emotions bubbled up as tears rolled down her cheeks. She didn't bother wiping them away.

In a voice barely above a whisper, she reassured Tia, 'You're in good hands here. You'll be fine and I'll be waiting for you. Ben, too. We'll be back together as a family very soon.' Their eyes locked, and Tia seemed to comprehend her words, filling Lauren with a sense of relief. Before she could continue, the door swung open, and Cali had returned.

'Sorry, Lauren. You'll have to leave now. Someone will phone you as soon as the op's over and let you know how it went.'

Lauren hurriedly swiped away the tears from her wet cheeks before turning to face the nurse. 'Thank you,' she said, her voice a little wobbly.

After one last glance at Tia, Lauren left the treatment room and headed straight through the reception area. She kept focused on the front door, deliberately ignoring the full waiting room.

She walked as if on autopilot until reaching her car,

knowing that if she stopped for even one second she'd break down.

As soon as she was back inside the car, her tears returned; they flowed freely throughout the entire drive back to work. By the time she'd reached the station she was completely cried out. She stayed in the car for a few minutes, composing herself and fixing her make-up so no one could see how distraught she'd been.

She refused to let anyone see her in such a vulnerable state, not when it would undermine her whole reputation.

The drive to St Austell took Matt and Jenna just over an hour via the A30, which meant they weren't able to enjoy the stunning coastline. Matt hadn't yet visited this particular shopping centre, but his parents had been a couple of times and had raved about it. He didn't enjoy shopping, full stop, so he knew he certainly wouldn't be *raving*. He pulled into the car park, which was already over half full, but he managed to secure a space close to the entrance.

'The management offices are on the first floor. We'll take the escalator,' Jenna said, pointing over to the left once they'd walked inside the centre.

Although it wasn't even ten, there were already plenty of people around.

'Is it always this busy?' he asked while they were standing on the escalator looking over to where most of the shops were situated.

'It's the only decent mall in the area, and even then it's not massive compared to others up country. When I get the chance, I go shopping in Basingstoke. The shops there are amazing.'

The centre management office was to the right of the escalator and when they walked through the door there was a woman sitting behind a desk.

Matt extended his warrant card so the receptionist could see. 'DS Price and DC Moyle. We'd like to speak to the manager please.'

'Maggie isn't here but you can speak to the assistant manager, Steve.' The woman crossed the reception area to an open door, lightly rapping her knuckles against the frame. 'The police are here,' she announced.

From the room emerged a man who looked to be in his fifties, squeezed into an ill-fitting navy suit that had clearly seen better days.

'I'm Steve Arden. How can I help?'

'We're investigating a missing person and her last known location was here yesterday. We'd like to view your CCTV cameras to see if we can spot her.'

Arden's eyebrows arched slightly. 'Finding her among the centre's visitors is likely to be a tall order. But of course we'll cooperate. Do you know approximately the time she visited, so we can narrow the search?'

Matt turned to Jenna, as she was the one who'd spoken to the missing woman's husband.

'I believe she was here in the afternoon. Any footage from two onwards should help,' Jenna said.

'Did she go to any specific shop or café we can check first?' Arden asked.

'Her husband mentioned shopping for a dress, but he didn't specify the shop. So, we'll need a comprehensive look,' Matt said, his eyes returning to the man.

'Understood. Follow me.' Arden led them into a room filled with two desks adjacent to one another and a row of screens. Each screen was a mosaic of four smaller panels, a live feed of every nook and cranny of the mall.

Matt's eyes scanned the screens. 'How many cameras in total?'

'Ten on each floor of the centre, with additional ones scattered outdoors.'

'And the multi-storey car park?' Matt queried.

'We've got cameras on each floor, and at the entrance and exit.' Arden took his seat at the desk, and with a flick of his wrist brought one of the feeds to life. 'This is the main entrance. I'll replay from two o'clock.'

'Jenna, you're up. I don't know what the missing woman looks like.' Matt stepped slightly to the side, allowing the officer a full view of the screen. She perched herself behind Arden, her eyes firmly glued to the images in front of her.

After a few minutes of watching the comings and goings at regular speed, Jenna leant forward. 'Could we speed this up a bit? I should still be able to recognise her. Otherwise, at this rate, we'll be here all day.'

Complying with Jenna's request, Arden increased the speed of the footage. It was a blur of shoppers darting in and out of shops until Jenna's voice cut through the room, sharp and urgent. 'Stop! There she is. That's Freya Kempston.'

Arden promptly halted the footage, their attention focused on a lone woman walking out of a bookshop.

'Right, keep going and we'll see where she goes to next,' Matt said.

Freya Kempston headed straight for one of the department stores. Twenty-five minutes later, she re-emerged, the cameras catching her as she drifted through various other shops, eventually settling in a ground-floor café. She chose a seat near the entrance that kept her within the camera's range. For twenty minutes she sat alone.

'She keeps glancing at her watch. Waiting for someone, perhaps?' Jenna suggested.

'Yes, that's what I was wondering,' Matt said, his eyes glued to the image on the screen.

Their attention stayed fixed on Freya as she eventually

pulled out her phone, keying in a number and holding a brief conversation. After ending the call, she stowed away her phone, rose from her seat, and prepared to leave.

'Perhaps she was contacting the person she was supposed to meet? If they've cancelled, that would explain why she's leaving,' Jenna said, keeping her eyes focused on the screen. 'What time does the footage say now?'

'Three forty-five,' Arden said.

'Let's continue. See where she goes next,' Matt suggested.

They tracked Freya through the centre into the car park. A man approached her and they stopped for a chat.

'She seems to know him, judging by the body language,' Matt commented.

The pair chatted for a while and then walked together. When she reached her car, she got in and drove away. The camera followed the man as he strolled further along the same level before getting into a van.

'Could they have planned to meet elsewhere?' Jenna asked.

'Let's see if he heads off in the same direction as she did. The name on the van is Turner's Car Repairs. Do you know anything about that place?' Matt asked.

'I do actually,' Jenna said, turning to face him. 'Our insurance company instructed us to take the car there after an accident – I met the owner. The guy in the footage could be Gareth Turner although I'm not one hundred percent sure, because I've only ever seen him wearing a cap and overalls. If it isn't him, it could be someone who works there.'

They returned to watching the footage. The van exited the car park, heading in the same direction as Freya's car.

'He's going the same way,' Jenna commented. 'But as they both live in St Ives that's hardly surprising, especially if they take the A30, which is the most direct route.'

Matt nodded. 'The meeting might be totally innocent, but I think our next move should be visiting Turner at his workshop.'

THREE

TUESDAY, 5 MARCH

Matt pulled up outside Turner's Car Repairs, which was on the Penbeagle Industrial Estate situated on the edge of St Ives. It was in stark contrast to the narrow winding lanes and white-washed fisherman's cottages they'd passed on their way through the quaint town.

Turner's business was situated in a single metal-clad unit with a large concrete drive on which stood two cars. The roller door to the unit was open three quarters of the way up, and when Matt and Jenna approached they were able to see inside. A red car was hoisted up on a ramp and next to it, chatting, were two teenage boys standing beside a much older man. None of them looked like the person they'd seen in the footage.

'Police,' Matt said, as they marched in. He held out his warrant card and the older man took a step forward to take a look. 'We're looking for Gareth Turner.'

'He's out the back,' one of the young men said, pointing towards an open door at the rear of the workshop.

'Thank you.'

Jenna and Matt headed across the workshop, through the open door, and into a cramped kitchen area that had a worktop with a kettle on it, a small microwave, and a fridge. The strong aroma of coffee permeated the air. Sitting at an old Formica table, on a dirty white plastic chair, was a man with a mop of curly dark hair, cradling in his hand a chipped mug which he was holding close to his lips. A half-eaten Cornish pasty was on the table in front of him, next to an open car magazine.

He glanced up and frowned. 'Who are you?'

'DS Price and DC Moyle,' Matt said, extending his warrant card. 'Are you Gareth Turner?'

'Yes. Why?' Turner set the mug on the table with a soft clunk and the chair groaned in protest as he pushed himself up to his full height. He was a solid, imposing figure, towering six inches above Matt, making him at least six foot four.

'We're investigating the disappearance of Freya Kempston. You know her,' Matt stated, leaving no room for doubt, even if he was pushing his luck, considering Jenna couldn't positively identify him and the footage they'd seen didn't prove his friendship with the missing woman one way or another.

Turner's frown deepened, and he slowly shook his head. 'No. I don't think so.'

'Then how come you were seen talking to her yesterday at the shopping centre in St Austell?' Jenna said, in a no-nonsense tone. 'And don't deny it, because you were caught on CCTV.'

Turner's eyes darted around the small kitchen, avoiding direct eye contact with Matt or Jenna.

'Was I?' His tone was nonchalant, but a trace of anxiety seeped through.

Matt's jaw tightened. He despised these mind games. Why was Turner being so evasive? What was he hiding from them?

'Yes. You were, in the car park. Now, let's start again. You were with Freya Kempston yesterday?'

Turner shuffled uncomfortably, shifting his weight from one foot to the other. 'Oh. That Freya. I forgot that was her first name. She's one of my customers.'

SALLY RIGBY

'But you knew the name Kempston. So why did you say you didn't know her when I initially mentioned her name?' Matt said.

'I didn't hear the surname at first. I'm a bit deaf from all the machinery here. I just heard *Freya* and thought I didn't know who you meant.'

Was that the truth?

'What were you doing at St Austell yesterday? Why weren't you at work?' Matt probed, unrelenting.

'Who are you, my mother? I own the business and if I want to go shopping then I will. The place wasn't left unattended.' Turner's defiant retort echoed around the kitchen.

'How many staff do you employ?' Jenna asked.

'I've got one excellent apprentice and one older mechanic who works part-time.'

'We saw three men when we walked into the workshop,' Jenna said.

'I'm doing a favour for a mate of mine. His lad wanted some work experience to see if he'd do okay as a mechanic. From what I've seen so far, he doesn't have the right attitude. And he hates getting his hands dirty.' Turner's voice held a touch of annoyance.

'What time did you go to St Austell?' Jenna asked.

'I left here after lunch to look for a birthday present for the wife. She wants a watch which they sell at one of the department stores over there.'

'Did you manage to buy it?' Jenna asked, her tone softening.

'No. They weren't in stock.' Turner's brow furrowed in frustration. 'Now I've got nothing for her birthday, which is tomorrow.'

'That must be annoying,' Jenna said. 'How much time did you spend with Freya?'

'I wasn't *with* her, like you're making out. We bumped into each other in the car park and chatted for a couple of minutes.

22

Then I went to my van and she went to her car. That's all there was. Which you probably already know if you saw us on camera. Talk about bloody Big Brother.'

'What did you talk about?'

'You know, the usual. I asked how she was. She asked about me. I mentioned her car, to see if it was going okay. Nothing really. It was just chit-chat.' Turner briefly clenched and unclenched his fists.

Why was he being so evasive?

'You and Freya both left the car park and drove in the same direction. Was that planned?'

A baffled expression flitted across Turner's face. 'Of course we went the same way. We both live in St Ives. You're asking stupid questions,' he said, giving a frustrated sigh.

Jenna cleared her throat. 'Enough of that. Did you come straight back here after you'd been shopping?'

Turner's gaze darted away from Matt and Jenna. 'Not exactly,' he muttered.

Now they were getting somewhere.

'Where did you go?' Matt demanded, his tone sharp and slicing through the tension.

Turner shrugged, looking as if he was trying to make out the question wasn't important. 'I don't want to say.'

'For goodness' sake,' Matt snapped. 'We need an alibi for you because you're the last known person to have seen Freya Kempston. Now, we want the truth. Where were you yesterday afternoon?'

Turner sighed heavily, running his fingers through his hair before responding in a low voice. 'Look, I drove out to the ocean and sat by myself, thinking about things. I have a lot of business and personal issues to work through and it's impossible to do it here or at home because of constant interruptions. I often go to the beach when I'm wanting some peace and quiet. I promise that it was nothing to do with Freya Kempston.'

'Did you go straight home or did you come back here to the workshop first?' Matt asked, wondering if the story could be true.

'I came back to make sure everything was locked up, because they're not the greatest at checking everywhere,' Turner explained. 'By the time I arrived they'd all left for the day. After that I went home and had dinner with my family and then we watched telly together until it was time for bed. It was the same as any other Monday evening.'

'When you were sitting by the ocean thinking through your problems, did you see or speak to anyone?' Matt pressed. 'Someone who could provide you with an alibi for that time?'

Turner sighed. 'There were a few people walking along the shore and several children running around, but I didn't pay much attention to them. I can't imagine that they'll remember me, either, because I was tucked away sitting on a rock.'

'I'd have thought being on a rock might have made you more noticeable,' Jenna said.

'Not really, because I was towards the back. Now if that's it, I must get back to work. There's an alternator that needs fitting before the car's owner returns in a couple of hours and I don't trust anyone else to do it.'

'That's it for now, but we may need to speak to you again,' Matt said, wanting the man to understand that it might not be over.

Matt and Jenna turned and left the confines of the small kitchen, Turner's footsteps echoing behind them. The curious eyes of Turner's employees bored into them as they navigated themselves through the workshop until they reached the car.

'Now what, Sarge?' Jenna said, looping the seat belt over her body and clicking it into place.

'We head back to the station and update the DI on what we've learnt so far,' Matt responded, turning the key in the ignition and starting the engine.

24

He pulled out behind a white van and headed out of the industrial estate, turning onto the road going from St Ives to Penzance.

'Do you believe Turner, Sarge?' Jenna asked, turning to face him.

He tossed a glance in her direction. 'I think so. But he doesn't have an alibi, which we need to keep in mind. I'm certainly not going to dismiss him from our enquiries yet, for sure.'

'Yeah, I agree.'

They drove in relative silence for the ten minutes it took to reach the station and once Matt entered the team's office his gaze instinctively gravitated towards Lauren's room to check if she was back from the vet's. He caught sight of the top of her head behind the computer screen, so he hurriedly approached and tapped lightly on the door.

'Come in, Matt,' came Lauren's subdued voice.

He stepped inside, gently closing the door behind him. He couldn't help but notice, even though it was through the glasses she wore for computer work, that her eyes were red-rimmed. She'd been crying. Not a sight he'd ever expected to see.

'How's Tia?' he asked, crossing his fingers, hoping that the situation hadn't got any worse.

'I can't talk about it,' Lauren said, her voice tinged with weariness as she waved a dismissive hand. 'What happened in St Austell?'

'We spoke to the centre management, who showed us CCTV footage from when Freya Kempston was there. We caught sight of her shopping, and she also spent some time alone in a café,' he explained.

'Do you think she could have been waiting for someone?'

'That's what we wondered, too,' Matt answered thoughtfully. 'We also observed her speaking to a car mechanic from St Ives in the car park before they both left. It could have been something and nothing, but we decided to visit his workplace, anyway, to check. He's Gareth Turner from Turner's Car Repairs, the owner of the business, and he doesn't have an alibi for the time following Freya's departure from the centre. He claims to have left St Austell and gone to the beach for time to *think*.' He made quote marks with his fingers. 'Having said that, my instinct tells me that he was telling us the truth. But we'll keep him on the back burner and re-interview him, if necessary.'

'I agree with your decision. Now I think we should speak to Freya Kempston's husband.' Lauren removed her glasses and placed them gently on the desk.

'Shall I go with Jenna?' Matt asked, making a concerted effort not to stare at the red rings encircling Lauren's eyes in case it embarrassed her.

'No,' his boss said firmly. 'I'll go with you. Freya's husband already knows Jenna, and that familiarity might influence the nature of the questioning. It's more appropriate for him to be interviewed by people he doesn't know. That way we can be objective when gauging his body language. Unfortunately, as you're no doubt aware, it's not unheard of for someone to report a family member missing only for it then to be discovered that they themselves were involved in their disappearance.'

Matt nodded in agreement. 'That's so true, ma'am. I've been a part of a few investigations where that has happened. Are you ready to leave now?'

'Give me five minutes,' Lauren requested, her voice carrying a touch of vulnerability. 'I need a second to gather my thoughts. I'll call you when I'm ready.'

Understanding her need to be alone, Matt gave a subtle nod.

'Of course, take your time. I'll get the address from Jenna

and will be ready whenever you are.' With that, he quietly exited the office.

It would probably do Lauren good to get out of the station and think of something other than the trauma Tia was going through.

FOUR

TUESDAY, 5 MARCH

Freya Kempston lived in a modern detached property with an integral garage. It was nestled in the middle of a sprawling estate on the outskirts of St Ives. Matt parked his car in the driveway behind a silver Renault Clio and they strolled up the drive to the front door, the soft crunch of gravel under their feet.

Matt rang the bell and the door swung open almost immediately, revealing a man in his early forties. He was dressed casually in a pair of well-worn jeans and a dark-blue crew-necked jumper.

'Mr Kempston?' Lauren asked, her tone firm, yet gentle.

'Yes, that's me.'

'I'm Detective Inspector Pengelly and this is Detective Sergeant Price. We're here about your wife.'

'Have you found her?' he asked, a spark of hope in his eyes.

Lauren shook her head. 'Not yet. May we come in?'

He nodded and stepped to the side to let them pass into the hallway. 'We can sit in the lounge.'

They followed him through the door on the left and into an open-plan space which served as a lounge, dining area and kitchen. The lounge was carpeted while the rest of the space had wooden floors. The kitchen was very modern, with white glossy units shining against the black worktops.

'You have a lovely home,' Matt observed, scanning the tastefully decorated interior. Leigh would have loved it. Before she'd died, they'd been discussing updating their home in Lenchester.

'Thanks. We recently had it remodelled,' Kempton replied.

'Let's sit. We need some details from you about Freya,' Lauren said, taking charge of the conversation. 'When was the last time you saw your wife?'

'Yesterday, as she left for St Austell. I've tried reaching her countless times, but her phone goes straight to voicemail. I've left message after message.' He nibbled at his lower lip. 'She's never disappeared like this before.'

'Did she take anything with her? Like a suitcase, or her passport, maybe?' Matt probed, his eyes never leaving the man.

'No,' Kempston said, shaking his head. 'I'm pretty sure all she had was a handbag hanging over her shoulder. On her way out she said that she'd see me later.' He paused a moment. 'Oh, and she did add that she wasn't sure when she'd be back, depending on how long the shopping took.'

'Was she there to buy anything specific?' Lauren asked.

'She mentioned looking for a dress for a wedding we've been invited to. She also wanted to buy a magazine rack for this room.' He gestured towards a sleek, light-wood unit located under the wall-mounted television, currently showcasing a few ornaments. 'She thought it would fit right there.'

'What about her passport?' Matt asked, returning to his previous question.

'I keep both our passports in the safe.'

'Which is where?'

'Hidden behind my workbench in the garage.'

'Have you checked the safe since Freya's disappearance?' It was the first place Matt would have looked if he was in this situation.

Rubbing his neck, a crease of discomfort appeared on Kempston's face. 'Yes, I have... Her passport's still there. Right next to mine.'

Interesting. Did that mean Kempston had considered the possibility that his wife might have left him?

Lauren's brow furrowed. 'Did Freya mention whether she'd planned to meet anyone in St Austell?'

Kempston shook his head, his eyes taking on a far-off look. 'She was a bit vague. She said she might catch up with one of her friends who works at the shopping centre, but there were no definite plans.'

'Do you have the name of this friend?' Matt queried.

'No. I don't know her, or which shop she works at.' The man shrugged, his palms upwards, in a gesture of helplessness.

'Are you meant to be working today?' Lauren asked.

Kempston looked up at the ceiling as if searching for his answer. 'No. We both took this week off.'

'In that case, why didn't you accompany your wife shopping yesterday?' Lauren asked, her question hanging in the air like an accusation.

Kempston's shoulders slumped, his eyes dropping to the floor. 'I was planning on doing some decorating. We're refurbishing the second bedroom. I wish I had gone with her...'

'Did she ask you to join her?' Matt asked, leaning forward.

'No, she didn't. She knew I wanted to get on with the decorating.'

'What does Freya do for work?' Lauren asked.

'She's a freelance virtual assistant and works from home. She's exceptional at her job – so much so, that she often has to turn work down due to her packed schedule.'

'And your profession?' Lauren continued.

'I'm a project manager for a company in Penzance.'

'You reached out to one of my officers this morning, despite being instructed by the police to wait until Freya had been missing for over twenty-four hours. What prompted that?' Lauren asked.

Kempston's face blanched, his hands nervously interlaced. 'It's just... I was extremely worried. Freya always lets me know if she's going to be late, and we maintain regular phone contact. She wouldn't not inform me of her whereabouts. I'm certain something's happened to her.'

'Do you have any children?' Matt asked, his tone gentle.

A shadow of pain flickered across Kempston's face, sadness in his eyes. 'We don't, regrettably. I do have a child from my previous marriage, but... we're estranged.'

'Do you recall what Freya was wearing yesterday?' Matt asked, extracting a worn notebook and pen from his pocket.

'Jeans, a white T-shirt, and a navy blazer,' Kempston replied promptly.

'And how would you describe her?'

'She's about five foot six inches tall with short dark hair. She's American,' he added.

'How long has she been residing here in the UK?' Lauren asked.

'About five years? Our paths crossed when I was in the States, supervising a project. We fell for each other and decided to return here...' Kempston's voice softened as he recalled the time. He paused for a moment, his gaze unfocused. 'Well, I returned alone initially to sort out our living arrangements. I was still married to my first wife back then.'

'Was that in Cornwall?' Matt asked.

'No. My ex-wife and our son still live in Kent,' Kempston clarified.

'Does Freya often visit the States?' Lauren asked.

'She aims to visit once a year to spend time with her family. Both her parents are still alive, and she has a brother over there, too. Whenever feasible, I accompany her.' His voice sounded wistful, likely evoking memories of their shared travels.

Matt decided to steer the conversation in a different direction. 'Would you mind if we take a look at your bedroom? It's a long shot, but we might glean some clues or insights that will aid us in our search for Freya.'

Kempston's eyebrows knitted together in slight confusion. 'Well, I suppose you can. But I highly doubt you'll find anything useful. Freya isn't the secretive type or one to conceal things from me...'

Except she didn't disclose the person she might be meeting or when she'd be back.

That rather indicated the contrary.

'It will give us a better understanding of Freya as a person. The more we can find out, the easier it will be to locate her,' Matt reassured him.

'Okay,' Kempston finally agreed. 'I'll lead the way.' Despite the uncertainty in his voice, he rose from the chair and headed out of the room.

They trailed behind him, their footsteps echoing in the quiet as they climbed the stairs and went into the generously proportioned bedroom.

With swift and practised movements, Matt and Lauren pulled on disposable gloves.

'We'll take it from here. Go downstairs and we'll join you when we've finished,' Lauren instructed.

'Why are you wearing gloves?' Kempston's voice sounded uneasy.

'To avoid contaminating the bedroom with our fingerprints,' Lauren said, with a dismissive wave of her hand.

Kempston's eyes widened slightly. 'Do you suspect that I've harmed Freya?'

'This is standard procedure whenever we conduct a search,' Matt said, his voice calm. 'Please go downstairs and wait for us, Mr Kempston. We won't be long.'

Once the man had left, they began meticulously searching the bedroom. Matt headed over to the bedside cabinet on what seemed to be Freya's side of the bed because of the bottle of perfume there. He pulled open the top drawer and sifted through its contents. His hand eventually landed on a small notebook. Flipping it open, his eyes skimmed the contents: page after page of handwritten notes.

'I've uncovered a journal of sorts here, ma'am. It doesn't appear to be a diary because very often there are no times and dates written down. It's more like somewhere Freya jots down her thoughts and feelings.'

'Are there any entries of particular interest?' Lauren's voice echoed from the other side of the room, her attention momentarily diverted from the wardrobe she was inspecting.

Matt's finger traced the scrawly handwriting on the page, his eyes narrowing as he focused on one particular entry. 'Here's one. It says *"I'm finding things really hard today. The only thing that makes me feel better is knowing I'll be with X on 4/3"*. That's yesterday's date.'

Lauren walked over to him. 'Who's X?'

'It doesn't say, look. She only refers to the person as X.' Matt held out the relevant page for Lauren to see.

'Was the journal hidden?'

'Not exactly, ma'am. It was under some other things but not hidden, as such. Maybe she used the X in case her husband read it? If it's an affair, she could explain that away much easier than if she'd used an actual name. She could say it was someone at work who was causing her issues and she'd used the X in case her journal got in the wrong hands?'

Lauren frowned. 'It's definitely something to consider. I wonder who she was meeting? And don't the words *be with* suggest she was planning to go somewhere with this person? Or am I over-analysing?'

'It does,' Matt said, nodding in acknowledgement. 'And it

certainly negates her husband's view that she doesn't keep secrets from him.'

'We'll ask him when we go back downstairs.' Lauren was silent for a couple of seconds, staring absent-mindedly at the bed. 'That's a strange pillow,' she said, pointing at it. 'Why is it shaped like that?'

Matt stared at the pillow, a memory hitting him. 'Leigh had one like it – she had a bad back. It's ergonomically designed for people who sleep on their side. The contour fits their shoulder.'

His thoughts drifted to Leigh, but he quickly pulled himself back. He couldn't allow himself to dwell on the past in the middle of an investigation. Even though nine months had passed since his wife's death, the grief was still as raw as if it was yesterday.

'Hmm... maybe I should get one. There's nothing else note-worthy here. Let's go back downstairs and question Mr Kempston about the journal.'

Anthony Kempston was seated in the lounge, perched anxiously on the easy chair he had been sitting on earlier.

'Did you find anything?' he asked, springing to his feet when he saw them.

'Are you aware that your wife keeps a journal in her bedside drawer?' Lauren asked in a casual tone.

'She's always scribbling things down. She has notebooks scattered all over the place because her memory isn't great. Why, what did you find?'

'An entry saying that she was going *be with X* on yesterday's date. Do you have any idea who this X is, and what the intended meeting was about?' Matt held out the journal and pointed directly at the entry.

Kempston paled. 'I... I... don't know... Unless...'

'Unless what?' Lauren asked.

'Could it be the friend who works at the shopping centre?' he suggested, sounding helpless.

'Does Freya often refer to her friends as "X"?' Lauren asked.

Kempston shook his head. 'Do you think that she ran off with this X person? Is that why she didn't come home?'

'At this stage, we can't be certain,' Matt said. 'What did she mean when she wrote that things were *really hard*?'

'I don't know.' Kempston shook his head.

'Was she referring to your relationship?' Lauren asked, making direct eye contact with the man.

'I've no idea,' Kempston answered, a helpless expression on his face.

'What were you doing yesterday afternoon after four, which was the last time your wife was captured on the CCTV footage at the shopping centre?' Matt asked.

'I was here at home, decorating. I've already told you that's what I was doing all day.'

'Can anybody vouch for you?' Matt pushed.

'Look, if I had anything to do with Freya's disappearance then why would I contact you?' Kempston asked, his voice anxious. 'No one can vouch for me because I was here alone.' He paused for a moment, seeming to remember something. 'I did speak to my mother on the phone at around four. We chatted for half an hour. I remember because the TV programme she wanted to watch was about to start and so we said goodbye.'

'We'll need her details so we can contact her to verify that,' Lauren said firmly.

'This is ridiculous. You should be focusing on finding my wife. Something's happened to her and you're wasting time suspecting me.' His eyes darted from Matt to Lauren and back again.

'Mr Kempston, we're just doing our job. We have to speak to everyone who knows Freya, including you,' Lauren said, her tone conversational but with a steely edge.

Kempston glanced down to the floor, appearing embarrassed. 'I'm sorry. I know that you want to find her. And I want the same. It's just that I'm so worried about what might have happened. What if...' He sighed. 'I can't think that. Please do check with my mum. She'll confirm that we were on the phone at four yesterday. Here's her number.'

With the number in hand, Matt and Lauren exited the house, leaving a flustered Mr Kempston behind.

'What's your take on this, ma'am?' Matt asked as they climbed into the car.

'He appeared genuinely shocked when we mentioned this mysterious X. But it could be a well-rehearsed act.'

'I agree. And let's not forget that he could have been anywhere at the time he spoke to his mum. So that's not a concrete alibi.'

'Exactly. Our next steps are to delve deeper into Freya Kempston's life.'

FIVE

TUESDAY, 5 MARCH

When they returned to the station, Lauren left her belongings in the office and then popped to the bathroom. When she got back, she picked up her mobile phone from the desk with a sense of urgency. A quick swipe, a hasty scan of the screen and her heart sank. No messages. She was hoping for some news about Tia's operation, a glimmer of reassurance in the gloom, but the silence was deafening.

She toyed with the idea of phoning the clinic, but quickly dismissed it because she didn't want to bother them unnecessarily. They were a very busy practice and they'd given their word that they'd contact her as soon as Tia had come out of the operating theatre. She clung to that promise, even though it did nothing to ease her worry. Of course, she'd been out of the office for a mere five minutes, so it was unlikely, almost ridiculous, to think that they'd call her in the short time that she'd actually been away from her phone.

With a resigned sigh, she pocketed her phone and stepped through the door into the main office, heading towards the whiteboard. The hustle and bustle of the office swirled around her, but she was so lost in thought she was unable to take in what everyone was doing.

She sucked in a breath and drew herself up to her full height. 'Okay, team,' she began, her voice crisp and authoritative. She waited until there was silence and everyone was facing in her direction. 'We've just returned from questioning Anthony Kempston, Freya's husband. When we searched their bedroom, we came upon this.' She stuck a photo onto the whiteboard showing the relevant page from the missing woman's journal. 'Freya was due to meet someone yesterday. Someone who's only referred to as "X" in her journal. And... it appears that she was looking forward to it, as you can see from her note.'

'So you're saying that she might have run off with a lover,' Clem said, his eyebrow arched in a questioning manner. 'Was it Gareth Turner, the man she met in the car park? I know he denied it, but it would account for him suddenly having to go to the ocean to do some *thinking*.' Clem did quote marks with his fingers.

'It's a possibility,' Lauren said, scanning the team. 'And we're certainly not going to dismiss it. Anthony Kempston denied all knowledge of this X.'

'Of course he would. Do you reckon he followed her to this meeting and then... well, you know... Took matters into his own hands?' Billy said, holding up two fingers to his temple and pretending to fire a gun.

'We're not excluding him from our enquiries, but there are other avenues to consider, too. I want scrutiny of CCTV footage from the whole geographical area. Check Freya's car after she left the shopping centre. She may have taken a back route where there aren't any cameras. We need to map her movements from four yesterday afternoon.'

'I'll do that, ma'am,' Billy said, already pulling his keyboard closer to him.

'Excellent. As for X, I want a thorough check of Freya's

social media. Tamsin, that's your area of expertise, so start on it straight away. Also, I want someone to look into her finances to see if there have been any large transfers of money either in or out of her bank accounts. Find out if she has any joint accounts with Anthony or whether they're all her own. Look for anything unusual.'

'Leave that with me, ma'am,' Clem said, nodding his agreement.

'Thanks. Also, her upcoming appointments should be checked – hairdresser, dentist, doctor, whatever. It's possible that she confided in one of them.'

Jenna nodded, a spark in her eyes. 'If it's a confidante we're after, then my money's on her hairdresser. She goes to the same salon I do, although I'm not sure who she sees. I'll get in touch with them now and find out if she'd mentioned anything to one of the stylists.'

'Great. After that, please could you contact Anthony Kempston's mother to confirm whether or not they had a phone conversation between four and four thirty yesterday? Sergeant Price has the number.'

'Yes, ma'am,' Jenna said.

'If you need me, I'll be in my office,' Lauren said, turning to leave.

But not before noticing a knowing glance between Jenna and Clem. Usually, she'd stay to monitor the team's work for a while. To make sure they were doing what she'd asked. But today she couldn't. Today, she was waiting for a different kind of news and if she tried to act like normal they'd see right through her. She was better off away from everything.

Lauren retreated into her office, pulled out her phone, placed it on the desk and then sank into her chair. Her gaze fixed on the device, willing it to spring to life. But despite her efforts the silence, much like the tension in the air, remained unbroken.

She couldn't simply sit and worry. There had to be something she could do to distract her, even if it was only for a short time. Her eyes fixed on the pile of admin tasks that had accumulated on her desk. Papers, folders and sticky notes all vying for her attention. Some of it related to budgetary requirements, and report metrics. Some HR responsibilities. Admin wasn't her favourite part of the job, but it offered a welcome distraction, a way to focus her mind on something other than the constant worry pitted in her stomach about Tia.

Lauren pulled a folder towards her, but not before her mind wandered back to Freya Kempston. She wasn't unduly worried about this missing woman. It was still very early days, and there was no hard evidence to indicate that there had been any foul play. The woman could have simply decided to take a breather from her life, maybe going away for a few days. She wouldn't be the first person to do so, nor the last. It didn't mean they wouldn't investigate her disappearance, but Lauren wasn't prepared to lose any sleep over it just yet. She had more pressing concerns, and—

The shrill ring of the phone sliced through her thoughts like a knife. She practically lunged for the device, grabbing it with her hand, her heart thumping like a drum in her chest.

She stared at the screen.

It was the vet.

She took a deep breath, steeling herself for whatever he had to say, and answered the call.

'Lauren Pengelly speaking,' she said into the phone, her voice steady despite the wildness of her heartbeat.

'Hello, Lauren, it's Elliot,' came the soothing baritone voice. 'I'm calling to let you know that Tia's operation went well. She's now in recovery.'

A wave of relief washed over her, leaving her slightly light-headed. 'Thank goodness. That's great news. May I come to see her? When will she be allowed home?' The questions tumbled out of her mouth.

'We'd like to monitor her here for a few days,' Elliot explained, his professional tone cutting through her relief. 'She's resting and will likely continue to do so for the next few hours. We don't want to disturb her. You can drop by tomorrow morning on your way to work.'

Tomorrow?

Lauren's heart clenched at the thought of Tia alone and in unfamiliar surroundings. And what about Ben; he was going to be devastated, too.

'Okay. Thanks,' she said, her voice barely concealing her disappointment.

'Keep in mind, though, that it's unlikely you'll be in the same room as Tia when you visit. We don't want to stress her. You'll have to check on her through the window,' Elliot added.

The news was a blow. Lauren wanted nothing more than to hold Tia, to comfort her, to be there for her. But she knew they were doing what was best for her precious pet.

'Yes of course, I understand. My main concern is Tia's well-being,' she managed to say, her voice quivering slightly.

'Tia's not out of the woods yet, which is why we're keeping her here. But the signs are promising, so far. I know it's hard, but try not to worry, Lauren. She's receiving the best possible care. We'll see you tomorrow morning,' Elliot reassured her, before ending the call.

'Thank you,' she said into the silent phone, her voice echoing in the quiet room.

The call might have ended, but Elliot's words hung in the air. Lauren fought back the tears threatening to spill over. It was crazy. She hadn't cried this much in her entire adult life. She couldn't even remember the last time she'd allowed herself such a display of emotion.

But as she sat alone in her office, all she could think of was life without Tia, and how devasting that would be.

A tentative knock on the door drew her back from her thoughts. She glanced up. Matt was standing awkwardly in the doorway. His face was a mixture of concern and trepidation. She motioned for him to enter, her hand waving him towards the chair in front of her desk.

'Sorry to bother you, ma'am,' Matt began, his normally confident voice hesitant. 'But I thought you'd want an update on the Kempston case.'

Matt sat, his eyes flicking between Lauren and the desk, clearly uncomfortable. After a moment, he spoke. 'Before we discuss the case, if you don't mind, I want to ask about Tia. Have you heard anything from the vet, yet?'

Lauren's heart fluttered at the mention of Tia. 'Yes,' she replied, her voice barely above a whisper. 'The operation was successful, but they're keeping her in for observation. She's...' Her voice broke, an avalanche of emotions threatening to spill over. She sniffed back her tears, took a deep breath, and forced herself to continue. 'It's tough. Harder than I thought it would be.'

Matt's face softened, his eyes full of sympathy. 'I can only imagine, ma'am. If you'd rather, we can talk about something else—'

'No, it's okay,' she cut him off, steeling herself. 'I've got it together. They're still concerned about Tia and, reading between the lines, the next few days are critical. I can't see her until tomorrow morning, and even then it's only through a window.'

Matt winced, the pain clearly shared. 'I'm really sorry, ma'am. If you need some space, I can take care of the investigation for now,' he offered, rising to his feet.

'No,' Lauren snapped, sharper than she'd intended. She caught herself. 'Sorry, I didn't mean... Please sit. Wallowing in

42

self-pity isn't going to help anyone. There's nothing I can do for now, so I'll focus on work. At least that's something I can control. Give me an update on the case.'

Matt nodded, a look of understanding in his eyes. He took his seat again, shifting to work mode. 'All right, then. So far, we have no leads on who X might be. But that's hardly surprising. The Kempstons have two joint bank accounts: an everyday account and a savings account. They're clearly not living from hand to mouth each week, but they're not particularly well off, either. There have been no unusual transactions recently. Nothing to indicate that anything untoward has been going on.'

Lauren took a moment to process this, her detective brain kicking into gear. 'And what about the CCTV footage? Do we know where she went after leaving the shopping centre?'

'Her car was spotted on the ANPR cameras on the A30 between St Austell and St Ives, but nothing after St Agnes. That's about a thirty-minute drive from there to her home. She could have left the A30 and taken back roads somewhere.'

'Why would she have done that?' Lauren asked, her mind spinning with possibilities.

'If she had planned to meet someone,' Matt suggested. 'This person X.'

'I agree. And we can probably assume that wherever she met them was fairly close to home.'

'Yes, ma'am.'

'It hasn't even been twenty-four hours since she was last seen, so I think we should continue our search, but we don't need the entire team working on it. We have other cases demanding our attention, too.'

Matt nodded his agreement. 'You mean the graffiti at the train station?' he asked, a faint grin playing on his lips, but his eyes were wary, as if he were testing the waters.

'Yes. I do realise that we're not exactly inundated with the sort of high-stakes crimes city forces have. But every crime, no matter how small, deserves to be investigated thoroughly.'

'I said the same thing to the team earlier, ma'am,' Matt said.

A wave of gratitude washed over Lauren and she offered him a small smile. She was grateful for Matt. For his quiet understanding and support. His concern for her was evident in his words and actions.

She appreciated the effort he was making to keep her focused on work while she was struggling through such a difficult time.

SIX

THURSDAY, 7 MARCH

Lauren stared at the computer screen, not really focusing on her email inbox, which was full, each subject line a stark reminder of the responsibilities needing her attention. But her thoughts were elsewhere. With Tia, who was still unwell. It had been two days since her operation, yet it seemed like an eternity.

That morning she'd stopped by the surgery, as planned, her heart heavy with apprehension. The concerned expressions on everyone's faces, from the receptionist on duty to the nursing staff and Elliot the vet, confirmed her worst fears. Tia still wasn't out of danger. They informed Lauren that Tia had had a restless night and they were keeping a constant eye on her.

Lauren was allowed into the small sterile room where Tia was resting, a sight that had tugged at her heartstrings. Her faithful friend, once so energetic and full of life, was listless and barely registered Lauren's gentle strokes. Tia's eyes opened briefly, a flicker of recognition in them, before they closed.

It was heartbreaking to see Tia in such a bad way but Cali the nurse had assured her that any pain was being managed with medication, and that had contributed to the drowsiness. Elliot had promised to keep her updated throughout the day, suggesting she try not to worry in the meantime. It was advice that felt as hollow as it was well-intentioned. Of course she was going to worry. It was like her life was on standstill.

Shaking her head, Lauren forced herself to attend to the neglected email inbox. Many of them were from DCI Mistry. A never-ending demand for figures, statistics, and reports. He was definitely a hands-off boss, preferring to keep his distance and allowing her the autonomy to manage her team. That she was more than happy with, but his obsession with budgets and figures, while important, often seemed to overshadow everything else.

In her mind, being a DCI meant taking a more rounded approach. Ensuring that cases were run efficiently and budgets were kept to, while making sure that no stone was left unturned when it came to solving cases. So that when prosecutions got to court there was sufficient evidence to ensure a successful outcome, and that criminals weren't let off on a technicality, as often happened, especially if a hot-shot barrister was involved.

She hadn't yet gone into the office for the morning briefing. She usually held it between eight thirty and nine, briefing the team on new cases, followed by a recap on the progress of existing cases. As far as she was aware, nothing else had happened in respect of the missing Kempston woman, nor had any other incidents occurred. It was quiet, even for them.

A knock on the door jolted her from her thoughts. Glancing up, she saw Matt standing there, concern etched in his features. She waved him in, bracing herself for another round of updates and decisions.

'Morning, ma'am. How are you? How's Tia?' Matt's voice was gentle and soothing. A contrast to the whirlwind of thoughts in her head.

'Not good,' Lauren managed to reply, her words slicing through the air like a knife.

Matt's eyes flickered with sympathy. 'I'm so sorry. Why

don't you go home. I can oversee the Kempston inquiry. There have been no new developments. In my opinion, she's disappeared on her own volition to be with X, whoever they might be. It's the only answer.'

'Your theory definitely makes sense,' Lauren said, nodding. 'But me going home isn't an option.'

She knew all too well that staring at the four walls of her home would only amplify her worries about Tia.

The silence.

The empty dog bed.

Ben was with Lauren's elderly neighbour, Betty Field, during the day, so he didn't get too lonely. It was the first time Lauren had ever asked anyone for help, much preferring to keep to herself, but this time it wasn't practical. And Betty loved Tia and Ben, and often brought round bones for them to chew on. It shouldn't be too onerous for her because the dogs slept most of the day now they were older.

'Are you sure?' Matt asked.

'Yes. I need to be here. We have work to do. I'll be in shortly to do the morning briefing and—'

The shrill ring of the phone on her desk cut through her sentence. She picked up the receiver, pressing it to her ear. 'Pengelly speaking.'

'Ma'am, there's a Mr Hughes at reception. He's asking to speak with someone regarding his missing wife,' Hicks, the desk sergeant, said.

Lauren's eyes widened. Another missing woman? The coincidence was too stark to ignore.

'Thank you, Sergeant. Someone will be down there shortly.' She replaced the receiver with a click, her gaze resting on Matt, who mirrored her expression of concern. 'We have another missing person case. A woman. I'm not saying they're connected, but two disappearances in one week is too unusual for us not to consider it.'

'Do you need me to go?' Matt offered, already rising from his chair.

'We'll go together.'

They hurried to the main entrance. A man sat hunched on one of the chairs. He seemed to be in his forties, dressed casually in dark jeans, a plain T-shirt and a denim jacket.

Lauren headed over to him. 'Mr Hughes?'

'Yes, I'm Rory Hughes. My wife, Yvonne... she didn't come home last night after work,' he said, his voice anxious.

'I'm DI Pengelly and this is DS Price,' Lauren said, introducing them and gesturing to Matt. 'We'll find a more private place to talk. You can tell us everything there.'

She ushered him into one of the interview rooms, where they all took their seats. Matt pulled out his notebook and pen, ready to jot things down.

'Okay, Mr Hughes. Please start from the beginning,' Lauren urged, her voice encouraging.

'Yvonne went to work yesterday. She had the two-till-ten shift at the supermarket near our home. I was at work so didn't see her leave. I came home, made dinner, and went to bed around nine, as I usually do. I have to get up early in the morning, so I don't wait up for her. It wasn't until my alarm rang at five that I noticed she wasn't there.'

'And you don't wake up when she comes in?' Matt asked, his pen poised.

'No. Never. I'm a deep sleeper. Once my head hits the pillow, I'm out for the count until my alarm goes off.'

'Did you try calling her? Or check your phone for any messages she might have left?' Lauren enquired, leaning in slightly.

'Yes, of course. I did both. My calls went to voicemail and there were no messages on my phone.'

'Has she ever not come home straight from work before?'

Lauren's tone was cautious, her eyes scrutinising his every reaction.

'Well...' He hesitated, his gaze shifting away for a few seconds.

'Mr Hughes?' Lauren prompted, locking eyes with him.

'Occasionally, she'll go out for a drink after work with her colleagues, but she's always home before midnight.'

'But if you're asleep, how can you be certain?' Lauren probed, her brows furrowing slightly.

'Because she tells me the next morning,' he replied matter-of-factly.

'Does she usually tell you in advance if she's planning to go out for a drink after her shift at the supermarket?'

'Most of the time, yes. But there have been instances when she hasn't. She doesn't go out regularly... maybe once a month when she's working the late shift. She says she's too wired to head straight home and sleep. Going out for a drink relaxes her. I totally understand. It's not like I go straight to bed as soon as I get home from work. I like to unwind, too. But she's never stayed out all night before. Never. Honestly.'

Lauren leant back in her chair, her fingers tapping on the table. 'We typically wait twenty-four hours before launching an investigation into someone's disappearance unless they're classed as vulnerable. More often than not, the person turns up. It could be that her car broke down, or she might have had one too many and decided to stay overnight with a friend or at a hotel.'

'But she would have called me,' the man insisted, his voice trembling slightly.

'Unless she lost or misplaced her phone,' Lauren suggested as an explanation.

'Are you saying you won't look for her? That I have to wait until ten tonight when her shift would've ended?' The distress in his voice was palpable.

'Have you tried contacting the supermarket?' Lauren asked, ignoring his outburst.

'No. I came straight here. I thought that was best,' Hughes said, his fists clenched and resting on the table.

'Do you know the names of the people she goes drinking with from work?' Lauren asked.

'No,' Hughes said, shaking his head. 'Yvonne doesn't talk much about her work.'

Really? That surprised her. Was there a reason for that?

'How long has Yvonne been employed at the supermarket?' Lauren asked.

'I'm not sure exactly, it's at least three, maybe even four years. The job fits well around our family life; that's why she stays there.' Each question seemed to add a new layer of worry on Hughes' face.

'Do you have any children?'

'Yes, a boy. He's fourteen. Spencer.'

'Does he know that his mum's missing?' Lauren might not have children herself, but she could imagine how awful it would be for him to not know where his mother was.

'No. Yvonne usually sleeps in when working the late shift and he doesn't see her before leaving for school. He's pretty self-reliant. I didn't want to alarm him unnecessarily...' His voice cracked slightly.

'Is he usually awake when Yvonne comes home from work?'

'He's like most kids and spends all his spare time in his room. We never see him after dinner until the next morning. He wouldn't know whether she was there or not.'

'Do you have work today?' Matt asked, his eyebrows drawn together in sympathy.

'Yes, but I called in sick. I work in Newlyn at the fish market. I've been too anxious about Yvonne to focus on anything else. Are you going to help find her, or do I need to wait until tonight and come back?' he asked, desperation in his voice.

'We'll make enquiries and speak with her colleagues at the supermarket,' Lauren said calmly. 'Do you have a recent photo of Yvonne that we could use?'

'Yes,' he said, pulling out his phone to show her a picture. 'This was taken at a friend's birthday party a couple of weeks ago.'

Lauren observed a pretty woman in her early forties with wavy red hair spilling over her shoulders. She was smiling and holding up a glass as if toasting someone.

'Did you take this photo?'

'Yes. We had a lovely evening. It was the first time we'd been out for ages, and she'd been looking forward to it.'

'I'll give you my card. It has my email address on it. Please forward it to me.' Lauren extended her hand, offering him the small card. 'Do you have any idea what Yvonne was wearing yesterday?'

'I'm not certain. She wears her uniform for work, but she keeps a change of clothes in her car for when she goes out afterwards.'

'The same clothes every time? Or does she take fresh clothes with her when she's planning to go out?' Lauren asked.

'I'm not sure, because I'm not here when she leaves. All I know is that she always has an outfit to change into.'

'What car does Yvonne drive?' Lauren asked, her mind already formulating a plan of action.

'An old red Ford Fiesta. I can't remember the registration number, but it does have a stripe down the side.'

'We'll get the details and keep you updated on our progress. If Yvonne turns up, please contact us immediately. We don't want to waste resources on trying to locate a missing person who actually isn't.' As Lauren spoke the words she felt a twinge of regret. She hadn't meant to come across so cold and detached. But the harsh realities of their job often demanded it.

'I understand,' Rory Hughes murmured, his gaze dropping to his hands, which were now clasped tightly in his lap. 'Thank you for believing me.'

'Mr Hughes,' Lauren said, leaning in slightly across the table, her voice softening. 'We don't for one moment think you're fabricating this. But police procedures are based on past experience and, as I've explained, it's not until after twenty-four hours have passed that we usually consider it more likely a person has genuinely gone missing, for whatever reason.'

'What do you mean?' he asked, uncertainty in his voice and lines of worry etching deeper into his features.

Lauren paused. She understood his confusion, his fear. She'd seen it many times before.

'Sometimes people disappear and don't wish to be found,' she began, her tone measured, trying to cushion the impact of her words. Her mind was already racing with the different scenarios she'd dealt with during her career. 'Others, well...' She offered him a tight-lipped smile. 'We don't need to go into that now.'

The panic in his eyes was evidence that the gravity of the situation had hit him. That hope was slipping away. She felt a pang of sympathy for him, but she knew she had to maintain her professional demeanour. They had a long day ahead.

SEVEN

THURSDAY, 7 MARCH

Matt pulled up his collar to stop the drizzling rain from running down the back of his neck. He followed Lauren as she headed through the automatic doors of the bustling supermarket, the bright overhead fluorescent lights a stark difference to the miserable grey day outside. Lauren walked with purpose, as if she was determined to immerse herself in work and be distracted from worrying about her dog.

Lauren approached the customer service desk, her warrant card already held out in her hand so the man behind the desk could see it.

'DI Pengelly and DS Price. We'd like to see the manager.'

The man behind the desk barely flinched. 'That would be me,' he responded, pointing to the store manager badge pinned to his supermarket uniform. 'I'm Brent Gable.'

Matt squinted at the badge, only then noticing its existence. Judging from the slight raise of Lauren's eyebrows, she hadn't noticed it either.

'Is there somewhere quiet we can talk? We'd like to ask about one of your staff,' Lauren said.

'Come through to my office. I've been out here checking stock levels, but that can wait.'

They navigated the aisles, which weren't very wide and were full of people pushing trolleys, until reaching the rear of the store. They followed as he pushed through a pair of swing doors and turned left into a small, windowless office. The room was claustrophobic, with barely enough space for a desk and two chairs. The manager gestured for them to sit before circling the desk and sitting on his own chair.

'We're enquiring about Yvonne Hughes,' Lauren said, breaking the silence.

'Yvonne? What's happened?' The manager's eyes widened, a crease forming between his brows.

'She didn't return home after her shift last night,' Lauren revealed, her voice calm despite the gravity of the words.

The manager slumped back in his chair, his face drained of colour. 'I worked late last night and I definitely remember seeing her leave when the shop closed at ten. There were staff stocking the shelves until later, so there were people around.'

'We understand from Yvonne's husband that she occasionally enjoys a post-work drink with colleagues. Was that the case yesterday?' Matt asked.

The manager moved uneasily, his gaze darting away. 'I wouldn't know. I saw her leave through the front door and called goodbye but didn't see where she went after that.'

If that was the case, then why was Gable being evasive? Why were his movements awkward and his eyes avoiding theirs? Was there more to this story?

Lauren appeared to sense this, too. She leant forward, looking directly at him. 'Was Yvonne's behaviour out of the ordinary yesterday? Did you notice anything different about her?'

The manager's gaze flickered away from Lauren's intense

scrutiny and instead he looked at Matt while answering. 'I didn't really see her much because I spent most of the time in my office yesterday. From the little I did see, she seemed her usual self. But I'm probably not the right person to ask. Katrina Pick might know more. They're often working the same shift. I'll give you her details.'

'Is Katrina working today?' Matt asked, jumping on the new lead.

'No. It's her day off,' Gable said, shaking his head.

Matt glanced at Lauren, noting the slight frown. Every second counted in cases like this. 'Would you say that Yvonne's a reliable worker?'

The manager's response was immediate, his head bobbing up and down vigorously. 'Absolutely. One of the best. She never phones in sick, is always happy to help customers and doesn't complain if she's asked to do anything. I could do with a dozen like her. It would make my life a hell of a lot easier, for sure.'

Lauren nodded, but Matt noticed the slight tightening of her lips. In all probability, whatever had happened to Yvonne would have nothing to do with how reliable she had been at work.

'We'd like to see the CCTV footage showing when Yvonne left the supermarket,' Lauren stated, leaving no room for argument.

'Ummm, yes, I suppose that's okay,' the manager said, his tone hesitant. His gaze darted between Lauren and Matt. 'Or should I ask for some sort of warrant?' he added, his voice tailing off.

Lauren's expression hardened, her patience visibly waning. 'Mr Gable, Yvonne is missing and we need your help. So please show us what we need.'

Lauren's voice was stern and, judging by the expression on the manager's face, it did the trick.

'Sorry, yes. I'm sure it will be okay.' Gable nodded, a nervous laugh escaping his lips. 'I won't tell my boss, then no one will know.'

Matt exchanged a glance with Lauren. Time was of the essence, and they had to act fast. The manager's hesitance was a delay they couldn't afford.

'Thank you,' Lauren said.

The manager's fingers danced over the keyboard with an assured agility, belying the tension in the room. After a few moments, he swivelled the monitor around so they could see the footage.

'Look here,' he said, pointing to the screen. 'That's Yvonne. She's exiting through the front door, making her way across the car park to her car. She's alone. And there she is, driving out and turning right, presumably heading back home.'

'You know her address?' Lauren asked, leaning forward and studying the screen, her tone cool.

'Yes,' the manager confirmed without hesitation.

Lauren's gaze didn't move from the screen, but Matt noted her eyes narrowing slightly. 'And do you know the addresses of all of your staff?'

'Not all of them. But Yvonne's I do.' Gable's shoulders lifted slightly in a shrug. 'I had to drive her home once when her car was at the garage being fixed.'

Matt cast a glance at Lauren.

'What were you doing on Monday afternoon from four o'clock?' Matt asked, scrutinising Gable's face for any sign that the question concerned him.

'I was here at work, why?' Gable's tone was almost defensive.

'Did you leave the premises at all?' Matt pressed.

'No.' Gable exhaled a sigh of frustration. 'I'm currently short-staffed, which means I'm always here. One of my assistant managers is on holiday and the other is in hospital. It's a right bloody carry-on. I've been working seven days a week for the last fortnight and, let me tell you, the wife isn't happy. If it wasn't for the overtime, she'd probably have divorced me by now.' He gave a shallow laugh.

Despite the manager's assurances, Matt wasn't totally convinced.

'Well, if you could provide us with Katrina's details we'll contact her. We may need to speak with you again.' His tone was firm, making it clear that the investigation was far from over.

Back at the station, Matt followed Lauren into the bustling office, the happy chatter of the team all around them.

'We've just returned from the supermarket where Yvonne Hughes was last seen,' Lauren began, slicing through the hum of activity. The room fell silent, as it usually did when the team were aware of her presence. 'We've reviewed the CCTV footage and confirmed she departed at the end of her shift. Her husband mentioned that she occasionally goes out for a drink after work, but we don't know if she did last night. When she turned out of the car park it was in the direction of her home, but we don't know which pub they go to, so she could've been heading there. The manager mentioned one of Yvonne's colleagues who we'll be questioning shortly. Before that, though, I want some feedback on what we know so far regarding the investigation into Freya's disappearance. Jenna, what did you learn from the hairdresser?'

'I spoke to Aggie, who's my own hairdresser,' Jenna said, absent-mindedly twisting a strand of loose hair that had escaped her tie. 'And it turns out that she's also Freya's stylist. According to Aggie, Freya wasn't happy in her marriage.'

'Did she say why?' Lauren probed, her gaze sharp.

'Aggie was reluctant to say too much, ma'am, other than Freya's often complaining that Anthony is boring and that it feels like they're on the fast track to retirement, even though they're barely out of their thirties.'

'Did Aggie know anything about person X Freya was due to meet?'

'I didn't mention X by name... well, by letter... but it turns out that at her last appointment, Freya brought in a picture of a new style she wanted to try. Said she wanted a new look.'

'Did you ask why she wanted this change?' Lauren asked.

'Yes, ma'am. Aggie said she got the feeling Freya was going to see someone, but she couldn't confirm it, and she didn't ask in case Freya thought she was overstepping the mark. You know what hairdressers are like.'

'What do you mean?' Lauren asked, looking puzzled.

'Hairdressers can be like a sounding board for their clients. It's an unwritten rule that if you confide in them, it will remain between the two of you.'

'A bit like therapy, you mean?' Matt said, remembering Leigh's special relationship with her hairdresser.

Not that he understood the whole stylist/client thing. He went to the barber four times a year, if that. But one of the main things his mum had worried about when they'd moved to Cornwall was finding a good hairdresser. Mind you, judging from Lauren's response, she wasn't one to use her hairdresser as a confidante.

'Sort of, Sarge,' Jenna said, chuckling.

'Do we have any more on Freya's social media activity?' Lauren asked, moving the conversation on.

Tamsin shook her head, her fingers resting over her keyboard. 'Nothing out of the ordinary, ma'am. Shall I research Yvonne Hughes' profiles?'

Lauren nodded. 'Yes, we should definitely look into her

online presence, too. As it stands, we have nothing linking the two disappearances, but we can't rule out the possibility they're connected. Sergeant Price and I are going to visit Yvonne's colleague, Katrina Pick, in the hopes of unearthing something useful. After that we'll circle back to the husband. I want the rest of you to continue with the research, but don't neglect your other cases. Billy, any progress on the graffiti front?'

Billy sighed, leaning back in his chair with an air of defeat. 'The culprits seem to know exactly where the cameras are placed, as I'd predicted. I reckon they're approaching the station from the rear and keeping out of sight. I've suggested to the station manager that they install some more cameras in areas close to the graffiti. Whether they will or not is anyone's guess.'

'It's probably a funding issue,' Clem said. 'Over the last four years budgets have been considerably reduced and that has had an impact on staffing and—'

'Not now, Clem,' Lauren said, cutting him off, her tone sharp. 'We don't have time.'

'Sorry, ma'am,' the older officer said, a resigned expression on his face.

'What else is going on today, apart from these missing women?' Lauren asked, her eyes scanning the room.

Matt frowned. This was Penzance; they weren't exactly drowning in cases.

Clem cleared his throat, breaking the silence. 'I have a road safety talk at the local school this afternoon, ma'am.'

Lauren's eyebrows shot up. 'Why you? It's not typically a job for a member of CID.'

Clem shrugged, a sheepish grin playing on his lips. 'The teacher coordinating it is my sister, and she specifically asked for me.'

Lauren gave a frustrated sigh. 'It's not exactly a good use of your time. But I suppose as it's already arranged you can go. If your sister asks you again, though, you're to direct her to uniform.'

'Understood, ma'am,' Clem said, nodding.

Lauren turned to Matt. 'Right, let's go.'

Matt grabbed his jacket, watching as the room returned to its previous hum, each officer buried in their work.

EIGHT

THURSDAY, 7 MARCH

Matt walked beside Lauren down the corridor and out into the station car park. She was staring straight ahead and showing no inclination of wanting to talk. He had something he wanted to discuss but was going to wait until they were outside and away from the confines of the station in case they were overheard.

'You were a bit harsh on Clem, ma'am,' Matt said, finally breaking the silence once they were well away from the front door. The rain had stopped, but the wind hadn't, and he shivered, wishing that he'd brought his warmer jacket to work that morning. He still hadn't got the hang of the Cornwall climate. Would he ever?

'No, I wasn't,' Lauren retorted. 'We work in CID and that means we don't go out on foot patrol or traffic duty. If any member of the team wants to do that, they can transfer to uniform and I'll replace them with someone who is more suited to work with us.'

'You also shot him down when he was talking about funding. Now, I realise that we had work to do, but sometimes for the good of the team we should allow the members to do what they're good at.'

'Are you questioning my authority?' Lauren turned and glared at him.

'You know I'm not,' he said quietly. 'Clem's a good member of the team and I think you were a little hard on him. I know things are difficult because of Tia but—'

'This has nothing to do with Tia,' Lauren said, lowering her voice.

He shrugged and didn't pursue it.

They climbed into her car and took the road from Penzance to St Ives. He stared out of the window as they entered the town and drove along the seafront. It was a place where it seemed time had stood still, with small shops, restaurants and bars overlooking the ocean. Cobbled lanes twisted and turned, leading away from the harbour. Matt opened his window slightly, allowing the scent of freshly caught fish to waft in.

Lauren drove along the narrow streets, eventually stopping outside a grey pebble-dashed terraced house in Treverbyn Road, which was fairly close to the supermarket. Before they could even mount the worn stone steps leading to the front door, they were greeted by a woman in her early fifties. Her dyed black hair was at odds with her pale complexion.

'Are you the police?' the woman asked, a guarded expression on her face, her eyes betraying a hint of trepidation.

'Yes,' Lauren responded with a curt nod, flashing her warrant card with practised ease.

'I'm Katrina Pick. Brent phoned and said you want to ask me about Yvonne. I was planning to meet up with a friend, but I cancelled because I didn't know when you'd get here.'

Matt observed the look of surprise on Lauren's face. They hadn't expected Gable to jump the gun and contact Katrina before they did. Then again, they hadn't told him not to.

'May we come inside?' Lauren asked, her voice softening slightly.

'Sure, but don't mind the mess because I haven't got round to doing any cleaning today. That's the trouble when you've still got kids at home. They expect everything to be done for them. And it's not like they're young. They're in their teens and out working.'

'How many of you live here?' Matt asked.

'Me and my three boys. The old man left us years ago. Thank God. He was a right bastard.'

Katrina led them into a small, cluttered room at the front of the house. The scent of stale coffee and vaping fumes filled the air. Piles of magazines littered the coffee table. Lauren and Matt shifted the clutter to make some space before sitting on the old sofa, while Katrina perched on the edge of a faded brown chair, examining her nails, clearly nervous.

'What do you want to know?' Katrina asked, a wobble in her voice that she wasn't able to conceal.

Lauren leant forward, staring directly at Katrina. 'You're friends with Yvonne,' she began, her tone light, almost casual. 'Do you have any idea where she might have gone after work yesterday?'

Katrina's gaze faltered, her eyes darting to a spot just over their head. 'She told me she was meeting a friend,' she admitted, her voice low and her words measured.

'Did she say which friend?' Lauren pressed, urgency creeping into her voice.

Katrina shook her head, her dark hair shimmering in the light. 'No, she kept that very close to her chest. She nipped to the bathroom at about nine forty-five and got changed. But she had her uniform on over the top so I couldn't see what she was wearing. She said she was going out for a drink. I didn't ask about it. Yvonne's a bit of a closed book. She'll only tell you what she wants you to know, if you get what I mean.'

Matt watched Katrina closely, noting the minute changes in her expression and the way her hands twisted in her lap. He could see the strain on her face, the uncertainty in her eyes. What was she holding back?

'Has she ever talked about her marriage?' Lauren asked, shifting the focus to a more sensitive topic.

Katrina went a pale shade of pink and ran her tongue along her bottom lip, her eyes flickering to the floor. 'Yeah, sometimes,' she admitted, her voice barely above a whisper. 'She told me it's not that she doesn't love Rory, because she does. But she's really bored sometimes and misses going out and having fun.'

'Has she ever talked about leaving him?'

'Not to me. But I don't think she would because they've been through a lot together.'

'What do you mean?'

'She miscarried several times before conceiving Spencer and they weren't able to have more children. He's special to both Yvonne and Rory.'

'Do you think she's having a relationship with someone else?' Matt asked, his eyes boring into Katrina.

The question seemed to catch Katrina off guard, and she shifted uncomfortably in her seat. 'I don't know. It's not like we're best friends who tell each other everything. We're work friends, that's all. She does like to go out for a drink after work. Sometimes a few of us will go out for a drink together. Other times I know she's gone out on her own and I assumed it was to meet a friend. It's happened more often, recently.'

'Does she regularly do the two-to-ten shift?' Matt asked, trying to put the pieces together in his mind.

'Yes, because she's volunteered to. Over the last four weeks she's done nothing but that shift. I know because I mainly do that shift, too, because it fits in with the kids.'

'Do you think she might be seeing someone from work?' Matt asked, wondering about the manager and his reactions when being questioned.

'Maybe, I suppose? There's Dale Cooper. She's always

saying how nice he is. He's the fruit and veg manager. They do seem quite friendly at work.'

Ah. Now they were getting somewhere.

'Was Dale working last night?' Matt asked, trying to keep his voice steady and not show his anticipation at being able to connect some of the dots.

Katrina nodded, a hint of reluctance in her expression. 'Yes, he was. And I did see him and Yvonne having a chat together during one of her breaks. Not that you heard that from me, mind,' she added. 'I don't want to get Yvonne into any trouble.'

'Katrina,' Lauren said sternly. 'Yvonne's missing. I don't think this is the time for worrying about getting her in trouble. Do you understand?'

Katrina blushed again and lowered her head. 'Yes. Sorry. But I do know Dale and Yvonne didn't leave together after work because I saw her leave and she was alone.'

'When you go out after work is it usually to the same pub?' Matt asked.

'Yes. We go to the Three Donkeys, which is about a five-minute drive from the supermarket.'

Matt glanced at Lauren, who was nodding.

'Yes, I know it,' she said.

'Have Dale and Yvonne ever gone out for drinks together after work in the past?' Matt asked.

'Not together, as such. But there have been several times when they've been the last two in the pub after everyone else has left. Most of us go for one drink to unwind a bit and then go home. Yvonne and Dale usually stay for another one or two.'

'How do you know that? Is it because you're the last but two to leave, yourself?' Lauren asked, frowning.

'I don't know until the next time we work together, because she tells me.'

'And have you ever asked Yvonne if there's anything going

between her and Dale?' Lauren pressed, keeping her focus directly on the woman.

'We've laughed about it, and I tease her. But I've never asked her outright if she's seeing him on the side. I wouldn't do that. We just have a bit of fun about him, that's all.' Katrina paused a moment, looking thoughtful. 'You don't think she could have run off with Dale, do you?'

'Do you?' Lauren asked, pushing the question right back.

Matt observed the indecision crossing Katrina's face. Was it because she knew something and wasn't prepared to admit it, or was she simply confused?

'I don't think she'd ever leave Rory and Spencer,' Katrina finally answered. 'But whatever's going on, there's got to be a reason for it. Rory seems like a good guy, but you never know what goes on behind closed doors, do you?'

'No, you don't,' Lauren agreed.

Matt glanced at Lauren and she nodded. They had enough and needed to interview the husband again.

'Thank you very much for your assistance. If you think of anything else that might be of use, please let us know,' Lauren said, holding out her card for Katrina to take.

The moment they stepped out of the terraced house, the wind whipped around them. They headed down the stone steps towards Lauren's car, their footsteps echoing in the quiet street.

'Well,' Matt started when they were out of earshot of the house, breaking the silence. 'What do you think of Katrina's answers? If you ask me, there's something she's not telling us. Did you see how she reacted when I mentioned Yvonne might be having a relationship?'

Lauren tilted her head, considering. 'Or maybe she was just surprised by the idea. We mustn't jump to conclusions. But there's definitely more digging to do.'

'The fact that she did give up Dale's name makes me

wonder if she was giving us a red herring instead of telling us the name of who Yvonne was really seeing.'

'Do you think she'd be so devious? Because I didn't get that impression,' Lauren said, her brows furrowing.

Matt stood there quietly mulling over what Lauren had said. Katrina didn't come across as someone who would be like that. But, then again, if Yvonne had sworn her to secrecy, then she wouldn't be worried by her friend's disappearance because she already knew about it.

Or was he tying himself up in knots?

'You could be right. This pub... Would Yvonne have turned right when leaving work if she was going there?'

'Yes, that's the quickest route. We need to talk to Cooper, and soon. But not before we chat again to Rory Hughes.'

'Yes, ma'am. He should be our prime concern, especially if he's aware of Yvonne's behaviour. He's the one person who might be able to shed more light on this.'

'Agreed,' Lauren said. 'We need to know more about her home life and the real state of her marriage.'

'But we must tread carefully, ma'am. We're dealing with people's lives here and we can't go in all guns blazing. There could be considerable fallout from taking everything Katrina said at face value.'

He'd felt dutybound to say that, considering the way Lauren had been behaving because of how stressed she was. She had to rein herself in or it could have far-reaching consequences.

Lauren stared at him as if reading his mind. 'Matt, I understand what you're saying. I intend to be subtle when dealing with Rory Hughes – you have no worries on that count. We'll ask about Yvonne's habits. Her friends. Her routine. We'll see how he reacts and watch his body language. If he's hiding anything, it will show.'

'Thanks, ma'am. I didn't mean to question your ability to work properly, it's just that—'

'Matt, it's okay,' Lauren interrupted. 'I get it. I'm under some stress and you're concerned that it's affecting my work. Well, it isn't.' She paused a moment. 'Okay, maybe I'm a bit snappy with people, but in the main it's not interfering.'

Was she referring to the way she'd spoken to Clem, and admitting that she'd been in the wrong? Matt would never know, but the main thing was that she realised there could be an issue, and he was happy with that.

'Thanks, ma'am. You know, if you let the team know what you're going through, that could make a big difference.'

Lauren stared at him as if weighing up his words. 'Easy for you to say. But... I'm not sure whether it's the right thing to do. We'll discuss it later.'

'Okay, it's your decision, but I don't think you'll regret telling them. It might even let them see you in a more positive light. And that could...' He paused a moment, taking in Lauren's stony expression. 'Sorry, I'm going too far.'

'You think?' she said. But a slight smile played at the corners of her lips. 'Come on, let's get going.'

As they climbed into the car, Matt couldn't help but feel a surge of anticipation. The investigation was beginning to take shape. But he wasn't foolish enough to believe that it could be solved that easily; he was well used to cases having the most surprising and unanticipated results.

NINE

THURSDAY, 7 MARCH

Lauren pressed the bell and waited. The door opened a moment later and Rory Hughes stared at them. His eyes were filled with uncertainty and his face creased with worry.

'Have you found her?' Hughes asked, each word coming out like he was gasping for air. He raked a hand through his hair.

Lauren shook her head. 'Not yet, Rory. We'd like to ask you some more questions,' she replied, her tone gentle, but firm. It was a delicate situation, and she had to tread carefully.

Hughes visibly swallowed hard, his Adam's apple moving up and down. 'Yes, of course, come on in.' He stepped aside to make room for them.

He led them into the small porch of the 1960s semi-detached. Coats hung from the hooks on the wall with several pairs of shoes and boots neatly placed below. It was a typical family home.

'Thank you,' Lauren said.

'I was about to make a coffee; would you like one?' Hughes asked.

Lauren and Matt both accepted, and they followed him through to the lounge, which had stairs going up one side, and on to the dining area which led to the kitchen. Normally she'd have refused the offer of a drink, but she wanted Hughes to be as relaxed as possible. It would make discussing the sensitive subject a little less strained. It would also give them a chance to observe his body language when he was in a more comfortable situation.

The kitchen was small, and Lauren and Matt stood in the doorway while Hughes prepared their coffee. Once they had their drinks, they sat around the square dining table, which was situated by the French doors overlooking the small but well-manicured back garden.

'Rory, we'd like to ask you about your relationship with Yvonne,' Lauren said, noticing his slight change in posture and how his fingers tightened around his coffee mug.

'Umm... It's good. We've been married for seventeen years. Obviously, we're way past the initial honeymoon stage, but what we have is solid. Why are you asking?' His confusion was evident, but Lauren wasn't going to back down now.

Drawing in a deep breath, she steeled herself for the next difficult question. 'During our investigation, we've received information suggesting that Yvonne is feeling restless in your marriage. It seems that this could be the reason behind her going out drinking after work. Are you aware of this?'

Hughes paled, his eyes widening with shock. 'W-well, like I said,' he stuttered, his voice barely above a whisper. 'We're settled in our ways. B-but she's never mentioned being fed up.' He seemed to shrink within himself, the very idea of his wife's boredom catching him off guard. 'I suppose... she does complain occasionally because we don't go out much. But that's normal, isn't it, when you've been together for as long as we have?'

A wave of sympathy washed over Lauren, but she wasn't going to let up. 'I'm sorry to have to ask this, Rory. But can you think of any signs that might suggest Yvonne has been seeing someone else?'

Hughes' face distorted in disbelief as if it was a foreign concept, one he'd never expected to be associated with his wife. 'An affair?'

'Yes, or possibly she's been spending lots of time with someone in a more friendly, non-romantic way. At this point, we can't be sure how far things might have progressed,' Lauren explained, her voice as kind as she could manage, trying to cushion the blow of her words.

Hughes seemed to retreat into his own world, his gaze distant and clouded with confusion as he grappled with the enormity of Lauren's words. 'I... I don't know. Lately, she's been taking on a lot of late shifts at work, but she told me that was because they have staffing problems at the supermarket... but... an affair? I know our routines keep us apart much of the time... and I suppose our weekends have been busy as well. On Saturdays, she usually visits her parents, while I take Spencer to his football matches. He's part of a local team. Sundays we're usually together, but our time is often filled with gardening and odd jobs around the house. You know... like most couples... An affair? I don't believe she'd do something like that. Not to me. And definitely not to Spencer.' His voice trailed off, the quiet hum of the kitchen appliances the only sound filling the room.

Lauren shared a loaded glance with Matt. Was there any link at all between this case and Freya Kempston's disappearance? On the surface, it seemed not, considering who the women were, but they were faced with two confused husbands. Both of whom seemed genuinely surprised that their wives could disappear without a trace.

'Is there anything at all, past or present, that you can think of which might have played on Yvonne's mind and been a catalyst to her going missing?' Lauren pushed.

Hughes avoided looking at Lauren and Matt. 'Well... something happened a couple of years ago... Look, I'm not proud of it,' he muttered.

Lauren's eyes widened. 'What?'

'There was this woman at work, and we... you know... at the Christmas party. It was a bit of harmless flirting and a kiss under the mistletoe, but a few months ago Yvonne found out about it. Do you think she's trying to pay me back for what I did?'

'I don't know. How did Yvonne find out about this incident?' Matt asked.

'She saw a memory social media post from someone I work with. I was in the photo with my arm around this woman. She confronted me about it and I told her the truth.'

'What was her reaction?'

'She was angry. Accused me of wanting to have fun with everyone except her. But that's not true. It was a one-off thing after I'd been drinking. I thought she understood. But it looks like she didn't.' He hung his head, as if ashamed of his actions.

'Can we look at your bedroom, in particular at Yvonne's belongings?' Lauren requested firmly, making it appear more like an order than a question. 'Hopefully you'll be able to tell us if there's anything missing or different from usual.'

'Yes. It's upstairs.' Hughes rose from his seat, his movements mechanical, as if he was acting on autopilot.

They followed him up the stairs, the air thick with tension. Lauren studied Hughes from behind. If he had anything to do with his wife's disappearance, he was certainly hiding it well.

'This is our room,' Hughes said, leading them into a square room which had a bed flanked by two bedside tables and a built-in wardrobe. 'Yvonne keeps her clothes in the small third bedroom which we've turned into a dressing area. Would you like to look there first?'

'Yes, that's a good idea,' Lauren agreed, her eyes briefly scanning the bedroom. It was immaculately kept, with no signs of a struggle or hurried departure. The bed was also made neatly, with cushions strategically placed on top. 'Don't the cushions drive you mad?' she asked, wanting to find out who was the neat fiend in the house.

'No. We stack them on the chair over there while we're asleep.' He nodded to the chair by the window.

'It looks like a show home,' Lauren continued, giving a sweeping gesture around the room.

'It's how Yvonne likes it. She's very fussy. I don't mind. I enjoy seeing the house looking pristine.' Hughes turned to leave the room and led them towards bedroom three.

When they stepped inside, they were met with an array of clothes hanging on two freestanding rails running along each side of the room. Under the window, a shelving area was filled with shoes of various styles and colours. A chest of drawers stood by the door, completing the set-up. Again, perfectly neat and tidy.

'She has a lot of fancy clothes,' Matt said, a note of surprise in his voice.

Matt had echoed Lauren's thoughts. Why would someone who was bored because she didn't go out much, and who worked at a place where they had to wear a uniform, have so many dressy clothes? It made no sense. When would she get to wear them?

'They go back years. Yvonne never likes to throw anything away,' Hughes said, a hint of affection in his tone.

That made more sense.

Lauren pulled on a pair of disposable gloves and moved towards the rails, her fingers brushing against the fabric as she flicked through them. 'Are all of her clothes here? Can you tell if there's anything missing?'

'I'm not sure,' Hughes admitted. He walked over to the far rail, which was filled with dresses, and began sifting through them. Suddenly he paused, pulling out an empty pink padded hanger. 'She bought a new dress several weeks ago and it's not here. We had a few words about it at the time because it was so expensive and we've been trying to save up for a holiday abroad in August. But she insisted that it was on sale and she couldn't resist it.'

'What was it like?' Lauren asked.

'It was pink with sequins and it had thin shoulder straps. It was quite flashy really, but Yvonne said she'd get a lot of use out of it and that it will be nice to wear when we're on holiday.'

'Perhaps she took it back to the shop after you argued about it?' Matt suggested.

'We didn't really argue. We don't do that. Sometimes the occasional niggle, that's all. And she can't have taken it back because she's already worn it... when she went to her younger sister's hen party a couple of weeks ago.' Hughes' eyes clouded with uncertainty.

'Could her sister have borrowed it?' Lauren asked.

'No. It wouldn't have fitted. They're nothing like each other in build,' Hughes said, shaking his head.

'Is everything else here?' Lauren asked, turning her attention back to the room.

Hughes looked around, and then pointed to a gap in the shoe storage area. 'The shoes that she wore with the dress aren't here, either.'

'I'm impressed that you actually know the contents of your wife's wardrobe, because I certainly wouldn't,' Matt said.

Hughes shrugged, a hint of red colouring his cheeks. 'I don't know everything that's here, but you asked me if anything was missing and I remembered the dress because it was new.'

Lauren studied him, her intuition tingling. If Matt was right that most men wouldn't even know if anything was missing, maybe he knew because he'd seen her in it and decided to take action. It was certainly something to consider.

'You mentioned earlier that you slept through from nine

o'clock on the night Yvonne went missing. Is there any way you can corroborate that?' Lauren asked, staring directly at the man.

'Of course not. I was alone and Spencer was in his room,' Hughes said, a look of confusion crossing his face, his brows knitting together.

She'd expected that answer, but still had to pursue it.

'If you'd decided to go out, would Spencer have known?' Lauren pushed.

'No. Unless he wanted to speak to me... but he never does.' Hughes shrugged. 'We're... Yvonne and me... we're always saying that the house could be on fire and Spencer still wouldn't notice. Once he's wearing his headphones and playing video games with his friends, he's totally unaware of anything else.' He ran a trembling hand through his hair. 'This can't be happening... It can't,' he muttered.

'What about Yvonne's passport, where's that kept?' Matt asked, moving the conversation on.

Hughes looked directly at him, as if coming out of his dark thoughts. 'Our passports are kept together in the drawer by my bed.'

'Could you check to confirm it's still there?' Lauren requested, wondering whether there was a possibility, however remote, that the woman had taken off overseas somewhere.

Hughes left the dressing room and they followed him back to the couple's bedroom. The room was charged with tension as he fumbled to pull open the drawer. He rummaged around amidst a pile of socks until his fingers closed around three passports held together by an elastic band. He slipped off the band, opened each passport to check and then handed one to Matt.

'This is Yvonne's,' he stated, his voice wavering. 'She hasn't taken it, so she hasn't run away if that's what you're thinking. Which means... something's happened to her. I know it has. This isn't like her at all. Please believe me. You're wasting time here talking to me when you should be out looking for her. Before...' His voice trailed off.

'Rory, this is all part of our investigation. We must consider every possibility, however remote it might be,' Lauren reassured him. 'From our discussion with you and based on information we've received from one of her work colleagues, it's most likely that Yvonne went out after work for a drink wearing her new pink sequined dress. But what we don't know, yet, is where she went or who she was with. That's what we've got to discover. We need to be thorough, and questioning you is part of that.'

'Okay.' He nodded. 'I get it. But surely now you can see that her going missing is nothing to do with me?' He stared at Lauren, his eyes accusatory, but also filled with tears. 'What have you found out, so far?' he added.

'At the moment, our only solid information is that her car was seen leaving the supermarket, but we've no idea where she went after that. We're looking at CCTV cameras in town to see if we can trace her. We're doing as much as we possibly can to find her.'

Hughes dropped down onto the bed, burying his head in his hands. 'Why would she leave me and Spencer? Especially Spencer. He's her whole world. That's what I don't get,' he murmured. 'And taking no clothes other than a posh dress makes no sense, either.' He glanced up at Lauren. 'Surely you must see that too.'

Lauren watched him, noting his confusion and fear. He seemed genuine, but she wanted to confer with Matt for his opinion before ruling him out entirely.

'We're doing everything we can, Rory. We'll be back in touch with you as soon as we have any updates we can share. I promise.'

What she didn't disclose was that Yvonne was the second woman to have gone missing within a few days. At this stage there was no value in adding to the man's worries, especially as they had no solid evidence to link the two cases. Yet, the striking similarity to the circumstances of Freya's disappearance sat like a heavy stone in Lauren's gut, a nagging feeling that they were dealing with something far more complex than a pair of unrelated incidents.

TEN

FRIDAY, 8 MARCH

The familiar surroundings of the office greeted Matt as he walked in, his shoes clicking against the polished concrete floor. He shrugged off his waterproof jacket, draping it over the worn wooden coat rack in the corner. He was the first one there and the soft morning light filtered through the tall windows, casting long shadows on his desk. He loved this time of day, when he could go through his diary, and his mail, and prepare for whatever the day was going to bring.

He was a little later than usual because it was his mum's birthday and, with Dani's assistance, they'd prepared her breakfast in bed. They all congregated in the bedroom while his mum opened her presents and cards... again with Dani's help. His daughter loved pulling off wrapping paper and playing with the boxes gifts came in.

He headed over to his desk but before he had time to sit his attention was drawn to a bright yellow Post-it note strategically stuck on his keyboard. *MY OFFICE IMMEDIATELY*. The fully capitalised message screamed urgency. It had to be Lauren. No one else would leave it. A small frown creased his forehead as he glanced over to her office, catching a glimpse of her silhouetted form through the glass section of her door.

He briefly contemplated making a detour to the coffee machine, but the prospect of Lauren having spotted him caused second thoughts. He squared his shoulders, mentally preparing himself for whatever news awaited him, and made his way towards her office.

With a soft rap on the door, which was slightly ajar, he peered inside. 'You wanted me, ma'am?'

'Grab your jacket,' Lauren responded without even looking up at him. 'We're going to Pedn Vounder beach. Yvonne Hughes' car has been located there.'

His eyebrows shot up, his interest immediately piqued. 'Any sign of her?'

Lauren's gaze lifted from the files spread out on her desk and she looked directly at him, brushing a stray hair behind her ear. 'Not that I know of. Forensics are already there, so they'll be able to tell us.'

He hesitated a moment, his mind racing. 'Where's this beach? I haven't heard of it before.'

'It's sixteen miles south of St Ives and a twenty-minute drive from here. It's east of Porthcurno. You must have heard of that place? It's world famous. Home to the cable museum and also the open-air Minack Theatre that's set in the rocks.'

He nodded, remembering. 'Yes, we've been there. We took Dani to the museum. Fascinating. Although I'm not sure she totally appreciated it. Two's a bit young to understand these things. But she enjoyed playing with the Morse code and other exhibits. To think that a small town like that is steeped in so much history. It's incredible.'

'Yes, it is extraordinary and brings thousands of tourists to the area, especially in summer. Which can be frustrating when we're trying to do our jobs. But if it keeps the economy afloat, then we have to put up with it.'

Matt smiled to himself. He didn't have Lauren pegged as such a pragmatist when it came to local tourism. 'I doubt every person living here shares your view. Whose car shall we go in, ma'am?'

'We'll take two,' she said in a tone that indicated it wasn't up for discussion. 'I'm uncertain when Tia will be released from the vet. It probably won't be until this afternoon, but on the off-chance I receive a call, I want to be able to head over there immediately.'

Matt found himself momentarily distracted by the mention of Tia. It had been four days since Lauren's dog had been taken ill, and the fact that she wasn't yet at home was worrying. 'So she's doing okay?'

Lauren nodded. 'I called in there last night and they assured me that she's on the mend, but they wanted to keep her in one more night, to be sure there are no complications.'

'That's fantastic news, ma'am. I'm so pleased for you. It must be a great worry lifted off your mind.'

Lauren let out a long sigh. 'Yes, it certainly is. I can't wait to have her back at home with us. But how she's going to cope, especially when I'm at work, is still a big worry. My neighbour's very good, and she's offered to help whenever I need it, but I don't like imposing on her. Having Tia back will also be good for Ben. He's been so unhappy not having his sister around to play with. I didn't realise how emotional dogs could be. I knew about elephants and how they mourn the loss of their children... but...' Her voice trailed off, as if suddenly realising she was getting too personal and that they had work to be getting on with.

'You know that I'm happy to take over the case if you need to disappear at any time, ma'am,' Matt offered.

For a moment, Lauren's face was an unreadable mask. He could almost see the gears shifting behind her eyes while she processed what he'd said. Then it hardened, and the lines around her eyes became tight. 'I'm not going to shirk off my work,' she said, her tone hard. 'You should know better than to think that I would. We have a job to do and nothing will get in the way. Yes, I have a dog to think about, but I will make it work without affecting what's happening here.'

Matt held up his hands, palms forward as a sign of surrender. 'I wasn't implying that you'd slack off, ma'am. I know you better than that by now. This is an unusual situation, so all I'm saying is that if you need me, you only have to ask. Just like you were for me with Dani, remember?' He forced back a frustrated sigh, but really she shouldn't be so touchy when he only had her interests at heart.

A brief silence followed his statement and he watched her gaze soften and her posture slightly relax.

'Yes, okay,' she finally said, a trace of tiredness creeping into her voice. 'I'm sorry, it's been a difficult few days. And thanks for the offer. I do appreciate it, even if sometimes it might appear that I don't.' She paused a moment. 'Actually, I've changed my mind. We'll go in my car because if I do have to go to the vet, I can always drop you off here on the way.'

Had his offer caused the change in plans? He certainly wasn't going to ask, because it was down to her. She was his boss and didn't owe him an explanation. Although, he had to admit, her unpredictability was intriguing. One moment she'd have her guard up and the next she'd show an unexpected vulnerability. It was like watching a dance, one where he was always a step behind.

When Dani had been kidnapped, Lauren had shown her gentle and compassionate side. She'd even knitted his daughter a cute pink elephant, which never left Dani's side and had taken pride of place over Edna, another soft toy. And they'd been out together in the local park so Dani could play with Tia and Ben. Yet Lauren acted as if that had never happened. She was a mystery.

But despite her little foibles, he found himself liking her more and more as time progressed. He was getting used to working with her, learning to understand her peculiar ways. She was so different from DCI Whitney Walker, who he had the utmost respect for and had thoroughly enjoyed working with. But that didn't mean one boss was better than the other. They both had an overriding desire to see justice done. And that was all that mattered... although he'd pay money to see them both working a case together. He smiled to himself as he left Lauren's office, headed over to the coat stand and pulled on his jacket ready for them to leave.

The stunning cliffs of Treryn Dinas overlooked the crystal-clear turquoise water and the white sandy Pedn Vounder beach. It was a breathtaking sight, and one Matt could have stared at all day. The crashing waves beneath them echoed in the silence that enveloped the scene of the abandoned red Fiesta which was cordoned off with yellow police tape that was flapping in the sea breeze.

Several forensic officers were huddled next to it, their white suits glaring against the car's faded paintwork. A number of uniformed officers were combing the surrounding area.

As they approached the car, Lauren straightened her jacket, the expression on her face stern and focused. A forensic officer, a woman in her mid-thirties, glanced up at them and then stepped forward.

'Any sign of the woman who owns the car? Or signs of a tussle inside?' Lauren asked.

The forensic officer shook her head, her brows furrowed in concentration. 'No, the vehicle's owner is nowhere to be seen and there's no sign of anything untoward having happened in or around the car.'

'I see. What else can you tell us?'

'The car's perfectly clean, as if it was intentionally parked here and left by the driver. There was a bag in the back containing a supermarket uniform, which I'll take back with us for further analysis, and a pair of flat black shoes, which will also be examined.'

Lauren crossed her arms, her gaze drifting off towards the endless ocean. 'We know she changed before leaving work at ten because she was going to meet someone. Maybe this was the spot they met.'

Matt scanned the area. 'It's a perfect place because there are no cameras. Which would make it virtually impossible to find out who she was with and the time of the meeting.'

'Was there anything else found in the car?' Lauren asked, directing her question to the forensics officer, who was still standing next to them.

'In the glove compartment there's the car registration details and the logbook. Also, we found a receipt from Turner's Car Repairs.'

Matt exchanged a glance with Lauren, a silent understanding passing between them. 'She knows Gareth Turner?' he said.

'It can't be a coincidence, surely. It's not as if that's the only repair shop in the vicinity of where she lives,' Lauren said.

'And we know our view on coincidences,' Matt said, forgetting that he was with Lauren and not back in Lenchester where they were always rejected and, if anything, had become part of the team's banter. 'There's no such thing,' he added, not wanting Lauren to realise his mistake. When he'd first joined her team she made it very clear that Cornwall was different from Lenchester and that he compared the two places at his peril.

'I agree. There's a definite link. We'll bring Turner in for further questioning,' Lauren said. 'Anything else at all that we should know?'

'No,' the officer said. 'It's a very clean car. More than most, for that matter.'

'Do you think it was wiped down?' Lauren asked, her brow furrowed in thought.

'No, not clean like that. Just a well-kept car. It might be old, but it's been well looked after. And there's no sign of a struggle or any blood anywhere,' the forensic officer replied, her voice steady and professional.

'We know that Yvonne Hughes is a very tidy person, which is in keeping with that. Was the car locked?' Matt asked, a thought entering his mind.

'Yes, it was. We had to break in.'

Lauren's mouth dropped open. Had the same thought now dawned on her, too?

She glanced at Matt. 'So it looks like Yvonne Hughes had planned this meet-up in advance and she willingly left her car to be with this other person. Most likely in their car, assuming that this person was also driving. Given how she was dressed, it was probably someone special.'

'Shall I call ahead and ask uniform to bring in Gareth Turner, ma'am?' Matt asked.

Lauren nodded, her gaze once again fixed on the sea, as if searching for answers in the rolling waves. 'Yes. He's the only link we have between the two cases. Surely he must know something and we're going to find out what it is.'

She sucked in a breath. Where was Yvonne Hughes? Who was she with? And was Freya Kempston's disappearance in any way connected?

This case had certainly taken a darker turn.

ELEVEN

FRIDAY, 8 MARCH

A surge of anticipation rippled through Lauren as she strode into the oppressive interview room with Matt following behind. 'Good to see you again, Mr Turner,' Lauren said, her voice slicing through the silence as she placed the manilla folder she'd been holding on the table in front of her.

Seated at the table, Gareth Turner had his arms folded tightly across his chest and he wore a scowl that wrinkled his broad forehead. He stared directly ahead, not bothering to look at either of them.

Matt sat beside Lauren and she nodded in his direction, signalling that he was to start the recording.

'Interview on Friday the eighth of March. Those present: DI Pengelly, DS Price and...' Matt's voice was firm and authoritative as he gestured to the man sitting opposite to speak.

Turner grimaced, his bottom lip sticking out defiantly. 'Gareth Turner. And it's not *good* for me to see you again. Your men barged into my workplace, totally unannounced, and without giving any reason other than I'm required for questioning, made me go out to the police car with them for everyone in the vicinity to see.'

The complaint hung in the air. It was a common ploy for the accused to play the victim and it wasn't going to wash with Lauren. She didn't care if the officers were a little heavy-handed with the man. If he had anything to do with the disappearances of Freya and Yvonne he deserved it, and she intended to find out the truth.

'Were you handcuffed?' she asked, her tone sounding faintly curious, even though she couldn't care less.

Turner huffed out a breath and glared at her. 'No, but they still marched me off the premises like a common criminal *and* one of my customers witnessed the whole thing because he was waiting for his car. It's hardly a good look for my business if people think the owner's in trouble with the police. Is it?'

She agreed, but that was beside the point. Their concern was with finding Freya and Yvonne. And if he had anything to do with it then what happened to his business was immaterial.

'You can tell anyone who asks that you're helping with our enquiries and that should satisfy their curiosity,' Lauren said, her tone measured.

'Yeah, if you say so. Anyway, I've got an appointment with my accountant later so can we please keep this brief,' Turner insisted, his arms still folded across his chest in defiance and glaring in the vague direction of Lauren and Matt.

Interesting that he was now getting a bit antagonistic.

Was he hiding something?

It was common knowledge that one of the best forms of *defence* was to go on the *offence*. It was a strategy that Lauren had often used in tricky situations, with great success. But if that was his game, then he wasn't going to get away with it.

'I'd like to discuss Yvonne Hughes with you,' she said, leaning forward and locking her gaze on to him until he finally met her eyes and squirmed awkwardly in his chair.

'I don't recognise that name,' Turner replied, a slight twitch in his right eye.

'I see. In that case, why did we find a receipt from your garage in her car?' She scrutinised his face for any indication that he remembered.

There was a silence while Turner stared into space as if trying to recall why the receipt was there.

'What make and model was the car?' Turner asked, cocking an eyebrow.

'It's an old red Fiesta.'

She watched as his eyes momentarily flickered with understanding.

'I do remember servicing a Fiesta of that description recently. If the paperwork shows the car as belonging to a Hughes, then that's probably the one.' His fingers traced an imaginary pattern on the table. 'You've got to remember that we work on a lot of cars. Often, I remember the vehicle itself and not the owner.'

Lauren opened the folder and pulled out a photocopy of the receipt and slid it over to him. 'Is this from your garage?'

'Why didn't you show it to me straight away?' he asked, glancing down at the piece of paper.

'Are you saying that, apart from servicing her car, you've never had any interaction with Yvonne Hughes?' Lauren asked, ignoring his previous question and resting her palms on the table. She peered at him intently.

'I don't think so.' His shoulders lifted slightly in a shrug.

'You don't *think*?' Lauren challenged.

'For God's sake. That's just what people say.' He shook his head, clearly annoyed. 'I don't remember ever meeting Yvonne Hughes. I can't even tell you what she looks like, or anything about her. Okay? Now do you believe me?'

'It's important for our investigation to be certain, as I'm sure you will appreciate. Where were you last night after ten o'clock?'

'At home,' Turner stated, straightening up in his chair.

'And can anybody vouch for you?' Lauren continued, her eyes searching his for any signs of deceit.

'I was in bed asleep, next to my wife. Feel free to ask her if you don't believe me.' His chin tilted upwards with a hint of defiance.

'Was she awake the whole time, then?' Lauren asked.

'Of course she wasn't. She went to bed before me and by the time I went up at around nine forty-five she was already asleep,' Turner said, averting his eyes.

Which meant that he could have easily slipped out without his wife knowing.

'What you're saying is that she can't actually vouch for you being there. Moving on, I'd like to revisit your *accidental* encounter with Freya Kempston at the shopping centre on Monday afternoon.'

'I've already told you all there is to know. We literally bumped into each other in the car park and had a quick chat about nothing. You know, the usual pleasantries when you bump into someone.' Turner's hands fidgeted, betraying his unease.

'It's odd that you recall Freya Kempston as a customer but claim to have no recollection of Yvonne Hughes,' Matt said, tilting his head to the side slightly, a frown etched onto his face. His voice echoed around the room, the accusation not lost on either party.

Lauren, whose arms were resting on the table while she was contemplating her next move, shot a quick glance at Matt, nodding in agreement. The hint of a smile tugged at the corners of her mouth. It was a good point, and one that she'd overlooked. She silently praised her sergeant for his observation. They would pursue this further.

'Obviously I remember some of my customers,' Turner said defensively, his hand running through his hair in a nervous gesture. His eyes darted between Lauren and Matt, a hint of desperation creeping into his voice. 'It's just I didn't remember the owner of the red Fiesta. The woman you mentioned.'

'Is that because Freya's younger than Yvonne and you think she's more attractive?' Lauren asked.

'No. Of course not. Like I told you, some people you remember and others you don't. Freya's American and chatty.'

'So Yvonne wasn't *chatty*?' Lauren said, pouncing on his answer.

'That's not what I meant. Look, Freya Kempston always talks a lot when I see her, and that's why I remember her. That's all.'

'Are you certain you didn't sneak out while your wife was asleep to meet up with Yvonne Hughes for a drink?' Lauren pressed, moving their conversation back to the woman, the chill in her voice hinting at a suspicion she had started to develop.

'Look, I've said that my wife was asleep and I can't do anything to prove otherwise. What's this all about?' He gave a sigh, fatigue etching lines into his forehead.

'Freya Kempston and Yvonne Hughes are both missing and you're the common link. You were the last person to have seen Freya Kempston, in the car park. Yvonne Hughes has a receipt from your workshop which suggests that you know her, or at least had dealings with her, even though you claim that you don't remember her.' Lauren's tone was unyielding, the seriousness of the situation etched in her words. She kept a keen eye on the man's reactions, looking for any tell-tale signs of guilt.

'It's all a coincidence. What about the guy I saw Freya Kempston with when she was at the centre?' He avoided eye contact and shifted in his chair.

What?

Where did that come from?

'And you've only just decided to mention this? Why?' Lauren demanded, the exasperation clear in her voice. 'What *guy* is this?' She made air quotes with her fingers, clearly unconvinced.

He clicked his teeth together, a nervous tic that Lauren had observed several times during their conversation. 'Look, I didn't want to get involved. The last time we spoke, you only asked me about when I bumped into her in the car park. I didn't know that two women were missing. Or that you were going to start pointing the finger at me.'

'When and where did you see Freya Kempston with this man?' Lauren leant forward.

'She was in the café of the large department store. I'd been in there looking for my wife's birthday present. The watch I told you about. I saw Freya sitting there with that man.'

'Can you describe him?' Matt asked, his pen poised above his notebook, ready to jot down any details.

'From where I was standing, he appeared to be in his early forties, good looking, brown hair and wearing trendy clothes. You know the sort of guy. The kind who women want to be with.'

'No, I don't. You tell me.' Lauren knew exactly what he meant but wanted him to spell it out to her.

'The guy that walks into a pub and women straight away stare at him, even if they're with you. And men usually like them too. It's just a thing about them. I can't explain if you don't know.'

'We do know what you mean,' Matt said, nodding towards Lauren. 'Could you tell from their conversation whether they were in a relationship or just having a casual chat? Was it heated or friendly? Give us more details,' Matt urged.

'I only gave them a quick glance. They were sitting opposite each other, engrossed in what looked like a serious conversation. Maybe they were more than friends, I can't say. It could be that she was trying to end things with him. All I can tell you is it looked intense. I didn't hang around staring at them. Can I leave now?' Turner's last words were spoken almost in a whisper, desperation creeping into his voice.

'We'll need to speak to your wife to find out if she remembers you being in bed after ten o'clock. But don't mistake that as us dropping our suspicions. You're the only known connection between these two women. You're not to leave town. At least not without first speaking to me. Do you understand?' Lauren said, her tone conveying that it wasn't up for negotiation.

'If you do want to speak again, I'd appreciate you not sending uniformed officers to haul me out of my workshop. I have a reputation to maintain. Phone and I'll be here. I'm innocent. I've done nothing wrong, and you can't prove otherwise,' he countered, his voice rising slightly as he finished speaking.

They escorted Turner to the front entrance, and once he'd gone, Lauren turned to Matt.

'Well, what's your gut telling you about him?' she asked as they headed down the corridor towards the office.

Matt rubbed his chin, his brow furrowed. 'He's jittery, no doubt about it. He knows them both, too. But I don't get the feeling that he has anything to do with the women going missing. The man Turner saw with Freya... that's a lead we need to chase. But how does he fit into the larger picture, and does he know Yvonne Hughes?'

Lauren nodded. 'Agreed. The mystery man is our next focus, once we've identified him. Turner's description wasn't great, but if this man's as charismatic as he suggested, then surely someone might remember him. We'll comb through the CCTV footage from the department store to confirm Turner's story and hopefully get a better look at Freya's café partner.' She paused, looking at Matt. 'We also need to get a statement from Turner's wife, to see if she can confirm his alibi. She might have woken during the night and seen him there.'

Matt nodded. 'Yes, but that doesn't mean we discount

Turner. He could be leading us down a rabbit hole when in fact he's involved.'

'He doesn't strike me as being clever enough for that, but I take your point. He's not going to be let off the hook completely. For now, we need to get moving on this new lead.'

TWELVE

FRIDAY, 8 MARCH

'Right, eyes front,' Lauren commanded, her tone cutting through the chatter in the room like a whip as she walked back into the office with Matt. 'We've interviewed Gareth Turner and now have a lead.'

All the team members – except Billy, who was engrossed in something on his screen – stared directly at Lauren.

'Billy,' Matt called out as he headed over to his desk and hung his jacket on the back of the chair.

'What?' The officer glanced up.

Matt marched over to him. 'The DI's about to feed back on our interview with Turner and wants everyone's attention.'

'Sorry, Sarge.' He glanced sheepishly at Lauren, who was staring directly at them. 'Ma'am.'

Matt didn't ask what was distracting him, in case it wasn't work-related and he didn't want Lauren to find out. It was best she assumed he was on a work task... which he could well have been.

'Okay, now I have your full attention,' Lauren continued. 'Gareth Turner denies knowing Yvonne Hughes, although when informed about the receipt in her car he can now

remember her car being serviced at his garage. He's also remembered that he'd seen Freya Kempston in the department store
café having an intense conversation with a man he didn't
recognise.'

'That sounds very convenient. Do you believe him, ma'am?'
Billy asked, frowning.

Lauren paced back and forth in front of the whiteboard.
'He doesn't have an airtight alibi for when Yvonne Hughes
came off work because his wife was asleep, supposedly next to
him. But, that said, we've got nothing concrete to hold him on.
Sergeant Price and I are both of the same mind on that.'

Matt headed over to where Lauren was standing and
scanned the team. 'That doesn't mean he's completely off our
radar. But for now, we need to focus on other aspects of the
case. We should consider Freya and Yvonne for a moment. If
we're to believe everything we've been told, they both have
secret lives. It's possible that both were having an affair or some
other relationship,' Matt said.

'Do you think that could be our link, Sarge?' Jenna asked.

Matt turned to Lauren for her to answer.

'It's certainly worth considering.' Lauren turned back to the
whiteboard, a marker pen in her hand. She drew a pair of
arrows coming from Yvonne's and Freya's names, converging on
a circled word *affair* with a question mark beside it.

'Is it possible they were seeing the same man?' Clem asked.

'Not that we're aware of,' Lauren said. 'All we know is that
Yvonne might've been meeting up with someone from work, but
not necessarily, according to her colleague. She could be seeing
someone else.'

'The same man that Freya Kempston was with?' Clem
asked.

'That makes sense,' Billy said. 'So all we've got to do is find
him.'

'Let's take a breath,' Matt said, holding his hand up. 'For a start, we've only got Turner's account of Freya having an intense conversation with a man in a café. That's hardly evidence of an affair, is it? And remember that both Freya and Yvonne mix in totally different social circles. Live in very different areas of St Ives.'

'St Ives is a small place. They're bound to have some connection,' Jenna said. 'Even if it's only going to Gareth Turner's place.'

'It's certainly something to consider,' Matt said, staring at the whiteboard and the connections Lauren had drawn.

'I want to sidestep for a moment,' Lauren said. 'If we assume that the missing women were cheating on their partners, why would they do that?' Lauren's question prompted an array of speculative glances among the team.

'People cheat for countless reasons. Perhaps their relationships were struggling,' Jenna said, her voice steady and thoughtful.

'The latest census estimates the divorce rate in the UK to be as high as forty-two per cent. It's increasing all the time,' Clem offered, his voice in the lecture mode that Matt had come to recognise and which had him forcing back a smile. 'Although it's not as high as in the US—'

'But from what we've learnt so far, neither relationship had yet broken down,' Matt interrupted before they were drawn down the long road of divorce statistics. 'We know that Yvonne Hughes was reportedly bored in her marriage, and she had recently discovered that her husband kissed a woman at his work Christmas party a couple of years ago, but she didn't appear to have any plans to leave her husband. At least, none that we're aware of. It was more that she liked to go out for a drink after she'd finished work to unwind a bit and have some fun.'

'We mustn't forget that she did change to working the late shift on a regular basis, and she was definitely meeting someone the night she disappeared,' Lauren said. 'We believe that she might have even changed into her new pink sequined dress.'

'And Freya Kempston was looking forward to meeting someone on the day she went missing, remember. It could be the same man,' Billy said.

'Which is why we need to find the man that she reportedly met in the café,' Matt said, bringing them back to where they were meant to be focusing. 'Also, we mustn't forget that CCTV footage showed Freya visiting a café later on her own. Why would she go to two cafés in such a short space of time?'

'Maybe she was meeting two men,' Billy said, a playful grin creeping across his face.

'Or she could have been waiting for a friend. We don't know about that, yet,' Matt said, giving an alternative explanation.

'Let's revisit the CCTV footage from the shopping centre,' Lauren said. 'Now we know that Freya Kempston met a man in the café in the department store, we have more to focus on. I asked the manager to forward the footage to us. Has it arrived?'

'Yes, ma'am, I have it,' Tamsin responded from behind her desk. 'Give me a second and I'll pull it up onto the larger screen so we can all check it together.'

Matt and Lauren turned so they were facing the screen at the front of the room, both standing with their arms folded. After a few seconds the screen flickered and brightened, and then the busy shopping centre was on display. A constant stream of people moving around.

'Set it from two o'clock, but let's watch at double the speed until we see Freya entering the department store,' Lauren said.

A collective hush descended on the room as they watched the footage, their attention unwavering.

'There she is,' Jenna called out. 'Going into the store from the left-hand side.'

Matt squinted at the footage, spotting Freya moving

through the main entrance to the store, along with other shoppers.

'Turner mentioned that the man she was sitting with was attractive and well dressed. It sounded like he was quite envious of him. Let's see if anyone of that description enters the store. We'll watch it in real-time,' Lauren proposed.

'Unless he was already inside,' Matt added, frowning slightly as he considered the likelihood of that.

'That's certainly possible,' Lauren agreed. 'If we don't spot anyone of that description, we'll wait for Freya to exit the shop and see who leaves after her.'

The team studied the footage in silence, with renewed interest, watching the comings and goings of the shoppers. But no one matched the mystery man's description.

'Shall I speed forward to when she leaves, ma'am?' Tamsin asked, giving a frustrated sigh, which echoed Matt's feelings entirely.

'Yes, that's a good idea, because otherwise we could be watching for ages,' Lauren said, irritation creeping into her tone.

Tamsin fast-forwarded the footage and soon Freya could be seen leaving the shop, holding two carrier bags, one in each hand.

'It looks like she's by herself and has been shopping,' Jenna said.

'Let's continue watching for a couple more minutes and see who else comes out,' Lauren said.

They continued staring at the screen, but nobody of the man's description left the department store.

'Where the hell is he?' Billy muttered. 'Do you think we missed him? Maybe he isn't as fit as Turner suggested. He could be ordinary looking and so we totally ignored him when he left?'

Matt had considered that but then rejected it. 'Turner was very clear with his description so I think it's unlikely he could be completely wrong. Bearing in mind that no one even close to that description has left, I think what's more likely is that this man came out of the shop *before* Freya, because after their meeting she wandered around buying things. Hence the carrier bags she was holding,'

It seemed the most logical answer.

'Good point, Matt. Rewind the footage until say twenty minutes before Freya comes out,' Lauren said.

Tamsin followed Lauren's instructions, and they resumed their careful analysis, methodically scrutinising each male going in and out of the store.

'Wait!' Jenna's voice cut through the silence, sharp and urgent. 'Stop and rewind a couple of seconds. I think I've seen someone.'

The room froze in anticipation as Tamsin rewound the footage.

'Who is it?' Lauren enquired, as all eyes were focused on the screen.

Jenna rose from her chair, determination etched on her features as she marched to the front of the room. Her eyes narrowed as she examined the face on the screen, recognition flickering in them. Her finger pointed at the man leaving the store from the door furthest left, slightly shielded by three women leaving at the same time. 'That's Callum Scott. He's one of our neighbours,' she said with certainty.

A sense of excitement stirred among the team and there was a tangible shift in energy in the room. Matt's pulse quickened at the possibility they now had something to work on.

'What do you know about him?' Lauren asked, her attention immediately shifting to Jenna.

The officer turned away from the whiteboard and faced the team, her gaze clear and focused. 'He's a nice guy, in his late thirties and lives alone. Always friendly. Pretty unassuming, I'd say.'

'Would you agree with Turner's description that he's the

sort of man women are drawn to?' Matt asked. 'Because he made a big deal out of it. He also said that men like him, too.'

'I do sort of get what he means. He does have something about him that's attractive, in a non-threatening way,' Jenna said, giving a gentle shrug.

'What else can you tell us about him?' Lauren asked, tapping her fingers on the edge of the whiteboard, before writing his name under Freya's.

'Not much, I'm afraid, because I don't see him often and even then it's not in a social setting. He's more a passing acquaintance. I've occasionally seen him with a woman, but never the same one more than a couple of times. Maybe Freya's having a fling with him? It's possible, I suppose. But... surely they'd be more careful than to meet up at the St Austell shops where so many local people go. Meeting in the café is a huge risk. For a start, they were seen by Turner. And possibly other people, too.'

'That's what we need to find out,' Matt said, thinking that the officer could be right. It did seem strange that they'd be so brazen about it.

'Well, we need to interview him straight away and find out the truth. Jenna, I want you to ask him to come to the station,' Lauren ordered. 'We also need to speak to Dale Cooper, who works at the supermarket with Yvonne, because we know they're very friendly. We'll find out if Katrina was right and there's something going on between them. Our only common thread in these cases right now is that both women have been involved with someone else. But if it's two different men, as seems likely, then where does that leave us?'

A hush fell over the room as the team digested Lauren's words. They all stared at the whiteboard, at the photos pinned up of Freya Kempston and Yvonne Hughes. Two seemingly very different women with nothing of substance to link them.

'It's a bloody mystery, if you ask me,' Billy said.

'Thank you for your insight, Billy. I think we've all realised that,' Lauren said, glancing at the officer and rolling her eyes.

Billy's expression dropped, but not before he cast a glance in Tamsin's direction and pulled a face that, luckily for him, Lauren didn't notice. Matt felt sorry for him, being spoken to like a child by Lauren, but Billy had been there long enough to realise that making quips wouldn't endear him to their boss at a time when she wanted them all to focus.

'It could be someone who didn't like the women's behaviour,' Clem suggested, breaking the silence. 'But that would mean that this someone not only knows Freya and Yvonne but knows them well enough to have insight into their personal lives. And that's where the theory comes unstuck.'

'That's the problem,' Jenna said, giving a sigh. 'Freya Kempston's background is so different from Yvonne's that it's hard to believe there's a mutual contact. What are we missing?'

'Yeah, well maybe that's not the thing connecting them,' Billy said, his voice sounding eager. 'It might be a red herring. I think there's something else that we've missed, and we don't yet know what it is. So maybe we shouldn't be focusing on the fact that they both could be cheating on their partners.'

'You could be right, Billy,' Lauren said, nodding, her tone much warmer than before. 'But as these are the only leads we have, we need to pursue them. I want research carried out into Callum Scott and Dale Cooper while Sergeant Price and I go to the supermarket. Clem and Billy, you take that. Tamsin, continue looking into any potential links between the two women. By the time we get back I expect Scott to be here. Jenna, that's for you to deal with.'

'Ma'am, what shall I say if Callum Scott asks why he's being asked to come to the station? I don't want to alert him,' Jenna asked.

'Tell him we're questioning everyone who lives in the vicinity of Freya Kempston's house. Say that an officer called at his house when undertaking our house-to-house enquiries and there was no answer. Don't put him on his guard. Let him think that we've spoken to all the neighbours, so he's one of many being questioned. We want his cooperation. If he thinks we've asked him in specially, he may decide to ask for legal representation. And that will only delay matters.'

'Yes, ma'am. I'm sure I can convince him to come in for a chat. Like I said, he's a nice man, and has never come across as being aggressive or challenging.' Jenna sighed. 'I still can't believe that he's having a fling with Freya. It doesn't seem likely.'

'Well, you should know by now that things are never as they seem. Once you've arranged for Scott to come in, do some more research into Gareth Turner – in case we've missed something.'

The room sprang into action, and Matt grabbed his jacket and followed Lauren out of the office. Despite the link they'd uncovered being tenuous, he couldn't help feeling that they were on the brink of discovering the truth about what had happened to the women.

THIRTEEN

FRIDAY, 8 MARCH

Lauren and Matt headed through the automatic doors into the supermarket and navigated their way past the tempting jam doughnuts that were strategically placed in the entrance to persuade customers to buy them.

Lauren's stomach rumbled loudly, and Matt looked at her and grinned.

'You sound like I feel,' he said. 'I haven't eaten since breakfast. If we have time, shall we pick up something on the way back to the station? Maybe a sandwich or a salad.'

'Good idea, I'm starving,' she said as they headed past the bank of self-service checkouts and up to the customer service counter.

A young woman with bright cheeks and dark curls, many of which were escaping from her hair tie, stood behind it.

Lauren held out her warrant card. 'Good morning, we'd like to speak to Dale Cooper; is he working today?'

'Yes,' the woman said, giving a nod, her eyes wide as she studied Lauren and Matt. She pressed on the tannoy. 'Dale, please come to the customer service desk immediately. Dale, customer service desk.'

Lauren and Matt took a step back to clear the counter. Within minutes, a man dressed in the red-and-blue supermarket uniform hurried past the checkout queues and headed towards them, an apprehensive expression on his face.

'Are you Dale Cooper?' Lauren asked, stepping forward and bringing him to a halt.

'Yes, that's me,' he answered, frowning.

'I'm DI Pengelly and this is DS Price. Is there somewhere private we can talk?' Lauren asked, her voice firm.

'Umm... Yes. Sure. What's it about?' Cooper replied, his brows knitted together.

'We'd rather talk in private,' Lauren said, leaving no room for discussion.

'Okay. Mr Gable, the manager, is out. We can use his office.'

They fell in step behind Cooper until they reached the back of the shop and headed through the double door marked 'Staff Only'. He took them into the manager's office, which they'd been in before.

Cooper sat behind the untidy desk, which had several piles of papers in the middle, and Lauren and Matt took the two chairs opposite.

'We'd like to ask you about your relationship with Yvonne Hughes,' Lauren began, her tone relaxed but probing.

The colour drained from Cooper's face. 'What relationship?'

'Are you and Yvonne seeing each other outside of work?' Matt asked, leaning forward slightly in his chair.

'W-we're friends, that's all,' Cooper stuttered, his hands rubbing up and down his thighs. 'Sometimes we go for a drink after work, but that's all. And there's usually a gang of us.'

'But there are occasions when it's the two of you in the pub. When you've gone together, or you're the last to leave,' Lauren stated, attempting to lock eyes with him, but he wouldn't meet her gaze.

'Yes. But not like *that*. We get on well and like to chat. She's married. I don't want to get involved.'

Lauren observed Cooper, studying his reactions. His discomfort was apparent, but that didn't necessarily indicate he was guilty of anything.

'Explain what you mean,' Lauren demanded, ensuring that her tone reflected the need for an honest answer. 'What exactly don't you want to get involved in?'

'Her personal life.'

Lauren went on alert. Was he going to corroborate what they'd been told by Katrina Pick about Yvonne and her husband?

'We need more. What can you tell us about the state of Yvonne's marriage?' she asked, raising a brow.

He drew in a breath. 'All I know is what Yvonne's told me. She hates it at home. Her husband couldn't care less about her. He's always working, and when he's home he sleeps. They hardly ever see each other,' Cooper admitted, a hint of sympathy in his voice.

'Has she ever mentioned leaving him?' Lauren pressed, this time managing to make him look directly at her.

Cooper squirmed under her penetrating gaze. 'No. When I suggested she should leave and start her life over, she said she wouldn't because of her son. She did say that once Spencer leaves home she might change her mind. And...' His voice fell away.

'Continue,' Lauren pushed.

'She recently found out that he'd been with another woman and that upset her.'

'What did she tell you about it?'

'Not much. It was someone from work. I didn't ask for details because it seemed like she didn't want to talk about it.'

'So, would you say that you and Yvonne are simply friends

who go out for a drink occasionally?' Matt asked, the corners of his mouth pulling down into a grimace, his tone sceptical.

'Yes, I suppose so.'

'Does Yvonne think there's more to it than friendship?'

The question that Lauren had been about to ask. Clearly the pair of them were thinking along the same lines, which didn't put Cooper in the clear. If anything, it made him more suspicious.

'No... but...' Cooper glanced away, his hands twisting together in his lap.

'But what?' Lauren prompted, her interest piqued. She watched him closely.

'Well... I'm not certain, but...' Cooper hesitated, his eyes flitting nervously. 'I think Yvonne might have met someone.'

A prickle ran up and down Lauren's spine. Was this the clue that could break their case wide open? Or was Cooper trying to stop them from suspecting him?

'And what makes you think that?'

'Look, I don't want to get involved,' Cooper protested weakly, his resolve clearly wavering under their intense scrutiny.

'Dale,' Lauren snapped, her voice cutting through the tension and making him start in his seat. 'Yvonne's missing. And anything we can learn about her whereabouts is crucial. Tell us what you know and stop giving us the runaround, or we'll charge you with obstruction of justice.'

What was wrong with the man? Didn't he realise that this woman, who was supposedly his friend, could be in danger?

'Last night...' he started, his voice hardly audible. 'Yvonne and me... we went for a quick drink after work. We were on our own. But after twenty minutes she got a message on her phone and then... then she said she had to leave.' His eyes darted from Lauren to Matt.

'And?' Lauren pushed, knowing that there was more to this story, but for some reason Cooper was unwilling, or unable, to tell them without being coerced.

'She said she was tired and heading home,' he finally continued. 'But I didn't believe her. She... she blushed, turning bright red as she spoke. I think she was going to meet someone else... Actually, I know she did.'

'How do you know?' Matt asked, his brow furrowing.

'Umm... because... I followed her,' Cooper admitted. 'And I saw them together.'

Irritation coursed through Lauren and her fists clenched in her lap. 'For goodness' sake. Why the hell didn't you tell us when she was reported missing? Do you realise how much time we've wasted because of you holding this back?'

'I...' Cooper faltered, his face a mix of regret and fear. 'I didn't want to get involved.'

'You're *already* involved,' Lauren shot back, her annoyance growing by the second. 'I want you to start from the beginning. From the moment you were in the pub.'

'Okay. We left work at the same time, and drove our own cars to the pub,' Cooper began, a tremor in his voice. He glanced down at the floor, his eyes squeezed tightly shut, before audibly sucking in a breath and glancing up to face Lauren. 'Yvonne was dressed up, much more than I expected for going out drinking. She'd usually change into jeans or something casual... not a pink sparkly dress.' He paused, as if he was remembering the scene.

'Did you ask her why she was wearing such fancy clothes?' Matt probed gently, his tone a softer contrast to Lauren's clinical directness.

'No. I thought... Well, it sounds stupid now. It gave me this... this hope that maybe she was starting to see me differently, like... like I see her.'

'So, she isn't just a friend to you, as you claimed before?' Matt asked, keeping his voice low.

Lauren sat back in the chair as a signal to Matt to continue with his line of questioning, which appeared to be drawing out Cooper more.

'Okay yes, but she's married, and I won't cross that line,' Cooper admitted, his voice laced with regret, as he glanced up and met Matt's eyes. 'Like I told you, after she got the text, she left and said she was going home. Something didn't feel right, so I decided to follow her. She drove all the way to Pedn Vounder beach and parked her car next to another one.' He paused, a flicker of uncertainty crossing his face. 'She stepped out of her car, locked it, and climbed into the passenger seat of the other one. Then they drove off.'

'Did you manage to get a look at who she was meeting?' Lauren asked, not intending to tell Cooper that they already knew where Yvonne had driven to.

'No, it was too far away for me to see, and it was dark. There's not much lighting around there,' Cooper replied, running a hand through his hair.

'What about the car? Did you recognise the make or model?' Matt asked.

Cooper shook his head, resting his elbows on his knees. 'It was some sort of SUV, but I couldn't tell the make. Maybe a Mazda CX-5 or a BMW? Honestly, they all look the same to me. And with it being so dark, I couldn't tell for sure.'

'Did it look like she was being coerced into getting into this car?' Matt asked.

'No, not at all. If anything, she was keen to go. When she first got out of her car, she straightened her dress and sort of fluffed up her hair. There was nothing sinister going on. Apart from the mystery over who he was.'

'How do you know it was a *he* and not a *she*?' Lauren asked, her voice steady. Had he seen more than he was initially letting on? And, if so, why was he keeping it quiet?

Cooper's brow furrowed in thought. 'I don't know for sure. I just assumed it was a man.'

'Could Yvonne have seen you watching her?' Lauren asked.

'No. My car was hidden beside a tree. And she wouldn't have realised I was following her because I carefully kept my distance and made sure there were cars between us during the journey.'

'Even when you got to the beach? Because surely that would've been deserted?' Lauren said, frowning.

'It's very open around there so I stopped when I saw where she was heading. After a short while I drove in and parked. I'm sorry for keeping quiet when we were told that Yvonne had gone missing. But I honestly thought that she hadn't gone home for the night... or even that she had left her husband but... Do you think something's happened to her?' He shut his eyes briefly, then reopened them, revealing a flicker of worry. Maybe she'd been wrong. Maybe he didn't know any more than they did.

'That's what we're here to determine, Dale,' Lauren stated, her tone indicating the gravity of the situation. She stood from the squeaky office chair, smoothing out the creases in her trousers with brisk efficiency. 'We appreciate your cooperation. Your information could be vital to our investigation.'

'Is... is there anything else I can do?' Cooper asked, the expression on his face a mix of guilt and worry. 'I couldn't bear to think of anything terrible happening to Yvonne. You have to know that. I was wrong in keeping what I knew from you, I realise that now. But it wasn't for any reason other than to protect her.'

However misguided that might be.

'If anything comes to mind, anything at all, get in touch

with us straight away,' Matt said, offering a reassuring smile to Cooper.

They all left the office and returned to the main shopping area, where they were greeted by the low ring of the checkout scanners, and customers pushing their trolleys, oblivious to the fact that what could be a pivotal interview had just taken place.

After Cooper left them, Lauren and Matt exited through the automatic doors into the mild spring afternoon. A quietness fell over them as they headed back towards the car.

Lauren broke the silence. 'What do you make of Cooper's statement, Matt?' She pulled out her keys, and clicked the unlock button as they approached the vehicle.

'It's what we've been waiting for. Proof that Yvonne was seeing someone. But is Cooper right that she might have gone off with this person, whoever they might be? Because if so it's likely that her disappearance was nothing to do with Freya's.' Matt said, his voice thoughtful.

They got into the car and as Lauren started the engine she let out a sigh. 'I've no idea. But we definitely need to look into this unknown person. Pedn Vounder beach isn't exactly a typical place for a casual rendezvous, is it?'

'No,' Matt agreed. 'A quiet romantic spot, perhaps? Or somewhere discreet for something else altogether?'

As the car hummed into life and they pulled out of the car park, Matt's ominous comment left them silent, both lost in thought at its implications.

Lauren's fingers drummed rhythmically on the steering wheel. 'Once we're back at the station, I'll get the team to start digging into Yvonne's connections. Maybe the person she met isn't as unknown as we think.'

As Lauren's words echoed in the car, the atmosphere was filled with a renewed sense of purpose. They had a clear direction now: leads to pursue and questions needing answers. Every minute counted, and their drive back to the station marked the start of the next phase in the investigation.

Lauren's fingers kept up their rhythmic drumming, a silent metronome counting down the time. The supermarket was soon a speck in her rear-view mirror, a reminder of the ordinary world they had temporarily left behind. Their focus now was on finding out where Yvonne had gone, and whether it was linked to Freya's disappearance.

FOURTEEN

FRIDAY, 8 MARCH

'Ma'am,' Jenna called out, the moment Lauren and Matt entered the office, her voice echoing through the bustling room. The chatter and movement around them subsided as if a switch had been flipped. 'Callum Scott's in interview room three. When I contacted him and asked him to come in, I said we thought he might be able to help us with some enquiries. He was perfectly fine about it.'

Lauren and Matt turned their attention to Jenna, who was seated at her desk. 'Didn't he push you for more information?' Matt asked, his face a mix of curiosity and anticipation.

Jenna shrugged. 'I said that we'd been speaking to everyone in the area about an incident and he seemed to accept that. He didn't mention Freya at all.'

'Thanks. Is there anything else we need to be caught up on before we interview him?' Lauren asked, scanning the room so the team understood her query was addressed to all of them.

'I've discovered that Gareth Turner's being investigated by HMRC for tax fraud,' Jenna said after the others all shook their heads indicating they had nothing to report.

'Really? How did you find that out?' Lauren asked.

'You don't want to know, ma'am,' Jenna said, a conspiratorial smile on her face.

'Why not, are you a spy?' Billy asked.

'Let's just say I have a friend who works there. Anyway, it's nothing to do with our investigation, so I take it you don't want me to pursue it, ma'am?'

'No, we'll leave that for them to deal with.'

'At least now we know why he sits on the beach thinking,' Jenna said.

'True...' Lauren agreed, before turning to Matt. 'We'll speak to Scott now. I'll drop my stuff off in the office and come back for you.'

She strode into her office, her steps quick and purposeful. Once inside she hung her jacket on the back of the door and dropped her bag onto the desk. She swiftly reached for her phone, hoping to find a message from the vet. She hadn't had a chance to check earlier because of driving.

The screen blinked to life, revealing a text notification. A surge of relief washed over her as she read the words:

Tia's ready for collection anytime up until 6pm.

She hastily tapped out a response saying that she'd get there as soon as she could.

With a spring in her step, Lauren returned to the main office and walked towards Matt, who was engaged in conversation with Clem. He noticed her and came over to where she was standing.

'Let's go,' she said, trying to hold back the smile that wanted to plaster itself across her face, but not sure that she'd managed it.

They were silent until leaving the room and then Matt turned to her.

'You're looking a lot happier than a few moments ago. Have you had some news about Tia?'

'Doesn't anything get past you?' she said, the severity of her words mitigated by the soft chuckle that left her lips as they continued walking down the corridor.

'I think even the most unobservant person would have noticed,' Matt replied.

'Actually, yes. She can come home today. Providing I'm there before six o'clock to pick her up.'

A flicker of relief swept across Matt's face. 'I'm so pleased. And if anything comes up here, you're going to leave me to deal with it, I hope? Surely by now you trust me to take charge during your absence.'

'Yes, I will leave you in charge. And yes, I do trust you,' she admitted, with a shrug. 'But for now let's focus on the task in hand. Interviewing Callum Scott.'

They entered the interview room and Lauren's eyes were immediately drawn to the attractive man lounging back in his chair and appearing relaxed, showing no signs of tension. That was most unusual in an interview situation, so either he was a very good actor or he genuinely believed he had nothing to worry about.

Scott smiled at them. Now Lauren understood what Gareth Turner had meant about him. There was an indefinable quality about the man that was appealing. Unnerving, almost. And she'd always believed herself to be immune to charms like that.

'Good afternoon, Mr Scott,' Lauren said, her tone direct, determined not to let his appearance and manner interfere with the interview. 'I'm DI Pengelly and this is DS Price. We've asked you in because we'd like to talk to you about Freya Kempston.'

'Freya? What about her?' Scott frowned, confusion in his voice.

'She's missing. Didn't you know?' Matt asked.

'No.' He shook his head vigorously. 'That's awful. I've been away for work for a couple of days. I got back late last night and hadn't left the house when Jenna called. Why didn't she tell me?'

'Where did you go?' Lauren asked, her eyes focused on Scott, searching for any sign of emotion, and ignoring his question.

'I was visiting a client in Bath. I'm a software engineer, and on the team developing their new operating system,' Scott replied, his hands resting on the table.

Lauren leant forward, staring directly at him. 'Can anyone vouch for your whereabouts?'

'Why?' Scott questioned, his voice uncertain.

'Freya's been missing since Monday afternoon and you were one of the last people to see her. You were with her in a café at St Austell shopping centre,' Lauren explained.

'How do you know that? I didn't mention our meeting to anyone and, as far as I know, neither did she...'

A secret meeting. Interesting.

'It doesn't matter how we know,' Lauren said, a dismissive wave of her hand. 'We do. Can you confirm seeing Freya on Monday?'

'Yes. But when I left her, she was going to do some shopping. We weren't together for long.'

'And was it a prearranged meeting?' Lauren pressed further.

'Um...' Scott hesitated, a fleeting look of concern crossing his features. 'Look, I don't want to get involved. Anthony, her husband, is my friend and I don't want to say anything to cause him grief and—'

'Mr Scott,' Lauren interrupted, her voice firm. 'Freya's missing. If you have *any* information that can help us find her, we want to hear it, now. Do you understand?'

'Yes.' Scott nodded, his relaxed stance long gone. He was now sitting totally upright in the chair.

'Good. Now, this meeting you had with Freya. Had it been arranged in advance?'

Scott's shoulders slumped slightly. 'Okay. I'll tell you what I know,' he began, his voice tinged with a mix of regret and unease. 'A couple of weeks ago, I took my nephew to the Eden Project near St Austell. I saw Freya in the café, sitting at one of the tables with a man. She looked up and saw me. I waved, but at the time I didn't think she'd seen me because she didn't respond. It didn't register that she was actually *with* this man, if you know what I mean, because they didn't appear close. They weren't engrossed in conversation or holding hands or being intimate.' Scott paused, silence enveloping the room.

'But she was with him?' Matt asked, after Scott had remained quiet for several seconds.

'Yes. It turned out she was,' Scott confirmed, his gaze fixed on some distant point in the room. 'Freya contacted me and asked to meet, but it had to be away from where we lived and during the day. She didn't say what it was about other than asking me to please not tell anyone. I agreed and didn't push to find out what it was about because she seemed so het up. We arranged to meet on Monday, because that was the soonest I could find time, what with work being so busy. It was only when we met that I discovered the issue. Freya assured me that she'd only met this guy as a friend, and that it hadn't gone any further. She said it was nice to have someone to talk to who actually listened to her. She begged me not to tell Anthony because he wouldn't believe her and then he'd get jealous over nothing. That would lead to him becoming angry and she feared that happening.'

'Did you believe her?' Matt asked, his brow furrowed with scepticism.

Scott sighed, a conflicted expression crossing his face. 'I did about Anthony. He does have a temper when pushed... but... did I believe the meeting was as innocent as Freya said it was?' He paused, appearing to contemplate his response. 'She was seeing him during the day and so it wasn't like they were out at night in some quiet, out-of-the-way pub. Also, when I noticed them, they weren't being intimate, like I already said.' He gave a sigh. 'Freya and Anthony are my friends. Anthony and I go way back. I guess I wanted to believe her. I do know that Anthony can be unnecessarily jealous at times... Look, rightly or wrongly, I told her that she shouldn't be seeing someone behind Anthony's back, but that I wouldn't say anything. She made me promise. And I did.'

Lauren leant forward; finally they might be getting somewhere. 'Can you describe the man Freya was with?'

'He was sitting down, so I couldn't see how tall he was. He had light brown, slightly greying hair. He looked smartly dressed and appeared relaxed and comfortable in his own skin. I'd say he was in his late forties to early fifties. Just a normal guy.'

'And it definitely didn't appear romantic?' Matt asked. 'Are you absolutely sure they weren't holding hands?'

'I didn't stare at them, so I suppose I couldn't be one hundred per cent certain they weren't holding hands under the table. But, honestly, they looked like a couple of friends out enjoying each other's company. That's why I believed Freya.'

'Do you think Anthony might've guessed that she was seeing someone and followed her there?' Lauren asked, her mind whirring with possibilities.

Scott shifted in his seat. 'I can't answer that,' he said, his voice laced with apprehension. 'All I know is that he wouldn't have liked it. Freya was right about that.'

The weight of revelations and unanswered questions hovered ominously. The investigation was finally beginning to unfold.

'In Freya's journal there was an entry that mentioned meeting X on the fourth of March. The implication was that she was looking forward to it. Do you think you're X? And, if so, why would she be eager to meet you?' Lauren questioned, her voice tinged with suspicion.

Scott's expression was one of genuine confusion. 'It can't be me. I saw them together two weeks ago, and she contacted me straight away. Why would she be looking forward to seeing me? It makes no sense. It wasn't like some sort of social thing.'

Lauren's gaze intensified, searching for any signs of deception. But there were none. 'Can you tell us anything about the man Freya was with that might help in our enquiries? Because if it's not you, then we urgently need to trace him.'

'No. She didn't tell me anything about their friendship and I didn't ask,' Scott replied immediately, giving a shake of his head.

It wasn't sitting right; Lauren needed more details. 'Did she mention his name? Or say what he did for a living? Or where he lived? Surely she can't have said *nothing* about him?'

'I'm telling you, all she said was that he was a friend. She let nothing slip, and I didn't push for any details. Her sole purpose for wanting the meeting was to make me promise not to say anything to anyone, especially Anthony. And I kept that promise. Well... until now.'

'I can't believe you didn't try to find out anything about this man. Freya's your friend. Her husband's your friend. Yet you were totally disinterested in him, even though she was determined to make sure you told no one that she'd seen him. You can see how this is sounding a bit strange, can't you?' Lauren said, a frustrated sigh leaving her lips.

'Okay, it might seem odd to you, but I believed Freya and so didn't pursue it. I have nothing more to tell you. May I leave, now? I have work.'

Lauren's intuition nagged at her. Something wasn't adding up. Not least Scott's lack of concern for Freya's wellbeing. He hadn't seemed worried about it at all. It was a red flag, that was for sure.

'You can go but before you do, what car do you drive?'

'I have a VW Tiguan,' Scott said, his gaze meeting Lauren's.

The hairs rose on the back of Lauren's neck. An SUV. The type of car Yvonne Hughes was seen getting into. 'What colour is it?'

'Gunmetal grey. Why?'

Dark.

'Do you know Yvonne Hughes?' she asked, hoping to catch him off guard.

Scott frowned and shook his head. 'Not that I recall. Why are you asking?'

'It's part of our enquiries. We've finished for now, but we may wish to speak to you again,' Lauren said.

As they escorted Scott to the exit she exchanged a glance with Matt.

'I know what you're thinking, because I am, too,' Lauren said, once Scott had left the building. 'Even though he gave all the right answers, he wasn't bothered by Freya's disappearance. It was as if he already knew where she was and forgot that he should show some signs of interest.'

'My sentiments exactly,' Matt said, nodding in agreement. 'If he was such a good friend, then surely her being missing would worry him. I think he knows more than he's telling us.'

'The trouble is, at the moment we have nothing to hold him on other than a hunch,' Lauren said, clenching and unclenching her fists. 'Not only that, did you notice that his description of the man Freya met was very similar to himself? Now, why would he do that?'

'To make sure not to be caught out?' Matt suggested. 'At least he'd always remember what he'd told us.'

'Hmmm... maybe.'

'I'll ask Tamsin to search through the CCTV footage from the shopping centre again. Let's see if we can at least spot Scott in the car park so we can identify where he went after he'd seen

Freya,' Matt said. 'And in the meantime, why don't you collect Tia. Leave me to deal with this.'

Lauren pondered for a few minutes before deciding. 'Okay. But check if he was in Bath at the time he said. If he was absent from the area when both women went missing, then maybe he's taking them somewhere or has done something with them.'

'Consider it done,' Matt said. 'Off you go. I'll text if there's anything new to report.'

FIFTEEN

MONDAY, 11 MARCH

Lauren reluctantly left for work at ten minutes past eight in the morning, after walking and feeding Tia and Ben, grabbing a quick breakfast of toast and tea, and putting on a load of washing. She'd been so tied up with the case and Tia that, apart from the white shirt she was wearing, she'd run out of work clothes – always a dark trouser suit with plain shirt. Of course, she could always wear leggings, hoodie and trainers – her attire of choice when she wasn't at work – but she doubted that would go down well with her superiors.

She glanced over her shoulder as she got in the car and could see both dogs sitting on the sofa, resting their heads on the back cushion and staring forlornly out of the window.

Talk about guilt-tripping.

Over the weekend, Tia had seemed almost like her old self, apart from the raw pink shaved patches on her belly and paw, a reminder of the surgery she'd endured, and the fact that she had to wear a cone for another few days to stop her from tugging at the stitches.

Betty had agreed to check on the dogs every couple of hours. She was going to let them out into the garden for a short time and make sure there weren't any problems. Normally when Lauren was at work she'd leave the back door open for them so they could go in and out as they wanted. But she didn't want to do that yet in case Tia got her cone caught on a branch or got stuck somewhere.

Lauren drove to the station and was seated at her desk by eight thirty, already going through her emails. Although she'd stayed at home over the weekend, she'd kept in regular contact with those members of the team who'd been working, but there'd been no further news on the missing women, despite the press conference about Freya Kempston. She'd have to ask the DCI if they could have another one to let the community know about Yvonne Hughes. The problem was, she didn't want the media to make a link between the two disappearances until they were absolutely convinced there was one.

The sharp ring of the phone on her desk cut through her thoughts. 'Pengelly,' she answered, her tone brisk.

'Ma'am, I have a Mr Brendon Evans in reception,' Sergeant Hicks said. 'He's here to report his partner, Hannah Gifford, missing.'

Lauren's heart pounded in her chest. A third woman? That put a whole new complexion on the situation. It was now becoming near on impossible to write off these disappearances as mere coincidence.

'Thank you, Sergeant. I'll be down shortly.'

The phone clicked and she replaced the handset on the desk. She sucked in a breath, bracing herself for the onslaught. She'd planned on going home to see Tia and Ben at lunchtime, but no way could that happen now.

She headed into the office and stood in the centre of the room. She scanned the members of her team, who had all arrived and appeared involved in their tasks.

'Attention, everyone,' she announced, the tone of her voice

causing all of them to turn and look at her. 'We have a third missing woman. Her partner's in reception.'

'Bloody hell. We know what that means. Lots of late nights and no social life,' Billy said, giving a loud sigh.

Lauren stared at the officer, frowning. 'You do realise that it's part of the job. If you—'

'I think he was joking, ma'am,' Clem said, interrupting her.

'Oh. Well, okay then.' She glanced at Billy, who had a tentative smile on his lips.

'Sorry, ma'am,' the officer said.

'Matt, you're with me,' she said, moving on, not wanting to be sidetracked. 'I want you to hear this first-hand. Tamsin, I've been informed the missing woman is named Hannah Gifford and her partner is Brendon Evans. That's all I know for now. Start digging and see what you can come up with. Any information could be vital.'

'Yes, ma'am, I'm on to it,' Tamsin said, turning to her computer screen.

Lauren motioned for Matt to follow her out of the room and they headed down the corridor towards reception.

'How was your weekend, ma'am?' Matt asked, breaking the silence.

'I spent most of the time with Tia and Ben. So, very quiet.'

'I envy you that. It was chaotic in my parents' house, especially on Sunday. You've seen how small it is. Add in some visitors, as in a couple my parents invited over, and you can imagine what it was like.'

'Have you thought about finding your own place, now you're more settled?'

She shuddered at the thought of having to endure the overcrowding Matt faced on a daily basis.

'Not really. It's a bit soon. And it's much easier having Mum and Dad on the spot, so to speak, to look after Dani.'

'Yes, I get it,' she said. Although, if she was honest, she

didn't really, having chosen to spend most of her time since leaving university living on her own.

'How's Tia holding up?'

'Better than expected,' she said, her voice softening at the mention of her dog. 'She's recovering well. But hates having the cone around her neck. It's only for a few more days until her stiches come out. Honestly, it's a huge relief to see her almost back to her old self. She's even started bossing Ben around again.'

'I'm glad to hear that,' Matt said. 'Dani will be too.'

Lauren glared at him. 'I thought we agreed that you weren't going to tell her.'

Matt shook his head, scratching at the back of his neck. 'She overheard me telling my mum, so I had to explain that Tia was in hospital but she was going to be fine. You know how much Dani loves your dogs.'

Lauren did know. When she'd arranged to meet Matt and Dani at a local park a few times with the dogs it had been like a mutual admiration society. The dogs had played non-stop with Dani, not wanting to leave her alone, and vice versa. It was always a bit odd spending time outside of work with her sergeant, but she was fond of Dani and enjoyed her constant chatter and incessant questions.

'Tell Dani that Tia's doing well and looks forward to their next playdate,' Lauren said, hoping her words didn't overstep any boundaries.

'I trust you know what you're in for. Dani will be pestering me non-stop now about when she can see you and the dogs again,' Matt replied, chuckling.

Lauren shook her head in amusement, then returned her focus to the task in hand. 'If Hannah Gifford's the third missing woman, it's becoming undeniable that these cases are connected. We need to step up the investigation. I kept tabs on any updates over the weekend, but there were no sightings, no leads.'

'I agree, ma'am,' Matt said, his voice solemn. 'But we still have nothing substantial linking them.'

'Then we have to work harder until we do,' Lauren said. 'Leads aren't handed to us on a plate, they have to be searched for.'

'Of course, ma'am, I wasn't implying that we're going to sit back and do nothing.'

Lauren could have kicked herself. She hadn't meant to criticise Matt. She valued his input, especially his dogged persistence and refusal to be defeated.

As they reached the station reception, Lauren noticed a man anxiously pacing near the desk. His features were taut, and his eyes darted around the room.

'Ma'am, that's Mr Evans,' Sergeant Hicks said, gesturing towards the jittery man.

Lauren approached him, extending a hand. 'Good morning, Mr Evans. I'm Detective Inspector Pengelly and this is Detective Sergeant Price. Let's move somewhere quiet so we can discuss this in more detail.'

She led them down the corridor, stopping at the first door they came to. She pushed it open and stepped into the sparsely furnished interview room, with only a table and four chairs. She gestured for the man to sit down while she positioned herself opposite him, with Matt at her side.

'It's my partner, Hannah,' Mr Evans began, a tremor in his voice. 'She went to a nightclub on Saturday night with her friends... and she didn't come back.'

'Why did you wait until now to report it?' Matt asked, his eyebrows furrowing.

'Because she's... she's done it before. But never stayed away this long.' He shifted uncomfortably in his chair. 'She's gone out, maybe had a bit too much to drink, and then stayed with a friend.'

'Do you know the friend she went out with on Saturday night?' Lauren prodded gently.

'Yes, her best friend, Molly Swann.' His gaze fell to the table.

'And you didn't want to go with them?' Lauren asked, observing his body language. He seemed to shrink inwards, almost as though he wanted to disappear.

'It's... complicated,' he said, his voice almost a whisper. 'Hannah never wants me to go out with her. She says she wants to be with her friends and not me because she sees me at home.'

Really? What sort of relationship did they have?

'Have you contacted Molly?' Lauren asked.

'Yes. She claims not to know where Hannah is.'

'Did she seem concerned?' Matt asked, staring directly at the man.

He shrugged, avoiding their eyes. 'Not really. She said she was sure she'd come home when she was ready.'

Lauren and Matt shared a glance. That was weird.

'Do you think that Molly knows where Hannah is?'

'I'm not sure.'

'How long have you and Hannah been living together?' Lauren asked, wanting to get a full picture of this relationship.

'Nine years. We met at university and moved in together almost straight away. We've been a couple ever since.'

'What can you tell us about Hannah?' Lauren asked.

'She's twenty-nine and works as an event coordinator for a company in Truro.' His lips curled into a small smile. 'She's fun to be with and she likes a good time.'

'And would you say that your relationship is good?' Lauren asked, watching his reaction closely.

He paused. 'Yes. But she does get a little restless... She doesn't particularly like living here. Thinks it's too parochial.'

'If you could let us have Molly's address and phone number, we'll contact her,' Matt said, sliding over his notebook.

Evans pulled out a phone from his pocket, opened it and then, after staring at the screen, wrote down the details, and passed them back to Matt.

'What was Hannah wearing when she went out?' Matt asked, his pen poised above his notebook.

'I didn't see,' Evans admitted, a hint of guilt crossing his face. 'She called out that Molly had arrived and said they were going straight to the club. I was watching the telly and didn't go out to see her leave. I didn't even shout goodbye when she left. And now... If anything's happened to her...' His voice cracked.

'What time was this?' Lauren asked, gently, bringing him back on track.

'Um... a few minutes after ten, I think. Yes... that's right. I remember now. The news had started.'

'Do you know which club she was intending to visit?'

'She usually goes to Magenta in Penzance, so I assume it was there. But I don't know for certain.'

'Where do you live, Mr Evans?' Matt interrupted with his own query.

'In St Ives.'

A jolt of realisation hit Lauren. A third woman from St Ives. That's their connection.

'You say Hannah's done this before. How long did she stay away?' Lauren probed.

'She's only done it twice and the latest she returned home was the Sunday evening because of getting ready for work on the Monday morning. But... but she didn't come home last night, and she wasn't here this morning. I've tried calling her phone several times since Sunday morning, and there's been no answer. That's why I decided to come to you.'

'How long has Hannah known Molly?' Lauren asked, her mind whirring with questions.

'We've both known her since university.'

'Do they often go out together?'

'They go to Pilates together three times a week, at a studio in St Ives, and out dancing two or three times a month.'

Lauren leant forward, her expression serious. 'And you can't think of anything unusual that might have made her leave? Have you checked her belongings? Is there anything missing?'

Evans shook his head. 'No, I haven't, but I'll look when I get home.'

'Do you work?' Matt asked.

'I'm an architectural technician for a firm in Truro. I work from home three days a week, Monday, Tuesday and Thursday. The rest of the week I'm in the office.'

Lauren stood, signalling the end of the interview. 'Leave it with us, Mr Evans. We'll be in touch. Meanwhile, we'll check with Molly and visit the club. If anything comes to mind that could assist, don't hesitate to let us know.' She held out one of her cards. 'Could you provide a photo of Hannah that we can distribute? Email it to the address on the card.'

'Of course. I'll email it to you now.' He nodded and picked up his phone from the table.

Lauren glanced at the photo when it arrived and forwarded it to Tamsin. Whoever had taken the three women didn't appear to have a specific type.

'Thank you, Mr Evans. We'll do our utmost to find Hannah,' Lauren assured him, her voice steady and resolute, even though inside her thoughts were anything but.

SIXTEEN

MONDAY, 11 MARCH

Lauren and Matt escorted Brendon Evans to the entrance of the station and then went upstairs to speak to the team.

'Okay, everyone, we now have three missing women. The latest, Hannah Gifford, didn't return home after going to a nightclub with a friend. She's twenty-nine and an event planner.' She took the pen from the whiteboard and wrote up the woman's name. 'Tamsin, please will you put up on the screen the photo of Gifford that I forwarded to you, and also images of the other two women.'

'Yes, ma'am.'

In a few seconds the screen lit up and the photos were staring back at them.

'What stands out?' Lauren asked, scanning the room.

'Nothing,' Billy said after a few seconds. 'They're all very different in looks and age.'

'And in occupation,' Lauren said. 'So, what's that telling us?' she encouraged.

'Umm... that they were just random victims? They were in the right place at the wrong time,' Billy said. 'Or should that be the *wrong* place at the wrong time? Do you think they're dead, ma'am, and we now have a serial killer?'

'We can't exclude that possibility, but I don't want to jump the gun. Whoever has them might be keeping them somewhere,' Lauren said, not wanting the team to give up hope about finding the women alive, even if she was already assuming the worst.

'Experts on serial killers say that they usually have an "ideal victim" in their mind based on race, gender, looks, or something else about them,' Clem said.

'So, you don't think that's what we've got then, because our victims are different?' Billy asked, turning to the other officer.

'Research points out that often serial killings seem random at first because victims have something in common which no one realises straight away, apart from the killer themselves.'

'Exactly. Thank you, Clem,' said Lauren. 'There's almost definitely something linking the three of them that we're missing. And that's what I want you all to concentrate on. Look for anything, however inconsequential it might seem, that ties them together. Sergeant Price and I are heading out to the Magenta nightclub, where Hannah Gifford went on Saturday night.'

When Lauren and Matt stepped out into the station car park, grey clouds were hanging low in the sky, heavy with the promise of rain. It was a good job she hadn't left the dogs with the door open, because they couldn't care less about getting wet and would have stayed outside in it. And that wouldn't do Tia any good at all.

'Are you assuming that these women are dead?' Matt asked.

'It's been on my mind. What's your view? You've had more experience with serial killers than the rest of us put together.'

'They're all so different that it's not useful to draw any conclusions, ma'am. I agree that it's a possibility, but let's hope we're wrong.' He sighed and shook his head.

'Amen to that,' she said.

'Do you know this club, Magenta?' Matt asked, changing the subject.

Lauren nodded. 'I've heard of it, but never set foot inside. As you've probably gathered, I'm not that into clubbing. I much prefer to be outside walking or cycling.'

'I'd never have guessed,' Matt said, grinning.

'What do you mean by that?' she said, frowning at him.

'I'm teasing, ma'am. Of course I realise that about you. I'm not into clubbing either. I expect the same could be said for Jenna and Clem. Most likely it's only Tamsin and Billy who would go there. Not that I know the entire team's social life.'

'Oh. Okay. Anyway, back to Magenta. There's trouble there occasionally, but no more than any other similar establishment. The occasional drunken fight, that sort of thing. That's all I can tell you about it.'

'Do you reckon anyone will be there at this time of day?' Matt asked as they reached Lauren's car and got inside.

The thought had crossed her mind, but it was worth going to check.

'Only one way to find out,' she said, giving a tiny shrug.

'Shall we phone first?' Matt suggested.

'No. I'd rather we went there unannounced. It should preserve the scene if anything untoward happened there that we should be aware of.'

The roads were quiet now rush hour was over and it didn't take long to arrive at the club. Magenta was in the heart of Penzance town centre and was a curious addition to the quaint surroundings. It was nestled within a refurbished stone building and the entrance was framed by a solid oak door which was locked when they tried to enter.

'Let's drive around the back to see if we can get in that way,' Matt said, glancing at Lauren.

They returned to the car and drove down a narrow alleyway that led to the rear car park.

A silver Range Rover was parked near the entrance, the vehicle standing out in the otherwise empty area. There were two doors. Lauren tried one but it was locked. She had better luck with the second and she stepped inside into a dimly lit corridor, with Matt close behind. The smell of stale beer hit her and she screwed up her nose.

'Hello, is anyone here?' Lauren called out as they continued walking, her voice echoing in the emptiness.

A door opened and a man who looked to be in his late forties, dressed casually in chinos and a sweatshirt, stepped out in front of them.

'We're closed,' he said bluntly, gesturing with his hand for them to go back the way they'd come.

Lauren held out her warrant card and stared directly at him. 'Police. Who are you?'

'Oh... Right...' he said, giving an almost imperceptible roll of his eyes. 'I'm Jed Simmons, owner of the club. How can I help?' He didn't appear surprised at their arrival; the expression on his face suggested he viewed them as a necessary evil. Was he used to regular visits?

'We'd like to ask a few questions about a woman who was here on Saturday night. She's now missing.'

Simmons glanced at his watch. 'I'm expecting a delivery in twenty minutes. But we can talk until then in my office. Can I get you a tea or coffee?'

'No, thanks,' Lauren said, answering for the pair of them. She wasn't intending for them to stay long and didn't want to be sidetracked.

He ushered them into his office. An untidy room with boxes stacked high in one corner, several bottles of spirits on a table, and piles of beer mats wrapped in plastic on his desk, it was less an office and more a dumping ground.

'Take a seat,' Simmons said, nodding towards some easy chairs in the corner of the room.

'We're looking for a missing woman. Her name's Hannah Gifford. Here's a photo – do you recognise her?' Lauren leant forward and held out her phone for him to check the screen.

Simmons shrugged. 'Sorry, can't help you. We have hundreds of people coming to the club and I don't know many of them.' There was a casual indifference in his tone, as if the missing woman was simply another forgotten face in the sea of club-goers.

'Are you sure?' Lauren pushed. 'Look again.' She held out her phone for him to take, which he did. He studied the photo for longer this time.

A slight frown creased his forehead. 'I still don't know who she is. Maybe some of the bar staff or doormen might, but none of them are here. I'm not expecting anyone in until we next open, which is Wednesday night.'

They certainly weren't going to wait that long.

'Can you give me contact details for the staff who were working on Saturday?' Lauren asked, making it sound more like an order than a question because she wasn't prepared to take no for an answer. 'Addresses and phone numbers.'

Simmons nodded. 'Yes, their details are in a book I keep in the bar beside the cash register.'

'Before you go, I noticed cameras at the front and back entrances of the club. Do you have any inside?'

'We have four cameras in total. One facing the front, one facing the car park, one focused on the bar and one focused on the dance floor.'

'There's a door at the back which was locked when we tried a moment ago. Where does that lead?' Lauren asked.

'That's the rear door for patrons to leave if they want to go out to the car park. It's one-way. Once they're out, they can't get back inside without walking around to the front. Would you like to look at the footage from Saturday night?' Slowly he rose from his chair and crossed the room, navigating the clutter that littered his office.

Lauren nodded, her mind already racing ahead. 'Yes, that would be great, thanks.' She stood up and Matt did the same.

Simmons moved a stack of paper on the desk to one side, revealing a laptop that had seen better days. He flipped it open, his fingers dancing over the keys with practised ease. 'Okay, I've called up Saturday night's footage from all cameras. Which one do you want to look at first?'

'We'll sort it out. I'd rather you went to get the staff details and text them to the number on my card straight away.' She held out her card for him to take.

Once Simmons had left, Lauren and Matt turned their attention to the screen.

'Shall we start with the bar first?' Matt asked.

'Good idea. Hannah's bound to have gone to the bar at some time.'

Lauren called up the relevant camera and the footage flickered to life. She adjusted it to triple speed and they watched the hustle and bustle of the club scene whirring by.

'There she is,' Matt said, pointing to the screen after they'd been watching for a short while, scanning each face for a hint of recognition.

Lauren paused the footage, and her eyes locked on Hannah's image. 'I'll put it on normal speed to see what she does.' They both stared at the screen, watching the woman buy a drink and take a sip. Lauren paused it again. 'Why did she only buy one drink? Surely she would have bought one for her friend, too?'

'You'd have thought so, ma'am,' Matt said.

An uneasy feeling twisted in Lauren's gut. 'So where is the friend then? Although, we only have Evans' word for it that Hannah was picked up by Molly when she left home.'

'Well, we can't check because we don't know what Molly Swann looks like,' Matt said.

'Let's stay focused on the bar to see if Hannah's joined by anyone.'

They returned to watching silently, their eyes glued to the screen, as the antics of the club's patrons unfolded in front of them. Hannah stayed at the bar alone for a while and then headed away so they were unable to see her.

'Hang on a minute.' Matt's voice broke the silence as Hannah disappeared from view. He paused the recording, his finger pointing at a figure on the screen. 'Look who's standing at the end of the bar. We can just see him. It's Callum Scott.'

Lauren's eyes narrowed, her mind instantly alert. 'What's he doing there? Do you think he knows Hannah? It's a bit too much of a coincidence that he's there, don't you think?'

'It sure is. We need to bring him in again for questioning. He can't keep turning up like this.' Matt's voice held an edge of irritation, his eyes still fixed on the frozen image of Scott. 'Look, there's Hannah again, I can see her from the side. She must know him, if that's where she went to after heading away from the bar. Restart the footage.'

Lauren started it, but then Hannah disappeared and Scott remained at the bar, ordering some drinks, after which he walked away. Again, out of camera shot. 'I'll try the dance floor.'

She called up the footage but neither Hannah nor Scott were dancing.

'This is ridiculous,' Matt said. 'Why isn't the whole place visible on camera? Hannah and Scott could be sitting somewhere together and we can't see because of inadequate security.'

'Let's check the car park to see if Hannah left from there and, if so, what time,' Lauren suggested, her voice tense. She, too, was desperate for answers, her feelings echoing the frustration evident in Matt's voice.

She switched the feeds and the image of the club's frenzied interior morphed into the quiet tranquillity of the car park. The footage sped past, the scenes of empty cars and the occasional passer-by blurring together in a parade of unremarkable moments.

'Where the hell is she?' Lauren murmured, frustrated at their lack of progress, and wondering whether Hannah had left the club on foot, using the front entrance.

'There she is,' Matt called out a second later, pointing out a familiar figure emerging from the rear of the club. 'It's only one o'clock and she's on her own again. No sign of any friend. Or of anyone, for that matter. Let's track to see where she goes.'

They watched as Hannah headed over to a dark SUV. The driver's window rolled down and Hannah leant in, her body language casual as if engaging in a mundane conversation.

Lauren squinted at the screen, her brow furrowing. 'Not another bloody SUV. Since when have they been so popular? It's impossible to see the make, model or registration of this car. Who's she talking to? Scott has a Tiguan – could that be it?'

'I've no idea, ma'am. By the looks of it she's not going with the car's occupant.' They watched as Hannah walked away and headed back towards the rear entrance of the club.

'Let's see where the car goes, anyway,' Lauren said.

They watched in anticipation, except the car disappeared.

'Damn. It must have gone through the other exit, which is out of the camera's reach,' Matt said, exhaling heavily. 'Yet another problem with the security. But at least we know whoever was driving wasn't waiting for Hannah.'

They kept staring at the screen and watched as a taxi drove up, illuminating Hannah in its headlights. She lifted her hand, flagging down the driver, and slipped inside the back of the vehicle.

'Okay, so she's getting a taxi from Handy Cabs,' Lauren said, staring at the sign on the roof of the vehicle. 'We'll contact them and find out where they took her. And she's alone. No sign of a friend. Or of anyone.'

For the first time since they'd started sifting through the footage, she felt a tad optimistic that they might be getting somewhere.

Simmons returned to the office and headed over to where they were standing. 'I've texted you details of all staff who were working on Saturday night.'

'Thanks,' Lauren said. 'Can you also email me this CCTV footage. You can use the email address on the card.'

'Sure,' Simmons said, nodding.

'Do you realise that your security cameras aren't up to scratch?' Matt said, glancing up at Simmons. 'We should be able to observe everywhere, not just the bar and the dance floor. You need to update it. And part of the car park isn't in view.'

'Yeah, I know. It's on my to-do list. It's finding the time that's the problem. But seeing as if there's any trouble inside it's likely to be on the dance floor or beside the bar, it's not particularly urgent.' Simmons glanced at his watch. 'The delivery's due now. Is there anything else you want from me?'

'Yes, there is one thing. Do you know of a taxi company called Handy Cabs?' Lauren asked.

'Yes, they're based in St Ives. They're not very reliable, though. I tend to stick to Uber or use one of the Penzance companies.'

Interesting. Why would she call out a taxi from St Ives to take her home when there were other closer companies, or Uber, that she could use?

'Okay, thanks. We're leaving now. Don't forget to send the footage.'

'Will do,' Simmons said, giving a mock salute.

They left the dimly lit club and headed into the daylight. Lauren sucked in a breath of clean fresh air, relieved to get rid of the stale-beer smell that had been invading her nostrils the entire time they were there.

'I don't know how Simmons can tolerate working in such a disgusting environment,' she said, turning up her nose.

'He probably doesn't even notice it,' Matt said, giving a shrug.

'I suppose you're right. Come on, let's visit the taxi company to find out if they've got a record of where Hannah went and who, if anyone, she was with. Then we need to follow up on Callum Scott.'

SEVENTEEN

MONDAY, 11 MARCH

Lauren drove them along the B3311, the quickest route from Penzance to Handy Cabs in St Ives. Matt periodically glanced at Lauren. Her gaze was fixed on the road ahead, one hand on the steering wheel and the fingers of her other hand tapping absent-mindedly on her legs. Was she still anxious about Tia? Or was it the case that was preoccupying her? Or maybe it was both.

As they reached their destination, Lauren pulled into the kerb, parking adjacent to the Handy Cabs neon sign that lit up the entrance.

Lauren was out of the car before he'd even had time to remove his seat belt, and he followed as she led the way into the building. Her stride was determined, and as they got inside her hand reached into her pocket. 'Who's in charge here?' she asked, presenting her warrant card to the man behind the desk, who gave it a cursory glance before looking directly at them.

'That would be me. I'm Jim. How can I help?'

'We're looking for this woman.' Lauren held out her phone for him to see the screen. 'She was picked up from Magenta club in Penzance by one of your drivers at around one on Saturday morning.'

'Hang on a minute, I'll just check.' Jim stared at the computer screen on the desk, his fingers moving the mouse as he accessed the necessary data. 'We did have a fare that went from there to Penwith Road.'

'Which is where?' Matt asked, having no real knowledge of the surrounding area.

'Here in St Ives, a few streets away.'

'Do you have a record of who drove her?' Matt asked.

'Yeah. It was Sandy. She's here at the moment, in the staffroom; I can get her for you, if you like.'

'Thanks,' Lauren responded, with a sense of urgency in her voice.

Jim turned and went through a door behind the reception desk.

'Why call a taxi from St Ives to take her home? Why not use a local company or an Uber?' Matt asked.

'I've no idea. Perhaps Hannah knows and trusts the company. But the other issue is, why Penwith Road, because that's quite a distance from Trenmar Road where she lives. And—'

Lauren stopped talking when a woman in her fifties entered the room. She had an easy smile and her hair was loosely tied up in a ponytail. She wore a shirt with the company logo on it.

'Hi, I'm Sandy. You want to know about a fare I took on Saturday night from Magenta,' she said, her gaze shifting between Matt and Lauren.

'Yes, please, but first can I confirm it was this woman?' Lauren held out her phone and Sandy took a quick look.

'Yes, that's her. I remember because she told me she wanted to be dropped off at the corner of Penwith and Porthia Roads where she lived, but not right outside of her house because of her nosy neighbours who'd be spying on her. She also added that she didn't want to wake everyone up.'

That wasn't where she lived, either. Matt exchanged a glance with Lauren. Why had she gone there?

'Did you see her walk down Porthia Road after she got out of the car?' Matt asked.

'No, I didn't. I had another fare and drove off as soon as she'd paid.'

'Could she have gone somewhere else? Is there a twenty-four-hour supermarket close by?' he asked, trying to work out why she'd wanted to get out there.

'Here in St Ives, love?' Sandy laughed. 'You've got to be kidding. The area where I took her is all residential. No shops. And even if there were, they wouldn't be open at that time.'

'Do you often get asked to drop someone off at a distance from their house?' Lauren asked, frowning.

'It's not uncommon. We get all sorts here.' Sandy chuckled, giving a small shrug.

'Was the woman drunk?' Lauren asked.

'I could tell by the smell on her breath when she got into the car that she'd had a couple, but she certainly wasn't out of it. She spoke clearly and wasn't wobbly on her feet. I wouldn't have taken her in the car if she was drunk. Cleaning up vomit isn't my favourite occupation. Even if I have had to do it more times than I care to mention.' She wrinkled her nose in disgust.

'Did she chat much to you on the journey back from Penzance?' Matt asked.

'No, she was quiet. From what I could tell when looking in my rear-view mirror, she was concentrating on her phone. It did ping quite a few times, so I guess she was messaging someone. That's all I can tell you.'

'Okay. Thanks for your help,' Lauren said, turning to leave.

As they left the building, Matt's mind churned with the new information.

'Why would Hannah Gifford claim to live somewhere she didn't?' he asked, turning to Lauren. 'Also, who was she messaging? And where did she actually go?'

'You won't realise this, but where Hannah was dropped off is close to where Callum Scott lives. I bet she went there. Why else would she be in the vicinity of his home?' Lauren replied, her face set firm. 'We'd better get back to the station straight away.'

Lauren strode into the office, her steps purposeful and confident, with Matt close behind. The room fell silent as she positioned herself in the centre, commanding the team's attention. She paused, taking a moment to assess the atmosphere, her eyes scanning the faces of her officers, their anticipation palpable.

'Right, now I have your attention. I want to let you know that we have a potential suspect,' Lauren announced, her voice resonating with authority.

'Who is it, ma'am?' Billy said, ever eager for information.

Lauren met his gaze. 'Callum Scott. We saw him on some CCTV footage at the club where our third missing woman was last seen. And she took a taxi to very close to where he lives, which is nowhere near her place.'

'Callum?' Jenna said, her voice dripping with disbelief. 'No way could it be him. I'm usually a good judge of character, ma'am, and I'd never have suspected him of abducting women in a million years.'

Lauren fought the urge to roll her eyes. 'You should know by now that we can't always assume we know a criminal when faced with one. Scott was in the vicinity when two of the women disappeared. Add to that Hannah Gifford's taxi and that puts him right in the frame. Also, we saw her talking to somebody in a dark SUV in the car park of the club, but we couldn't make out the make or model of the car.'

'That also fits in with Dale Cooper's observation of the car that he saw Yvonne get into,' Clem added, pointing out the connection. 'Do you know what car Callum Scott drives, Jenna?'

Jenna nodded, her expression filled with uncertainty. 'Yes, it's a VW Tiguan.'

'In gunmetal grey. We asked him during his interview,' Matt added, his voice steady.

'I still can't believe it,' Jenna said, a pained expression crossing her face. 'Do you think that she spoke to him in the car park and then arranged to take a taxi back to his place?'

'She was picked up by the taxi soon after speaking to the person in the car, so it would appear that it had been pre-booked. Unfortunately, the taxi company didn't record the time the booking came in,' Lauren said, giving a frustrated sigh. 'Tamsin, see if you can pick up the SUV on the CCTV in town. I'll also forward the footage from the club.'

'Yes, ma'am.' Tamsin nodded, looking determined.

'We know that Hannah likes to go out on her own without her partner. Is that relevant?' Lauren posed the question.

'It depends on whether she is seeing someone on the side – and we believe that's our link,' Clem said.

'True, but it's all supposition at the moment,' Lauren said. 'Clem, arrange for uniform to bring Callum Scott in for questioning immediately.'

Clem acknowledged the order with a brisk nod. 'Yes, ma'am.'

'And while you're at it, do some digging into the man. See if there's anything we don't already know. Billy, I want you to contact the bar and security staff who were working on Saturday night at the club and see if they remember her,' Lauren instructed, her voice carrying a sense of urgency. 'I'll text their details. Ask them to come to the station straight away so you can show them her photo.' She reached for her phone and forwarded everything to him.

Billy nodded, his gaze fixed on Lauren. 'Yes, ma'am. Why don't I send the photo to them; it would be quicker.'

'No. I want you to see them in person so you can watch their reaction when they're shown the image. You can make sure they look carefully at it and also assess whether they're trying to hide anything.'

'Okay. Will do,' Billy said, his chest swelling.

Lauren couldn't help but notice the change in Billy's demeanour. Had her decision to assign him this task sparked a sense of pride within him? It was important to nurture the growth and development of her team members, and she hoped this opportunity would do just that.

'Jenna, contact Molly Swann,' Lauren directed, shifting her attention to the older officer. 'She's Hannah's best friend. Get her to come in for an interview.'

'Yes, ma'am. I'm on to it,' Jenna said.

'Ma'am, Scott's arrived. He's in interview room four,' Matt announced, poking his head around the edge of Lauren's office door.

Lauren glanced up from her desk, a determined look on her face. 'Good.' She set her pen down on the desk and rose from the chair. 'Okay, let's go. How's it going in there?'

Matt leant against the door frame, his arms crossed. 'We've been able to pick up the mysterious car on the CCTV footage in town. Initially, it was heading in the same direction as the taxi, but we lost it once he reached residential areas because there are no cameras there. But it's certainly possible for Hannah to have met the driver somewhere.'

Lauren nodded thoughtfully, her gaze distant as if she was

absorbing the information. 'Yes, that makes sense, especially if they know where the cameras are, and they don't want to be seen. But then why allow themselves to be noticed talking through the car window?'

'They might have believed the club's camera didn't quite reach the car.'

'True. Come on, let's see what Scott has to say for himself.'

Lauren headed around her desk to the door that led directly into the corridor and Matt joined her.

Entering the interview room, they found Scott sitting on one of the chairs, his face still and lips set in a firm line. His hands were clenched tightly on his lap, the knuckles white. Vastly different body language from the last time they'd spoken to him.

Did he realise that the noose was tightening, and they were getting closer to the truth?

'Why have you brought me in? I've already spoken to you about Freya. I can't tell you anything else,' he protested.

'We'll be recording this interview. Sergeant Price, if you could set it up, please,' Lauren said, clearly paying no attention to Scott's outburst.

'Yes, ma'am,' Matt said, nodding. He pressed the button on the recording equipment. 'Interview on Monday the eleventh of March. Those present: DI Pengelly, DS Price and...' He paused, looking expectantly at Scott.

'Callum Scott,' Scott filled in, his voice quieter now.

'Mr Scott, I understand you were at Magenta on Saturday night,' Lauren began, her tone professional and detached.

'Yes, I went with some friends,' Scott responded, his voice even but lacking the confidence they'd heard from him in the past.

'Do you recognise this woman?' Lauren asked, sliding over her phone showing Hannah Gifford's image.

Scott glanced at the screen, his top teeth biting down on his bottom lip. He shook his head. 'No. I don't know her.'

'Are you sure?' Matt said, his voice stern. 'Because there was a flicker of recognition in your eyes when you saw it.'

A wave of surprise washed over Scott's features, his eyes widening a fraction. 'Well, I don't actually know her,' he admitted, moving in his chair. 'But I do sort of recognise her. I know her friend, Molly. We spent some time together while I was at the club on Saturday. And a couple of times this person, whatever her name is, came over and whispered something into Molly's ear. I didn't hear what she said.'

'Her name's Hannah,' Lauren said, filling in the details, her eyes probing. 'Are you sure that Molly didn't introduce you?'

Scott's gaze faltered, his hands fumbling nervously in his lap. 'No, I don't think she did. Well... she might have done. But I don't remember. It wasn't like I stayed with Molly for long. After a while I went back to hanging out with my friends.'

Lauren leant forward slightly, her eyes unblinking. 'So, Hannah didn't come up and speak to you in your car before you left the club?'

Scott shook his head. 'I wasn't driving. One of my friends was the sober driver for the night.'

'We'd like contact details for your friend to confirm this. Did you all leave the club together?' Matt asked.

Scott nodded, his fingers tracing the edge of the table absent-mindedly. 'Yes, we left the club at about one thirty and went to get something to eat from the local drive-through burger place. Then my friend drove us home about half an hour later. It was a stag night.'

Lauren's phone pinged, and she glanced down at it. She then slid it over to Matt and he read the message that had come from Clem:

Callum Scott had an injunction taken out against him five years ago for stalking an ex.

145

'Mr Scott, is it correct that five years ago you stalked an ex-partner of yours?'

Colour leached from the man's face. 'Yes,' he muttered, his voice barely audible.

'Who was this woman?'

'Someone I worked with. She got it wrong. I wasn't stalking her. We'd dated for a few months and then she dumped me to hook up with someone else.'

'And you resented that?'

'She said I stalked her, but it wasn't true. I just wanted to speak to her to understand what had happened. We had a great thing going. I'd planned to propose, but...' His voice trailed off.

'But you interpreted your relationship differently from how she did,' Lauren said.

'Yes. But I don't see why this is relevant. It happened years ago.'

'We'll decide what's relevant in this investigation. We'll be confirming your alibi and may wish to speak to you again, so make sure you don't leave the area,' Lauren said with a slight nod.

They let Callum Scott go and returned to the office. When they entered, the place went silent, members of the team staring up at them expectantly. Matt didn't blame them — especially Jenna, who knew their suspect.

'It's unlikely that Callum Scott is the man Hannah was speaking to outside of the club. He was on a stag night and has an alibi until he was driven home by his friend at around two. That doesn't put him in the clear. Hannah could have been waiting for him when he arrived.'

'Is he in custody?' Clem asked.

'No. We have nothing concrete to hold him on. But I want his alibi confirmed.'

'I'll do that, ma'am,' Jenna said. 'I still can't believe he'd be involved.'

'Thanks. I'll forward the friend's details. Back to Hannah. We know she goes to Pilates three times a week, according to her partner. I want someone to check that's true. He said she goes with Molly Swann. Have you managed to get hold of her, Clem?'

'I've left a message on her voicemail to contact me,' the officer replied.

'Okay. I'm going to see the DCI regarding a press conference to talk about the three missing women.'

The weight of the situation settled in the room, the enormity of the investigation hitting them all.

EIGHTEEN

MONDAY, 11 MARCH

'Keep me informed of how the investigation's going,' DCI Mistry said to Lauren as they left the press conference and were making their way back to their respective offices. His words carried a sombre tone. 'Obviously, we don't know whether these women are alive or dead. But for them all to have gone missing in such a short space of time... I'm not convinced that this is going to have a happy outcome. We could have a serial killer on our hands.'

Lauren nodded, her expression reflecting how serious it was. 'Yes, sir. My team is working on it now. We have some common threads which we're investigating and—'

The shrill ring of the DCI's phone sliced through the air, interrupting her mid-sentence. His immediate reaction was to reach for the mobile, his eyes briefly darting from her to the screen and then back again. Without a word, he dismissed her with a casual flick of his hand, engrossed in the incoming call.

As Lauren observed his behaviour, a knot of unease tightened in her stomach. She couldn't help but overhear snippets of his conversation, and it sounded personal. It was unlike the

DCI to allow his personal life to intrude upon work. Was there a problem?

Shaking off her concerns, Lauren headed straight for the office, refocusing her attention on the task in hand. Her gaze landed on Matt, who stood by the whiteboard, facing the rest of the team.

'Ma'am,' Matt said, catching sight of her. 'We've managed to get hold of Molly Swann. She was in Exeter for the day yesterday and is on her way back this afternoon. She's going to call at the station on her way.'

Lauren sighed, a mixture of relief and frustration washing over her. Progress was being made, albeit at a painstakingly slow pace. Time was slipping away, and the chances of a positive outcome were growing increasingly slim.

'Did you explain to her what it was about?' Lauren asked, her voice tinged with caution.

'I told her there had been an incident at Magenta and we're contacting all patrons about it. She was happy to talk to us. I didn't want to mention anything about Hannah,' Tamsin responded.

'Good. We don't want her to be scared off in case it turns out that she has something to do with Hannah's disappearance,' Lauren affirmed. 'We've held the press conference and explained that three women are missing. We provided the names of Freya Kempston and Yvonne Hughes, but not Hannah Gifford. We won't do that until we're certain she's missing too. What time's Molly Swann due to arrive?'

'Anytime within the next half an hour, ma'am,' Tamsin answered. 'It depends on traffic.'

'Okay. Where are we on Scott's alibi?' Lauren asked, turning her attention to Clem, her voice betraying a mix of hope and trepidation.

Clem's response was immediate. 'It checks out, ma'am. The

friend said he was dropped off at home at just gone two. I also asked him if he noticed anyone hanging around and he said no. But that doesn't mean Hannah wasn't there. Scott could've given her a key.'

'If it's him. And even if he gave a key to Hannah, what about Freya and Yvonne? We can't place them anywhere near his house,' Jenna said.

Lauren clenched and unclenched her fists, an avalanche of conflicting emotions roiling within her. She wasn't ruling out Callum Scott, but it didn't sit right. 'That's true, but we'll continuing investigating. Has anyone investigated Hannah's social media presence?'

'Me, ma'am,' Billy responded. 'She's quite active on social media, posting photos of her outings and adventures. Interestingly, despite living with the guy, her partner's hardly ever in the photos. It's mostly Hannah with her friends, going out to various places. It's almost as if she presents herself as single. Do you think that's relevant?'

Lauren pondered Billy's observation, the gears of her mind turning. 'I don't know for certain, but it's something to bear in mind. We'll continue exploring that angle. Now, where do we stand with the CCTV footage?'

'No change, ma'am. We couldn't locate that SUV again after we lost it in town. It could be nothing, though,' Clem said.

'Except that it's been spotted twice,' she said, frustration in her voice. 'I want the footage in and around the shopping centre examined again. Look for any car matching that description.'

'There are bound to be several cars like that, ma'am. They're quite common. If we don't have any other more specific details it's going to be difficult,' Jenna said, a hint of doubt in her tone.

'Well, that's all we have, so let's get on with it. We need to pursue every lead, no matter how slim.' Lauren's patience had waned and her words echoed off the walls of the room with an unintended harshness. She caught a flicker of unease in a glance exchanged between Tamsin and Billy, and a pang of guilt pricked at her conscience. Her sharpness might have affected her team more deeply than she'd intended. However, she also knew that their vigilance and focus were crucial to the investigation, and if it required a stern reminder, she could live with that for now.

'Yes, ma'am,' Jenna finally said.

Lauren's gaze swept across the team, the tension unmistakable. But she was determined to leave no stone unturned in the search for the missing women.

The phone on the desk adjacent to the whiteboard rang, disturbing the silence. Lauren's hand shot out, reaching for it. 'Pengelly.'

'There's a Molly Swann here to see you,' the desk sergeant said.

'Thank you, Sergeant Hicks. We'll be down shortly.' Lauren replaced the handset. 'Hannah's friend is here. Matt, you come with me. The rest of you, keep searching, keep probing. Check the social media accounts for all three women. We're looking for any link between them.'

As Lauren and Matt left the office and headed towards the stairs, he turned to her. 'You were tough on Jenna in there.'

'I don't believe so,' she countered immediately. 'We need to drive this case forward. The DCI shares our view that we could be dealing with a serial killer. While we don't have any tangible proof to substantiate that yet, we can't afford to be complacent. This isn't the time for kid gloves.'

'The team is fully aware of the stakes and they're working as hard as they can,' Matt shot back, his voice firm.

A frown crossed Lauren's brow. 'Since your arrival I've tried to temper my approach and, frankly, I'm not convinced it's effective. They need to dig in, go that extra mile.'

Matt started to respond but seemed to think better of it. 'Well... never mind, it doesn't matter.'

His unfinished sentence lingered in the air.

'Matt, this is *my* team. You're a valuable addition, no doubt, but I prefer things to be run my way, with order and discipline. I'm not open to further debate on this.'

Silence fell over them until they reached the reception. A woman, probably in her late twenties, was seated upright on one of the chairs, her posture one of unease. As they approached her, Lauren was already mentally preparing for the conversation to come.

'Molly Swann?' Lauren asked.

'Yes,' the woman confirmed, a slight tremor in her voice. 'I was asked to come in.'

'Yes, one of my officers contacted you. Please follow me.'

They headed past the reception desk and down the corridor, soon arriving at interview room one.

'Are we recording this, ma'am?' Matt asked, once they were all seated.

She glanced at him, her eyebrows knitting together in mild surprise. 'Of course.'

Was this because of their earlier conversation? Did he now think he had to defer to her all the time? Which was ridiculous.

'Interview on Monday the eleventh of March,' Matt began. 'Present are DI Pengelly, DS Price and...' He glanced at the woman sitting across from them. 'Could you please state your name for the recording.'

'Molly Eve Swann,' she answered, her voice quiet.

'Thank you for coming in, Molly,' Lauren started, keeping her gaze fixed on the woman. 'We're investigating the disappearance of Hannah Gifford, a friend of yours we believe.'

Molly's mouth fell open in surprise. 'Why didn't anyone mention that when they called? I thought something happened at Magenta.'

Lauren held up her hands in a placating gesture. 'We didn't want to cause any undue worry while you were on the way here. Hannah's partner, Brendon, alerted us. He mentioned your name. You've all been friends for many years, we believe.'

'Yes, that's right,' Molly confirmed, her face losing some of its colour.

Lauren leant forward in her chair. 'What can you tell us about their relationship?'

Molly fidgeted a little in her seat before answering. 'Hannah often says he's boring and hates going out, but he doesn't mind if she does. I once asked why she stayed with him, and she said because they get on well together. They've known each other for a long time.'

'Do you know if Hannah's been seeing anyone else on the side?' Matt asked.

Molly shrugged, appearing a little uncomfortable. 'She likes to have a good time when we're out. There might be a few kisses on the dance floor, or a couple of harmless flirtations at the bar, but nothing serious.'

'Do you think that Brendon knows about this?' Lauren probed.

'I can't say for sure. There's nothing serious in what Hannah does. It's a bit of fun,' Molly insisted, her eyes pleading for them to understand.

'Do you and Hannah usually share a taxi home after a night out?' Lauren asked, breaking the silence that had followed Molly's last answer.

The woman blinked at the sudden question. 'Usually, yes. But on Saturday, I was... spending time with someone else.'

'Callum Scott?' Matt said.

Molly's eyes widened. 'Yes. I was with him for part of the night.'

'What was Hannah doing during that time?' Lauren asked.

Molly glanced upwards as if she was recalling the night. 'I didn't keep an eye on her particularly, but I remember seeing her dancing and also standing in a group with some mutual friends. We knew quite a few people there.'

'Why didn't you leave with Hannah when she got a taxi at one?' Lauren asked, her tone sharp.

'Umm... well... she mentioned meeting an old boyfriend and insisted that I needn't go with her.'

'We have CCTV footage showing her talking to someone in a dark SUV,' Lauren continued, her gaze locked on to Molly. 'But she didn't leave with him. Any idea who that person could be?'

Molly furrowed her brow, her expression reflecting genuine confusion. 'No, I'm sorry. It could have been someone we know who was at the club.'

'Let's circle back to this old boyfriend. Do you know who he is and where they were going to meet?' Matt asked, leaning forward, pressing for more information.

Molly shook her head, a touch of frustration seeping into her voice. 'I'm sorry. I wasn't really listening. The music's always so loud. We agreed to catch up at Pilates later in the week.'

'What time did you leave the club?' Lauren asked.

'Around two. I got an Uber straight home.'

'Can anyone vouch for you? Someone who can confirm your whereabouts at that time?' Lauren asked.

'No, I live on my own.' Molly's response was tinged with a hint of regret. 'But I can provide you with the Uber details.'

'Could Brendon have found out what Hannah was doing and gone out looking for her?' Matt's line of questioning shifted, exploring another possible angle.

'I don't think so,' Molly said, surprise evident in her voice. 'Brendon isn't the jealous type.'

'Was Hannah always like this, even when they first got together at uni?' Lauren asked, incredulity seeping into her words.

Molly sighed. 'Brendon has always been the serious one. But that's what she likes about him. They're good for each other.'

Seriously?

'Even though she has flings with other men?' Lauren asked, unable to hide her scepticism.

'Like I told you, it's harmless fun. She always says how much she loves Brendon.'

There was silence for a few seconds as Lauren and Matt absorbed the information.

'Is there anything else you can tell us that might help find her?' Lauren softened her tone slightly. 'We're worried. Two other women have gone missing. We held a press conference but haven't yet given out Hannah's name.'

Molly's mouth dropped open. 'Oh... I didn't know.'

'Weren't you concerned when you spoke to Brendon and he said that Hannah hadn't come home?'

'No. Because I assumed she was with the guy she mentioned... But I didn't tell Brendon that. It's not my business. I didn't want to get involved,' Molly confessed.

'Do you think he'd have been angry if he'd found out the truth?' Lauren probed further.

Surely the man would. How could anyone be prepared to put up with such treatment?

'I guess,' Molly said. 'He idolises her. I think part of the reason Hannah does what she does is because Brendon never questions her. But don't quote me on that. It's only my opinion.'

Lauren nodded, getting a picture of the missing woman, and not liking what she was hearing. But she wasn't there to judge what Hannah did in her free time. Lauren's role was to find her. Hopefully, before anything serious happened.

'Thank you for coming in to see us. You're free to leave for now. But we may wish to speak with you again, so please don't leave the area without first contacting us.'

NINETEEN

TUESDAY, 12 MARCH

Matt arrived at work having spent a restless night going over and over in his mind what had happened to the missing women. The only pattern emerging was that all three women might have been unfaithful to their partners, although even that was debatable because they had no concrete proof.

As he stepped into the office, he noticed that, as usual, he was first to arrive, apart from Lauren, who he could see through the glass door of her room. He hung up his jacket and headed towards her. He could see through the glass that she was already immersed in work. He gave a light knock on the door. She glanced up and beckoned for him to come in.

'Morning, ma'am,' he greeted, sitting on one of the empty seats across from her desk. 'You're in early. Is everything okay with Tia?'

'Yes, she's fine, thanks. It's working out well with Betty, my neighbour, which is a big weight off my mind. Do you want anything in particular? I have some admin tasks which need my attention before the morning briefing.'

'Only to say that I've been going over the case and there's one recurring theme. The women are all restless in their relationships and are possibly having an affair. The problem is their lives don't intersect. They hang out with different people. Have different social circles. So how are they all being targeted? There's a crucial link but it's evading us.'

'I agree. And it's what's been running through my mind, too,' Lauren said, nodding in agreement.

'I think we should bring Brendon Evans in for further questioning, especially now Molly has told us more about Hannah.'

Lauren picked up the pen on the desk in an absent-minded way and held it between her thumb and forefinger. 'Yes, we do need to question him further... But I think it might be best if we talk to him in his own environment. It might give us additional insights, and he may give us permission to search Hannah's belongings.'

'Has anything of use come from the press conference?' Matt asked, moving on quickly, aware that his boss wanted to get on with her other jobs.

'According to a text I had from Tamsin, who stayed late processing the calls, a few people reported seeing Freya at the shopping centre, but nothing yet has come in regarding Yvonne. We'll have the morning briefing as soon as everyone's here, which hopefully will be soon, and then we'll visit Brendon Evans. This is one of the days when he works from home, so he should be there.'

Matt raised an eyebrow. 'I wouldn't have thought he'd have been working with Hannah still missing.'

'Well, some people prefer to keep busy in times of stress. It could be his coping mechanism,' Lauren said, shrugging nonchalantly.

Matt returned to the main office and was relieved to see that within fifteen minutes the rest of the team had arrived. He appreciated them coming in early, aware that Lauren would have expected it of them. It had become apparent since he'd been there that mediating between his boss and the rest of the team was an important part of his role. He was determined to continue trying to subtly push Lauren into easing her micro-management tendencies. That way they might become a team that gelled together from top to bottom.

The team were chatting amongst themselves. They usually included him in their conversations, but they were discussing a programme on television the previous evening that he hadn't seen because it clashed with one of the nightly soaps his parents watched. His mum had suggested that they should buy a second TV, but he said no, it wasn't worth it. He'd much rather read in the evenings, anyway. But not crime novels. He much preferred non-fiction, particularly biographies.

'Glad to see you're all here,' Matt said, standing and facing them all. 'We're going to have the morning briefing shortly.'

'We assumed the DI would want to kick things off early,' Clem said.

'Any update on the missing women?' Jenna asked.

'Nothing new since last night. The DI will cover every-thing,' Matt responded as Lauren exited her office and strode purposefully towards the whiteboard – her designated spot anytime she wanted to speak to them en masse.

'Good morning, team,' Lauren greeted them.

'Morning, ma'am,' the team responded in unison.

'There are no significant changes from yesterday. The three women remain missing, and we're still trying to establish a link between them. Billy, you were assigned questioning the bar and security staff at Magenta. What did you learn?'

Billy, who'd been slouching in his chair, sat upright. 'I interviewed the two security guys who were working on the door on Saturday night and one of them recognised Hannah as a regular. He didn't remember her being with anyone. Neither of them witnessed any fights or other altercations involving her. I asked them about the SUV and neither of them could recall it, but that makes sense because they were stationed at the front door. The back door is only used for people leaving.'

'Why don't people go in that way?' Clem asked.

'Because it's not a door you can go in and out of. It's kept on the latch so it's a way out only, according to the doorman,' Billy said.

'Yes, we saw that door when we visited,' Lauren confirmed.

'I also spoke to one of the women who was working behind the bar that night. I couldn't get hold of the other one,' Billy continued. 'She recognised Hannah from the photo but also didn't notice her being with anyone or being involved in anything weird.'

'Good work, Billy.'

The officer coloured slightly. 'Thanks, ma'am.'

Matt nodded his approval at his boss acknowledging Billy. Perhaps she had been listening to his hints... however subtle they might have been.

'Tamsin, you've been searching through their social media pages. Have you found any commonalities between the three women? Shared events, locations?'

The officer shook her head. 'No, ma'am. There's absolutely nothing that I can find to link them.'

'I know that Turner's no longer a suspect, but do we know whether Hannah uses his garage for servicing her car?'

'I'll check, ma'am,' Tamsin said.

'Thanks. Hannah regularly attends Pilates at the Wellness Studio with her friend Molly Swann. Contact them to see if Freya or Yvonne go to classes there.'

'I've already checked that, ma'am, and neither of them are members,' Tamsin said, shaking her head.

Lauren gave a disappointed sigh. 'It was worth a try. But really I'd have been surprised if it was that easy. Jenna, Hannah works as an event planner in Truro. Find out the name of the company and get in touch with them. I want you to speak to her colleagues. They might have some idea of where she might be, or insights into her recent activities.'

'Will do, ma'am,' Jenna said, pulling her keyboard towards her.

'Sergeant Price and I are going to visit Hannah's partner, Brendon Evans. We intend to look around their home for any clues that might give us some idea of where she was planning to go after the club and with whom. It's possible we may receive more calls following the press conference, not that anything useful has come in so far. Tamsin, can you and Clem look through Hannah's finances, please. Let's see if the three women regularly shop at the same places. Or whether there have been any unusual transactions.'

'Yes, ma'am,' Tamsin and Clem said together.

'There must be a connection somewhere. We just haven't found it yet. Any questions before we leave?'

'No, ma'am,' the team responded, perfectly synchronised.

Matt couldn't help but frown at their collective response. This unified answering had become an ingrained routine. Like it was second nature to them. It was still a weird thing to witness, despite him having been working there for over six months.

'All right then. Keep me posted if you uncover anything significant. We'll be back once we've spoken to Brendon Evans.'

TWENTY

TUESDAY, 12 MARCH

'Have you got some news?' Evans asked the moment he answered the door to Lauren and Matt.

Weariness was etched on the man's face, the lines of concern leaving deep grooves. There was a heaviness to his posture, as if the weight of the world rested upon his shoulders.

'Nothing yet, Brendon,' Lauren replied, her voice gentle and comforting. 'We'd like to ask you more about Hannah. We've spoken to Molly and would now like to get a fuller picture from you. My officers are going to contact Hannah's workplace to see if anyone knows where she is. Have you been in touch with any of them?'

Matt noticed a slight tremor in Evans' hand as he clutched the door handle. 'No,' the man responded, his voice tinged with worry. 'I only spoke to Molly, as I told you. Come on inside, we'll talk there.'

They entered the hallway of the ground-floor maisonette, following him into the lounge. Evans gestured for them to sit, and Lauren and Matt settled themselves side by side on the brown leather sofa, while Evans perched on the edge of a matching chair.

Matt's gaze swept across the room, taking in the modest yet cosy living space. His eyes lingered on the abstract artwork adorning the wall. Leigh would have found it intriguing, but it was wasted on him. It looked like something Dani could've painted.

'This is a nice place,' Matt remarked, hoping to steer the conversation away from his own thoughts about Leigh. 'Have you lived here long?'

A weak smile tugged at the corners of Evans' lips. 'We've been renting it for the last five years since we moved to St Ives from Plymouth.' Evans' shoulders relaxed slightly as he settled back into the chair.

Curiosity prompted Matt to delve further. 'What made you move?'

Evans sighed, as if regretting what they'd done. 'Because of Hannah's job. She found a new one here.' There was a bitter-sweet tone to his words, tinged with unspoken complexities.

'But I thought you said she didn't like it because it was too parochial,' Matt probed, puzzled by their decision to move to a place they seemingly didn't want to be.

Evans let out another sigh. 'We didn't know that at the time. It was a good job offer, and we thought we'd like the area. We'd often visited Cornwall in the past and always enjoyed it.'

'And did Molly follow you here?' Matt asked, interested in the relationship between the three of them.

Evans shook his head. 'No, she was already here working. She comes from Newquay and her family still live here. That was one of the reasons why Hannah decided to take the job – to be close to Molly.'

'And what about your job?' Matt asked.

'I'm a graphic designer and can work from home. The head office, which I travel to twice a week, is easily accessible. It takes me under two hours on the train.'

Lauren leant forward in her chair. 'Molly told us that

162

Hannah enjoys a good time. That she likes going out and having fun. How do you feel about that?'

Evans glanced down briefly before meeting Lauren's gaze, a sense of resignation evident in his eyes. 'It's just who she is.' Sadness in his voice. 'We're very different, but that's what keeps us together. Look, I know what you're thinking, that she's probably hooked up with some guy, but I don't believe it. I'm not stupid enough to think that she doesn't, maybe, get together with a guy at a bar if she's been drinking, but that's all it is – a bit of fun.'

Matt shook his head, grappling with Evans' perspective. Was he truly okay with this? The notion seemed incomprehensible.

'So, would you say you have an open relationship?' Lauren persisted, her voice kind but unwavering.

Evans shook his head, a flicker of uncertainty crossing his features. 'No, not open in the sense that she goes out with different men regularly. All I'm saying is, if she does go out to a club she might have a bit of fun.'

Matt observed the mix of protectiveness and vulnerability in Evans' demeanour and exchanged a glance with Lauren. Judging from her expression, she, too, believed there was more to this story than Evans was revealing.

'But you don't know for sure that she hasn't gone off with somebody, do you?' Matt pushed.

He scrutinised Evans' face, searching for any sign of guilt. Yet what he saw etched on the man's features was pain, a sense of hurt mixed with a reluctant acceptance of the situation.

'But why would she have gone and left everything?' Evans' voice grew desperate. 'I had a look after we spoke, and nothing of hers is missing. Her passport's here. So are her clothes. She literally only has what she was wearing when she went out, including her handbag, which would have held her purse and phone. That's not someone who's gone off with someone or has run away, is it?' His pleading eyes locked with Matt's.

Matt nodded, absorbing the weight of the information and contemplating the implications of Evans' words. The man was desperately trying to make sense of Hannah's disappearance... as they all were.

'Brendon, we'd like to look through Hannah's possessions, to give us a better idea of what she's like and to see if there's anything out of the ordinary that you might have missed. Would you mind that?' Lauren asked, compassion in her voice.

As his boss spoke, Matt observed Evans closely, analysing his reaction. There was a genuine sense of bewilderment in his eyes, mirroring his and Lauren's confusion. It was becoming increasingly evident to Matt that the man wasn't involved in Hannah's disappearance.

Evans hesitated for a moment, staring at the floor. 'I'll show you our bedroom and you can have a look round,' he murmured, his voice a mix of resignation and hope.

They followed Evans into the corridor and entered the room opposite. Matt and Lauren pulled on disposable gloves, preparing themselves for the search.

'We'll see you back in the lounge when we've finished,' Lauren said.

Matt nodded in agreement, his mind racing with thoughts and theories. As they closed the door behind them, he turned to Lauren.

'It's all very odd. Evans clearly doesn't like the relationship they have but must love her so much that she gets away with it.'

Lauren nodded, her expression thoughtful. 'Do you think he could have cracked and done something to her? It wouldn't be the first time a put-upon partner had reached the end of their tether and reacted,' she speculated.

Matt considered her words, his mind running through what they already knew. 'It's a possibility, but how likely is it when we're already looking for two other women who have disappeared? It's doubtful that Evans knows Freya and Yvonne. He rarely, if ever, goes out, so when would he have had a chance to meet them? My gut's telling me that it's not him, but hopefully we'll find something in here that will help.'

Matt approached the wardrobe, opening it carefully. He began sifting through the contents, searching for any clues or items that stood out. Meanwhile, Lauren headed over to the dressing table, opening one of the drawers.

As Matt continued his search, his hand brushed against a long, purple roll tucked away in the corner of the wardrobe. He pulled it out, frowning in confusion.

'What's this?' he asked, holding it out for Lauren to see.

'That's a lumbar roll. She might use it at Pilates. I was recommended to use one once to give me some relief from back pain. They're great, and really helped...' She paused as if deep in thought. 'Oh... Bloody hell... That's it, Matt... Backs... It's backs.' Her eyes flashed with excitement and she turned to the door and opened it. 'Brendon, can you come in here,' she called out, her tone brimming with anticipation.

Within a few seconds Evans appeared at the doorway. 'Have you found something?' he asked, his voice anxious.

Lauren exchanged a quick glance with Matt before turning back to Evans. 'Does Hannah have a bad back?'

Evans nodded, his expression serious. 'Yes. She's had one for years. That's why she regularly goes to Pilates,' he confirmed, sounding puzzled.

Matt's mind raced, trying to connect the dots... except they already knew that Freya and Yvonne didn't go to Pilates with Hannah.

'And aside from the class, does she see anyone for treatment?' Lauren pushed.

'Yes, she does. She's recently been going to an osteopath in town. She said that he's really good and has made a huge difference to her back,' Evans replied with a frown.

Matt's heart pumped in his chest. Now he got it. He glanced at Lauren. Her eyes sparkled. Had they found their connection? They already knew that Freya had a bad back. Did Yvonne?

'Do you know the name of the osteopath?' Matt asked, trying to keep the tone of his voice neutral, so as not to alert the man.

Evans paused for a moment, his brows furrowing as if trying to remember. 'Umm... Yes... His name's Fergus Deakins and his consulting rooms are in the town centre... I think.'

Matt and Lauren exchanged a brief but significant glance. Were the pieces finally coming together? They already knew that Freya and Yvonne didn't attend Pilates. But did they visit Fergus Deakins, the osteopath?

'Thanks for that. We've looked through everything, and can't see anything that has given us an indication of where Hannah is. But we'll keep looking,' Lauren assured Evans. 'Is there anyone we can contact to be with you so you're not alone?'

Evans shook his head, a solemn determination in his eyes. 'Thanks, but no. I'd rather be on my own. I'll carry on with my work and wait for you to find her.'

As Matt and Lauren left Evans' home, the weight of the investigation settled heavily on Matt's shoulders. If the potential connection between the three women was having a bad back, then the osteopath, Fergus Deakins, was where they needed to check next.

'So, we've got Hannah with a bad back, seeking treatment from this osteopath Fergus Deakins,' Matt mused. 'And we know that Freya also has a back problem. The pieces are starting to come together, don't you think?'

Lauren nodded, her eyes reflecting the same intensity that Matt was feeling. 'It's a significant lead. If there's any foul play involved, then Deakins is most definitely a person of interest. We need to gather more information on him, his background, and his practice. We should also dig into his personal and professional life. When we get back to the station we'll get the team working on it. We need to know if there have been any complaints against him, or any signs of unethical conduct. Anything that raises suspicion.'

'But before we do that, first, we need to find out whether Yvonne has a back problem. And if she does, whether she visits Deakins. We also need to check with Freya's husband whether she's had treatment from him, too.'

'An osteopath doesn't just treat backs. They treat a wide range of conditions. Yvonne could have visited him for another issue,' Lauren reminded him.

She was right, he hadn't considered that. Probably because he wasn't a hundred per cent sure how an osteopath worked. The only physical therapist he'd ever visited was a physiotherapist after being shot.

'Good point,' he acknowledged. 'We'll ask her husband. There's no point in diverting all our resources into digging into Deakins until we know for sure that each woman visited him. We can't afford to waste time chasing a lead that doesn't pan out.'

'Yes, I agree. We'll make the connection first and then move forward. We'll get to the bottom of this. We have to. We owe it to the women and their families,' Lauren said, her determination matching Matt's.

An unwavering sense of purpose settled within Matt as they walked back to the car in silence. They were one step away from uncovering the truth and finding out what had happened to the three women.

TWENTY-ONE

TUESDAY, 12 MARCH

Lauren strode into the office with Matt trailing behind her. All eyes immediately fixed on her as she spoke. 'Right, everyone, I think we might have found ourselves a link between the three women. We need to check something out and act quickly,' she commanded.

'What is it, ma'am?' Clem asked, his eyes never leaving Lauren's face.

'Hannah goes to an osteopath in St Ives called Fergus Deakins because of her bad back. We also believe that Freya Kempston has back issues because, when searching her bedroom, we found that she uses a pillow ergonomically designed to help. But whether she receives any treatment for it remains to be seen.' Lauren's voice had an edge of urgency about it. 'Billy, contact Anthony Kempston and find out. Jenna, get in touch with Rory Hughes and ask him if Yvonne visited Deakins for treatment of any description. Tamsin, I want you to dig into Fergus Deakins – find out everything you can. I know that this link may seem a bit far-fetched, but it's the only lead we've got.' She paused. 'I have a budget meeting to attend, so may be unavailable for much of the day. Sergeant Price will run the investigation in my absence.'

The air crackled with anticipation as each person began fulfilling their tasks.

'Thanks, ma'am,' Matt said, turning to her.

Lauren smiled thinly. 'Follow me into my office. We need to discuss when and how you can provide your feedback,' she murmured in a voice so low he could barely hear.

Matt's forehead creased in a frown. What couldn't she say on the main office floor that required such secrecy?

He followed and closed the door behind them.

'What is it, ma'am?' he asked cautiously, turning to face her.

'I'm leaving for the budget meeting soon, but also need to take Tia to the vet to have her stiches removed. I didn't want the rest of the team to know,' Lauren said, her voice low, as if she was ashamed of what she was doing. 'I'll still be contactable.'

A heavy sigh escaped Matt's lips. There it was again. The guarded look that always crept into her eyes when personal matters were brought up. Would she ever realise that such personal information needn't be kept from the team? Maybe if they knew some details of her private life they would start believing she was human, too, and had her own vulnerabilities like everyone else.

'Don't worry, leave it to me. If Deakins turns out to be our link, then once we have more information about him I'll take one of the team and pay him a visit.'

'Take Jenna, unless he's unavailable, in which case you and I will go tomorrow morning.'

Matt nodded. 'Understood, ma'am. I'll be in touch. I hope it all goes okay at the vet with Tia.'

'Thanks.'

Matt returned to the office, his mind buzzing with possibilities. If Deakins was their link it could mean that they were on the verge of a breakthrough. The trust Lauren had placed in him, handing him the reins of the investigation and revealing her own apprehensions, wasn't a fact he took lightly. He was determined to live up to the faith she'd put in him.

'Sarge.' Jenna's voice sliced through his musings. He had barely crossed half the office space when she called out.

'What is it?' He walked towards her, his stride long and determined.

'Yvonne Hughes has knee problems and she's been visiting Fergus Deakins,' she reported.

Her words echoed in the room, silence enveloping the team as the implications began to sink in.

The rapid drumming of his pulse echoed in his ears, drowning out the lingering silence. His chest tightened as if a hand was constricting his breath, pressing into his ribs. Could this be the pivotal breakthrough that they'd been desperate to find?

'And Freya?' he questioned hesitantly, holding his breath as if the room was suddenly void of air. His muscles coiled with anticipation, his heartbeat thudding in his chest, echoing the rhythm of anxiety and excitement.

'Freya also has treatment for her back,' Billy said. He paused, as if enjoying the heightened tension it caused. 'And guess who she sees...'

'My money's on Deakins,' Clem said optimistically.

Billy shook his head, a long, audible sigh escaping his lips, his face crumpled in disappointment. 'No, it's not.'

A tangible sensation of deflation rushed through Matt and his heart seemed to drop into the pit of his stomach. 'Oh, for a moment there I hoped—'

'Only joking, Sarge,' Billy interrupted, a devilish smirk playing on his lips, mischief dancing in his eyes.

Groans of exasperation rippled through the team, followed by collective sighs that seemed to drain the tension from the room.

'Don't do that to me,' Matt retorted, rolling his eyes and shaking his head. But a chuckle escaped his lips, nonetheless. He enjoyed the banter, the camaraderie.

'Sorry, Sarge,' Billy responded, his face a picture of innocence, void of any real regret.

Matt didn't mind. Despite the seriousness of their case, laughter and levity were not only permitted but necessary. They helped to relieve tension, knit the team together, maintain their unity in times of stress.

'Okay, it's official. We now have three women linked to Deakins. All of them have been treated by him,' he announced, his voice bringing everyone back on track.

Billy's eyes sparked with anticipation, nodding eagerly. 'That's it. Deakins is our man,' he stated, his voice tinged with determination.

Matt's raised hand cut through the air, quieting the team. 'Hold on a minute, Billy,' he said, caution lacing his words. 'We can't rush in there all guns blazing and arrest Deakins. We have no proof that he had anything to do with the women's disappearance.' He paused, his gaze sternly sweeping across the faces of his team. 'Remember, every move must be carefully planned and calculated. We must be circumspect.'

'Yes, Sarge,' came Billy's deflated murmur. He slumped into his chair as if invisible strings holding him upright had been abruptly severed.

Noticing this, Matt quickly attempted to restore the officer's morale. 'That doesn't mean we won't go after him,' he said, softening his voice, his tone encouraging. He turned his attention towards Tamsin. 'What do we know about Deakins so far?'

Tamsin's face was a taut mask of concentration, a line of worry etching itself between her brows. 'He's forty-nine. He's only been practising in the area for three months. He rents a room in a health centre in St Ives. Before that, he was living and working in Cardiff.'

'Do we know how many osteopaths there are in the area?' Matt asked.

Clem was swift with his response, his eyes shining. 'There are four, including Deakins,' he declared. He fell into a thoughtful silence for a moment, before adding, 'They have been working in the area for twenty years, eleven years, eight years and a couple of months respectively.'

Billy's brow arched with genuine surprise. 'How do you even know about these osteopaths?' he asked incredulously. His eyes scanned Clem, bewildered. 'I mean, that's crazy even for you.'

Clem shrugged nonchalantly, his lips curving into an amused grin. 'A couple of months ago, my wife had a wrist problem, and I was on the hunt for a therapist. I came across him, and the other osteopaths,' he explained casually, although his tone carried a note of pride. 'She ended up going with a physiotherapist, though. And her wrist's now okay... in case you're wondering,' he added as if it was an afterthought.

Matt's jaw clenched as he mulled over the information that Clem had provided, and the room was silent while the team waited for him to respond. 'Okay. We need to know where exactly in Cardiff Deakins came from and why he decided to move here. I mean, what are the chances of all three women booking appointments with him if he hasn't been in the area for long?' he asked, scanning the team.

'It makes no sense,' Jenna said. 'Especially as we know there are four different osteopaths to choose from.'

'I agree. We need to find out what it was that made all three of them choose to go to him for treatment.' He drummed his fingers on the desk beside him. 'Tamsin, I want you dig deeper into Deakins' background and see what you can uncover. Anything at all, however small and inconsequential it might seem.'

'Yes, Sarge,' Tamsin said, nodding firmly, her features resolute. 'I'll get on to it straight away.'

Matt started pacing the room, his strides steady and slow. 'We need to pay Deakins a visit. But not yet. Before we go, we've got to be as prepared as we possibly can. Jenna, I'd like you to join me if the DI isn't available.'

'No chance of that happening today, Sarge,' Jenna said. 'According to Google, and his posted opening times, he doesn't open on a Tuesday.'

Matt gritted his teeth and halted mid-stride, growling in frustration. 'Okay, let's find out where he lives.'

Jenna shot Matt a look of caution. 'Maybe... but barging into his home unannounced is bound to alert him to our suspicions. Turning up without any valid reason could tip him off that we're on to him and he might do a runner. We've got to be careful. Let him think that he's not on our radar at all. That he's just helping us with our enquiries.'

Nodding in agreement, Matt clenched his fists and squared his shoulders. 'Yes, you're right. Let's wait until tomorrow morning when he's open. I'll go with the DI in that case. In the meantime, let's gather as much information about him as possible – forewarned is forearmed.'

TWENTY-TWO

WEDNESDAY, 13 MARCH

'Good morning, we'd like to see Fergus Deakins, please,' Lauren said in a firm and authoritative tone as they walked into the modern health centre and up to the reception.

The receptionist looked up from her desk. 'Do you have an appointment?' she asked, her gaze flickering between Matt and Lauren as if she was trying to work out what they were doing there.

'No, we'd like to speak to him on a police matter.' Lauren held out her warrant card so the receptionist could see.

'He's with a patient at the moment, but if you'd like to go downstairs to his waiting room, you'll be able to see Mr Deakins when they leave.'

Lauren's eyebrows furrowed. 'Can you phone and interrupt? This is important. We don't have time to wait.'

The receptionist pulled a face. 'I'm sorry, no. Mr Deakins never answers his phone, or any knock on the door, when he's with a patient. That's one of his strict rules. But... he always allows fifteen minutes between each appointment. So, there'll be time for you to speak to him then.'

'What time did this appointment start?' Lauren asked,

letting out a frustrated sigh.

Matt could sense her impatience and shared her sentiment.

'At nine. We allow forty-five minutes per appointment... Give or take a few minutes. Sometimes he runs over.'

They left the reception area and made their way over to the stairs adjacent to the lift. As they reached the waiting room, an eerie silence engulfed the space, with only the ticking of a wall clock breaking the stillness. Matt's eyes landed on the white door with a frosted glass section bearing the name Fergus Deakins, Osteopath.

'I hope we don't have to wait too long,' Lauren said, her voice cutting through the silence.

'If he allows fifteen minutes between appointments, then this one should finish by nine forty-five. So only twenty minutes,' Matt reasoned, hoping to offer some reassurance. They settled onto the chairs lining the walls, bracing themselves for the wait ahead.

As Matt reached for a magazine on the coffee table, he caught a glimpse of his boss's face in his peripheral vision. He turned to her, and his heart sank at the hostility she displayed.

'I'm not convinced that waiting until today was the best decision. You should have run it past me,' she asserted, her words disapproving.

'You left me in charge, and I believed this was the best approach to take, even though it delayed us overnight. We didn't want to arouse his suspicions,' Matt defended himself, standing his ground and meeting her gaze head-on.

Lauren's dubious expression remained unchanged. 'He's still going to be put on the back foot by us arriving here.'

'But not as much as if we'd gone to his home. By visiting here, during working hours, we can play it off as part of the wider investigation, given that we know our missing women are receiving treatment,' Matt reasoned, hoping to sway her perspective.

'Yes, but did you consider that another woman could have gone missing last night?' Lauren's reproachful tone intensified Matt's guilt.

'I hadn't thought of that, ma'am.'

Had he misjudged things? Clearly Lauren thought so. Did he agree?

'We have no idea whether they're alive or dead, and by not approaching him as soon as the link had been made, we could've put another woman at risk. And if he's not involved, then we've wasted more time chasing yet another dead end,' Lauren emphasised, her disappointment evident.

Matt's shoulders slumped under the weight of her words. What she said made total sense. But so, too, did his decision. It was a Catch-22 – whatever he'd decided, the other option was also a possibility.

'Ma'am, it's pointless going over this, because I made the decision and it can't be changed,' Matt asserted, his voice firm and projecting a confidence he didn't entirely feel. 'Have you ever visited an osteopath?' he asked, wanting to move them away from debating whether he'd made a mistake.

She appeared taken aback by the sudden shift in conversation, a look of confusion on her face. After a moment's pause, she replied, 'No. When I've needed treatment, I've seen a physiotherapist.'

Matt nodded, leaning back against the chair, his mind briefly drifting back to the memories of his own rehabilitation. 'Same for me,' he shared. 'When I was shot, I had a long period of rehab that involved a physio. Are osteopaths the same as chiropractors?' he asked, not knowing much about them, either.

'I'm not certain,' Lauren admitted, her expression thoughtful. 'But I believe the difference is that a chiropractor focuses on the spine, joints, and muscles, whereas an osteopath treats the entire body. And I think they use different approaches.'

The conversation lapsed into silence, both lost in their own thoughts as time seemed to stretch on endlessly. Finally, the door swung open and a flushed-faced woman emerged, offering a friendly smile in Matt's direction before disappearing.

'Right, let's go,' Lauren said, rising from her seat and making her way towards the door, with Matt following.

She tapped on the door three times and, without waiting for an invitation, opened it and stepped into the room. Deakins, who was wearing navy scrubs, was engrossed in his computer screen and didn't appear to be bothered by their presence.

'I'll be with you in a moment if you'd like to wait in the waiting room,' he muttered distractedly, still not looking up.

'Mr Deakins, I'm Detective Inspector Pengelly, and this is Detective Sergeant Price. We'd like a word with you. We're not here as patients,' Lauren stated, her voice echoing through the cold, sterile walls of the room.

Deakins swivelled around in his chair to face them. An attractive man with mid-brown hair flecked with grey, he looked younger than his forty-nine years. He smiled, appearing relaxed and not at all perturbed by them being there. 'How can I help?'

As Matt closed the door behind them, he surveyed the light and airy room. It was sparsely furnished, with a medical bed occupying the centre, a desk and filing cabinet against the wall, and a full-size skeleton on a stand in the corner. Prints displaying various bone structures adorned the otherwise bare walls.

Lauren perched on the chair beside Deakins' desk, and Matt swiftly dragged another chair over, placing it next to hers.

'We're investigating the disappearance of three local women and have discovered that all three have visited you recently for treatment,' Lauren stated firmly. 'Their names are Freya Kempston, Yvonne Hughes and Hannah Gifford. Do you recall their visits?'

Deakins furrowed his brow, momentarily staring up to the ceiling – an instinctive behaviour of someone deep in thought.

However, Matt remained sceptical. He knew that such body language could be easily manipulated by those who understood what it was supposed to mean.

After a long pause, Deakins nodded. 'Yes, those names do ring a bell, but I'll have to check my client list to make sure.'

Swivelling back towards his computer screen, Deakins positioned his fingers on the mouse and began searching through his records. Matt tilted his head slightly, managing to catch a glimpse of the screen and the long list of names that Deakins was scrolling through.

'You have a lot of clients, considering you've only been open a few months,' Matt commented, his gaze glued to the computer screen. Every name, every appointment could be another crucial piece of evidence.

'Yes,' Deakins replied, turning to look at Matt, his expression calm. 'When I first arrived, I ran a marketing campaign on social media and offered a free first treatment for anyone who booked during my initial two-week opening period.'

'That's a brilliant idea. You must have had a good response,' Matt responded, his tone purposefully non-committal.

Deakins beamed at him. 'Yes, I did. And sixty per cent of those who received the free treatment booked for further sessions. It was an incredibly successful way of getting my business off the ground. I only wish I'd known about it sooner,' Deakins explained, a self-satisfied tone to his voice.

Matt maintained his composure despite the flurry of thoughts racing through his mind. He couldn't dismiss the fact that Deakins' marketing strategy not only boosted his business but also conveniently provided him with opportunities to meet women – plenty of them. But even so, how would he have learnt so much about their private lives?

'Is offering free sessions a common practice among osteopaths?' Matt probed, keeping his voice deliberately neutral.

'It's common in America, but here in the UK, not so much, which is probably why it was so successful for me,' Deakins replied, his gaze drifting toward the open window that revealed a small rear garden.

'And this special offer is how Freya, Yvonne and Hannah found you, I take it?' Lauren asked, skilfully steering the conversation back to the reason for them being there.

Deakins returned his attention to the computer screen, resuming scrutinising the patient list. 'Yes, I can see that they did.'

'When was the last time you saw these women?' Lauren enquired, her voice coming across as if she was just making an interested enquiry, but Matt, knowing her as he did, could identify the suspicion behind it.

'Yvonne Hughes was last here three weeks ago, according to my records,' Deakins responded, nodding at the computer screen. 'She only needed four sessions in total, and her knee was significantly better than when she first arrived.'

'So, you remember the details of treatments but not your patients' names,' Lauren pointed out.

'Against Yvonne's name, there's a note indicating that her treatment has concluded, most likely because she showed improvement. I'm hopeless at remembering every little detail,' Deakins explained, giving a self-deprecating smile.

Matt frowned, intently absorbing Deakins' explanation. 'Do you only maintain a list like that? I would have thought individual records for each patient would be necessary.'

'Yes, I do have those, but I find it helpful to have this overall sheet so I can quickly review any treatments before a client's appointment,' Deakins replied, his tone unwavering.

'Surely it would be better to read a patient's entire notes before treating them. In case you do something that might harm them,' Matt asked, not convinced by Deakins' reasoning.

'If I have a busy day, it's not always possible. This

condensed version serves its purpose,' Deakins commented, a trace of defensiveness creeping into his voice. 'I only have my patients' best interests at heart. I'm a well-qualified professional. You can check.' He pointed to the certificates on the wall above his desk.

A silent exchange of glances passed between Matt and Lauren, their shared suspicions now more pronounced than ever.

'I apologise, it wasn't my intention to question your integrity. How many patients do you have on your books?' Matt asked, keeping his voice low and non-threatening, to placate the man.

'No problem,' Deakins said, appearing pacified. 'I have approximately eighty-five patients on my books. People start and finish treatment, and sometimes they come back if they have issues.'

'When did you last see Freya or Hannah?' Lauren asked.

Deakins glanced back at his screen. 'Freya is due in on Friday, and I last saw her four weeks ago. She's in a maintenance programme now. Hannah visited last Thursday. But I don't see how this has anything to do with them being missing,' Deakins responded, furrowing his brows in apparent confusion.

'Because they all visited you for treatment recently, we wondered if you could add anything to our investigation,' Lauren said, her voice relaxed and non-threatening.

'Oh, I see. Yes. Of course.'

'You don't seem to be bothered that three of your patients have disappeared,' Matt said, trying hard, but failing, to hide his annoyance with Deakins' nonchalant attitude.

'I'm sorry. I didn't mean to come across like that. It's awful that they're missing but... I don't know what you expect me to say. They're my patients, not my friends. I really don't know much about them. It's not like we chat when they visit. It's purely professional.'

'So, you don't know anything about their private lives or their families, then?' Matt asked.

Deakins shrugged. 'Sometimes patients do talk about their families while I'm treating them. But to be honest, I don't remember. I've got an awful memory, as I've already mentioned. Anything that isn't written down goes in one ear and out the other.' He gave a dry laugh, as if that was a comment he made on a regular basis.

'So, Freya, Yvonne and Hannah might have talked about themselves to you, but you don't remember the details,' Matt clarified.

'Yes, that's about the size of it,' Deakins said, shrugging. 'I'm sorry. You know I would like to help if I could but unless you want me to make up something then I'm afraid I can't.' He glanced at his watch. 'I do have another patient shortly.'

'Where were you on Monday, March fourth, during the afternoon?' Lauren asked, ignoring his pointed request for the interview to be over.

'I was here at work, and the reception staff upstairs can vouch for me,' Deakins replied, a note of certainty in his voice.

'Unless you left through the emergency exit in the waiting room,' Matt countered, locking eyes with Deakins.

'I didn't. I had patients,' Deakins said, his defensive stance faltering slightly.

'And what about last Saturday night?' Lauren pressed.

'I was at home. I finished work at five, went food shopping, and was home by six thirty. I didn't leave after that.'

'Can anyone vouch for you?' Lauren asked.

'No. Although... you can ask my elderly neighbour, Angie. She's always peering out of the window. She would have seen my car parked in the driveway,' Deakins suggested, a smirk tugging at the corners of his mouth.

'Do you live alone?' Lauren continued.

'Yes, since I was divorced from my wife just over a year ago.

My daughter goes to university, so I don't see her much. Occasionally, she'll visit,' Deakins responded, a flicker of regret crossing his face.

'Where's your wife?'

'I don't know, and I don't care,' Deakins replied with disdain, the look on his face a clear indicator of unresolved issues.

Matt seized the opportunity to dig deeper into Deakins' background while being cautious not to arouse suspicion. 'Before you came here, where were you practising?' he asked, his tone measured and composed, even though he already knew the answer.

'Cardiff,' Deakins responded matter-of-factly, as if the question was no big deal.

'You don't sound Welsh,' Lauren commented, her head tilting to one side as if she was curious.

Deakins shrugged nonchalantly, his gaze drifting away from theirs. 'I'm not. I was born in Scotland, but we travelled around a lot when I was young. Hence me not having a Scottish accent either. My father was in the air force,' he explained, reciting the statement as if it had become a rehearsed response over time. 'We lived in Germany, Yorkshire, in the Midlands... You name it, we lived there.'

'That must have been hard for you as a child,' Matt said.

'Not really. I got used to it.'

'What made you decide to move to Cornwall? It's very different from Cardiff's city life,' Lauren asked.

Deakins' shoulders tensed subtly at the question. 'I wanted to live somewhere quiet and away from the hustle and bustle. It's beautiful here. Why are you asking?'

'I was curious, that's all. Before we go, please could you tell us where you were on the evening of Tuesday, March fifth, after ten,' Lauren asked, her tone now laced with a more serious edge.

'I have Tuesdays off because I work on Saturdays. On the fifth, I spent the day out on a boat, fishing. I got home around nine or ten after stopping at the pub for something to eat,' Deakins explained.

'And can anybody vouch for you?' Lauren pressed, her gaze unwavering as she stared directly at Deakins.

'The pub was busy, and I doubt they'd remember me. But, again, you can ask Angie if she saw my car,' Deakins suggested dismissively, accompanied by yet another shrug.

'Thank you, we will,' Lauren acknowledged, her tone shifting slightly. 'Now, can you tell us what car you drive?'

'I have a Mazda CX-5,' Deakins responded, a brief flicker of confusion crossing his face.

'And what colour is it?'

'Midnight blue.'

Matt's mind immediately leapt to a dark SUV. The puzzle pieces were starting to come together, painting a picture that intensified their concerns.

'And—' Lauren began to speak, but Matt quickly interrupted, cutting her off.

'That's a cool model skeleton,' Matt said, redirecting the conversation, preventing Lauren from delving into sensitive topics that might raise an alarm with Deakins. He had a gut feeling that probing too deeply could trigger a defensive response from Deakins, potentially prompting him to do a disappearing act.

Deakins smiled, seeming to be amused by the change of subject. 'Yes, I like to have it here for my patients so I can demonstrate what's wrong with them on a life-like version of themselves,' Deakins explained, glancing at his watch. 'If that's all you have to ask, I do have another patient waiting, and if I'm late for her, then I'll be late for the next. It's a domino effect. I do hope you find these missing women. It must be such a worrying time for their families.'

Lauren stood up, and Matt followed suit. 'Thank you for your time,' Lauren said.

'It's my pleasure,' Deakins said, flashing a smile. 'I'm sorry that I can't tell you any more than I've treated Freya, Yvonne and Hannah, along with all my other clients.'

Matt and Lauren exited the treatment room, climbed the stairs, and made their way outside. Matt's gaze lingered on the building they'd just left as he turned to Lauren. 'Well, what do you think?'

'There's something about him that I don't trust,' Lauren replied, her expression contemplative. 'He's clearly aware of his attractiveness and uses it to ingratiate himself. And his interest in the women's disappearance didn't appear genuine. I felt that maybe...'

Her voice trailed off, and Matt nodded. 'Agreed. That's why I interrupted and asked about the skeleton. I wasn't sure if you were going to bring up the sightings of the dark SUV. If it is him, that might cause him to take off. It's better for him to believe he's just helping us. Then again, in my experience of serial killers, they like to stick around and see what the police are up to. They enjoy outwitting us,' Matt said, his tone grim.

'That's assuming we do have a serial killer on our hands. But I agree, we don't want to alert him any more than necessary. We need to dig deeper into his life, find out where his wife is. And we need to check with his neighbour. If his car was parked at his house during those key evening hours, then we can't place him at any crime scene,' Lauren said.

As they walked away from the osteopath's practice, Matt's mind filled with questions and suspicions. Unravelling the truth behind the disappearances would require careful investigation and relentless pursuit of the facts.

TWENTY-THREE

WEDNESDAY, 13 MARCH

'We've just returned from seeing Deakins, and there's definitely something fishy about him.' Matt's voice echoed in the otherwise quiet room.

He stood in front of the whiteboard, his mind still piecing together the disjointed facts they had about Deakins. Lauren had been called in to see DCI Mistry and she was going to join them shortly. In the meantime, he needed to progress the investigation.

'Sarge,' Tamsin called out, 'I've been in touch with South Wales Police because I had no joy in finding Deakins' ex-wife. According to them, she disappeared shortly after the divorce was finalised. The family reported her missing. They interviewed Deakins during the investigation, but they didn't pursue it because they didn't believe he had anything to do with it.'

'Why not?' he asked.

'They didn't say. I'm guessing he had an alibi. They did mention when she went missing she'd been seeing another man.'

Matt absorbed the information, his fingers drumming on the

empty desk beside him. 'What could they tell you about this other man?'

'Well, that's the thing. He was missing too.'

'And this wasn't a cause for alarm?' Matt shook his head in disbelief.

'No, Sarge. They said there was no evidence of any crimes being committed and assumed that they'd gone off somewhere together.'

'When did this take place?' he asked, pushing aside an annoying stray lock of hair that had fallen over his forehead. His mum had been nagging him to get his hair cut. But he never seemed to have the time.

'About a year ago.'

'And what about the daughter?' Matt asked, remembering that Deakins had mentioned her.

'I didn't come across a daughter. It was only him and his wife who lived at his old place until they split and then he was alone until moving here,' Tamsin said, a small frown on her face and surprise showing in her eyes.

'He told us that his daughter went to university, but he didn't get to see her much. See if you can find her.'

'Yes, Sarge, will do,' Tamsin assured him.

The room was silent as Matt continued. 'Deakins has a somewhat tenuous alibi for the times when Yvonne Hughes and Hannah Gifford went missing. He maintains he was at home alone, but his car was in the drive and his elderly neighbour would vouch for him because she's always looking through her window at what he's doing.'

'A curtain twitcher,' Billy interjected, his laughter bouncing off the wall.

The others joined in, and Matt grinned.

He turned to the young DC. 'You may well laugh, but they have proved very useful in many cases.' He paused a moment until the laughter died down. 'Someone needs to get in touch with this neighbour to confirm the alibi,' he said, his tone becoming serious again.

'I'll do it,' Clem volunteered, reaching for his phone.

'Sarge, do you think that Deakins' wife was cheating on him with this other man and that's why they divorced?' Jenna asked.

Matt paused, tilting his head back slightly as he absorbed the question. His fingers traced an absent-minded path along the rough stubble on his chin. 'It might be... ahhhhh... I see where you're going with this.'

'Where?' Billy asked, sounding confused.

'If Deakins is our man, then maybe he's got a thing about women who cheat on their partners,' Matt proposed.

Billy's face turned grim. 'But how would he know that Freya, Yvonne and Hannah were all doing that?'

A faint, dry smile played on Jenna's lips. 'You'd be surprised what people let slip when they're with a professional, Billy. Especially if the professional, in other words Deakins, asks the right questions.'

Jenna was right. Deakins was in a position of power over these women and could have elicited all sorts of information from them.

'Sarge.' Clem's voice cut through the contemplative silence that had enveloped the room. 'The neighbour confirms seeing Deakins' car in the drive on both Tuesday and Saturday evenings. She was in bed by ten thirty on both nights. Apparently, she gets up to answer nature's call around two to two thirty most nights, and the car was still there on both occasions. Because she checked.'

The information dropped like a pebble into Matt's pool of thoughts. 'And she's certain about her bedtime?'

Clem responded with a confident nod. 'Yes, she's adamant that she's always in bed by ten thirty. So, if Deakins was aware of her routine, he'd have an ample window to operate.'

'But there's no way he could know what time she gets up to use the toilet,' Jenna added, her face appearing doubtful.

'Most people won't stir for the first three or four hours of sleep, so he could probably bank on that... If it is him,' Matt said.

The office door opened, diverting their attention. Lauren strode in, her face stern. Without a moment's pause, she made her way to where Matt was standing. 'Get me up to speed,' she ordered.

'Deakins' wife and her lover vanished a year ago and remain unfound,' Matt began, outlining the main points. 'We're searching for evidence of his daughter, as Tamsin couldn't find any mention of her in her initial search. The elderly neighbour has confirmed his alibi, with the caveat that she was in bed during the hours we're interested in. We're also exploring a theory that Deakins targets women he believes are unfaithful. But, for now, it's all conjecture.'

The room remained in tense silence, the collective weight of their investigation pressing heavily on each officer present.

'Ma'am, I've got an idea.' Jenna's voice punctuated the silence, wavering just enough to betray her nerves. She shifted in her chair, her hand absent-mindedly rubbing at her lower back. 'Why don't I book an appointment to see Deakins? My back's been giving me trouble, so it's a plausible reason to request an emergency appointment. I can hint at some marital issues during the session.'

'Go undercover, you mean?' Lauren's question was more of a statement, her voice carrying a note of uncertainty.

Jenna nodded. 'Sort of, yes, ma'am. I'll use my maiden name.'

Matt studied Lauren's expression closely, his keen eyes catching the flicker of doubt dancing in her eyes. Yet, he found himself leaning towards Jenna's strategy. It was a tad on the risky side, but it held promise.

Lauren's lips curved upward into a rare smile, softening her stern demeanour briefly. 'I'll need to speak to the DCI to get his permission. But... It could work. Good idea, Jenna.'

A look of relief washed over Jenna's face at the acknowledgement, her tense shoulders visibly relaxing. 'Thank you, ma'am.'

'Don't thank me yet – we don't know whether we'll get the DCI's approval. If he says no, then we'll have to think again.'

'Of course he'll agree,' Billy said. 'It's a great idea. Then we can nail the bastard and—'

Lauren held her hand up, silencing the officer. 'Let's cool it. It's pointless getting excited without knowing whether he'll approve. And even then, this is serious. We should keep calm and approach it professionally. The DCI's in his office. I'll go and see him now.'

The moment she'd left the room, the team members burst into animated chatter. Although Matt agreed with Lauren, he didn't think it hurt for them to let off steam. He knew that when it came down to it the operation would be approached with utmost professionalism.

With a careful tap on the door, Lauren drew in a breath and gently pushed it open. The DCI's office was a familiar sight, a hub of authority and decision-making. She tentatively stuck her head around the door, her heart pounding with anticipation. Without his approval, their plans would be dead in the water. 'Sir, do you have a minute?'

'What is it, Lauren? I've only just seen you,' Mistry replied, frowning. He had the look of a man constantly burdened by the weight of the world, his shoulders squared as if ready to take on any challenge. Although, she knew that most of the challenges he faced were administrative.

Lauren took a moment to collect her thoughts, knowing the importance of the lead they'd discovered. 'We have a very strong lead now for the missing women,' she started slowly. 'He's an osteopath called Fergus Deakins who's new to the area and practises in St Ives. I'd like to send one of my officers in for an appointment with him. DC Jenna Moyle. She'll be undercover. We believe he has an issue with women who cheat on their partners and she'll let it slip that she's having problems in her marriage.'

Mistry raised an eyebrow at this. 'Is DC Moyle likely to be in any danger during the operation?'

'Not at this stage, sir, no,' Lauren reassured him quickly, having already predicted his concerns. 'She's going to use her maiden name and so won't be linked back to us. She hasn't been involved in any interview with him. It was just Sergeant Price and I who visited him at his clinic.'

'And what do you hope to achieve from this? Because you could well be putting a target on her back,' Mistry said, uncertainty in his voice.

Lauren had considered this, too. 'We'll make sure that she doesn't give her real address, and we'll also be giving her a phone specifically for the purpose. That way he won't be able to make contact without us knowing, nor can he discover where she lives.'

'Unless he follows her,' the DCI said.

'If she's going to visit him during his clinic hours then I don't see how that would be possible.'

The DCI seemed to consider her words, his gaze piercing and thoughtful. 'If you wish to go further than this one appointment you're to see me first. That includes another appointment, or if he suggests meeting her away from his consulting room.'

'Yes, sir,' she responded dutifully. 'So do we have your permission to go ahead with the first part of the plan?'

After a moment of contemplation, he gave a terse nod. 'Yes, you do.'

With a sigh of relief, Lauren exited the office and made her way back to the team's office. When she entered, she was hit by the weight of anticipation from them.

'What did the DCI say?' Billy was the first to ask, his voice eager.

'He's given his permission for Jenna to have an appointment with him. Jenna, we'll give you a mobile solely for this purpose and you're to give a fake address. We're not to take it any further than this first meeting without obtaining the DCI's approval. I want you to try for an appointment with him at the clinic for tomorrow, if that's at all possible.'

'I've actually gone online, ma'am,' Jenna said, a spark of excitement in her voice. 'There's an available appointment showing for eight forty-five tomorrow morning. Shall I book it?'

'Yes, definitely.' Lauren nodded approvingly, feeling a surge of momentum building. 'We'll sort out the phone and make sure that you've got everything you need. Go there straight from home and then come here as soon as you've finished for a debriefing.'

The room buzzed with anticipation and a shared sense of purpose. For the first time since this case began, they were finally making tangible progress.

TWENTY-FOUR
THURSDAY, 14 MARCH

The knock on Lauren's door was sharp and, glancing up from the computer, she saw Matt's outline through the glass panel.

'Come in.' She beckoned, her hand fluttering in a brief invitation before resuming its hold on the mouse.

Matt pushed open the door and stepped into the office, remaining standing. 'Ma'am, Jenna's arrived back from her appointment with Fergus Deakins. We're ready to listen to her feedback once you are.'

Lauren nodded, glancing back to the computer screen at the unfinished sentence in the email she was sending.

'Thanks, Matt. Give me a moment and I'll be with you.'

With a nod, Matt left, closing the door behind him. She hastily finished and sent the email before pushing away from the desk, her chair rolling backwards with a quiet rustle on the carpet. Anticipation coursed through her veins. A lot hinged on Jenna's feedback.

She stepped into the main office and marched over to where Matt and Jenna were huddled together in front of the whiteboard, their fellow officer's attention glued to them. As she approached, Matt turned and acknowledged her presence.

'Right, the DI's here. Let's hear what happened, Jenna,' Matt said, giving a nod.

Jenna glanced at Lauren before starting. 'Okay, I had my appointment with Deakins this morning. I told him that my back was playing up and he took down my details – I gave him a fake address and the burner phone number. Then he took a brief medical history and asked me to stand so he could evaluate my posture. It turns out that I naturally lean slightly to the left side. He then asked me to lie on the bed.'

'Did you keep your clothes on?' Billy asked.

'I removed my shoes and sweatshirt. But I kept on my trousers and shirt the whole time. Deakins did a lot of poking and prodding and pushing for about ten minutes.' A slight flinch crossed Jenna's face as she recounted the examination.

'Doesn't sound very professional,' Billy said, his arms folded tightly across his chest.

'It was,' Jenna said, her voice firm. 'It's just... You know.' She paused, her gaze distant as if reliving it. 'Because I was there undercover, it sort of gave me the creeps. If you get what I mean. But he didn't do anything inappropriate. It was like any normal examination.'

'I understand, Jenna,' Lauren said softly. 'You did well, keeping your cool.'

'Thanks, ma'am,' Jenna answered, lifting her eyes to meet Lauren's. 'Anyway, it turns out that I've got a problem with my lower discs which he said he can treat.'

Lauren's brows knitted together at Jenna's revelation, but her mind quickly shifted back to the reason they'd sent Jenna undercover in the first place. 'What did he talk about while he was treating you?'

'He asked about my job.' Jenna's voice was steadier, her words more sure-footed. 'I told him I was an administrator and sat a lot, which could be why my back was hurting. He agreed that could be the problem.'

'Did he ask anything more personal?' Lauren asked.

Jenna nodded. 'Yes, he asked where I lived and about my family. I told him that I have a daughter, but she lives far away, and we don't get to see her often.'

'Do you?' Matt asked, sounding surprised.

'No, Sarge,' Jenna clarified, amusement in her tone. 'I said that because of his comments about his own daughter. He latched on to my words and started talking about himself. He's divorced, lives alone, and misses his daughter, who's away.'

'And what was your response?' Lauren queried, her eyes not leaving Jenna's face.

Jenna shrugged slightly. 'I agreed and said how difficult it is when children leave home. I added that it underlines how monotonous life can be. It was a way to keep him talking.'

'That's an excellent answer,' Lauren said, nodding her approval. 'Did he ask more about that?'

'Yes. He wanted to know why my life was boring and I used that as a chance to say I've been married a long time and I miss going out and having a good time like I did when I was younger.'

'What did he say to that?' Matt asked.

'He said he could sympathise with my situation. I then told him that my husband is happy to sit in front of the television every night and that, more often than not, he falls asleep. I said it can get lonely.' She paused a moment. Scanning the room. 'Deakins then said in a light-hearted, jokey way, that maybe we should go out for a drink together to keep each other company.'

'What a creep,' Billy said, turning up his nose in obvious distaste, his reaction immediate and raw. His usual easy-going manner replaced by something much harsher.

'Yes, Billy, but it's also the point of Jenna going,' Lauren said, reminding him that it was the whole focus of the operation.

'I know that, ma'am. But that doesn't stop me from thinking he's a sleazy creep.'

'I understand,' Lauren said. 'But our aim is to discover what he's like. How did you respond, Jenna?' she asked, returning to look at the officer.

'I laughed, as if I thought he was messing around. I didn't pursue it but also didn't want him to think that I took offence at what he'd suggested.'

'Good. Did he mention it again during the appointment?' Lauren asked.

Jenna shook her head. 'No, he didn't. But he does want me to go back for a second session. He said he needed to do more work and didn't have time to do it then because he had another patient straight after. I know we're meant to let the DCI know, but I thought it would be suspicious if I didn't agree, so I've booked in for Monday. I can always cancel if the DCI doesn't agree.'

'That's okay. I'm sure DCI Mistry will be fine about it. What's your impression of Deakins?' Lauren asked, her mind already formulating their next steps, and wanting to better understand the man.

Jenna appeared to consider the question before answering. 'He seems good at what he does and is certainly knowledgeable. He showed me on the skeleton he had standing in the corner exactly where my discs are and what would be happening to them in my current state.'

'What about him as a person?' Lauren asked.

'Honestly, if I didn't know what we suspect him of, I'd say he was really nice. He smiled a lot and put me at my ease. He has a relaxed manner. He's an attractive man.'

'You've got to be kidding,' Billy said, making pretend vomit noises.

'That doesn't mean I fancy him! But I can see that some women would.'

'That's exactly right,' Lauren said. 'If he did persuade

Freya, Yvonne and Hannah to go out with him, then there has to be something that would make them agree.'

'Totally,' Jenna said, nodding in agreement.

'Okay, so now we have to wait to see if Deakins phones,' Lauren said, scanning the room and addressing the whole team. 'But while we wait there's work to be done. This isn't the time for us to become complacent.' She looked directly at Clem. 'I want you to drive out to the health centre where he works and keep an eye on any movements in and out of Deakins' practice. I don't want any direct confrontation, just observe and report back at the briefing each morning. We need to build up a clear profile of his routine, his clients, and any visitors he receives. Pay particular attention to any regular visitors, especially if they're female. Or if he goes out for lunch with anyone. He's open for appointments for the next three days, counting today, so let's see what he gets up to.'

Clem nodded. 'I'm on it, ma'am. Shall I go alone?'

'You can take Billy,' she said, nodding towards the other officer.

'Good. Let's go nail the creepy tosser,' Billy said.

'I said no confrontation, Billy,' Lauren warned.

'Just a figure of speech, ma'am,' Billy said, turning his head, but not before Lauren noticed the smirk. She hoped she wouldn't regret her decision to send him out with Clem.

'Tamsin, I want you to go through Deakins' background again. There might be something we've missed. An old case, a former partner, a disgruntled patient – anything that could be useful.'

Matt was already nodding before she finished. 'I agree, a second and more thorough look would be good.'

'And don't forget to locate this daughter... Unless she doesn't exist and he invented her to portray himself as a father figure. It would certainly make him seem more protective of women rather than predatory.'

'Yes, ma'am,' Tamsin said, turning away, her fingers already dancing over the keys on her computer.

'Jenna, your task is equally important. As you're the point of contact, we need you to keep us updated. If he phones, I want to know immediately. However early or late it might be in the day. We also need you to be prepared for Monday's appointment,' Lauren instructed, her gaze steady on Jenna.

'I will be, ma'am,' Jenna confirmed, her expression serious. 'But there's nothing for me to do, really.'

'You can help Tamsin, while we're waiting. Remember, everyone, communication is key here. We're a team, and this investigation depends on each one of us playing our part. This isn't just about uncovering the truth. It's about ensuring Jenna's safety.'

With that, the room broke into a flurry of activity.

Lauren turned to head back to her office but noticed Matt staring at her, his brow furrowed in deep thought.

'Something on your mind, Matt?'

Matt shrugged, 'I'm thinking about the case. It's a tough one. We've got *some* information, but it's a long way from anything substantial. Jenna's doing well, but we can't put everything on her.'

'I know,' Lauren agreed, her lips pursed in thought. 'But it's all we have. We need to work with what we've got and, right now, that's Jenna's appointment and the hope that Deakins will make a mistake.'

'Right,' Matt replied. 'But this kind of investigation can take a toll, especially on Jenna. We need to ensure she's still okay to continue with whatever direction it takes us.'

'Yes, I agree.'

'Shall I talk to Jenna today, to make sure she's holding up okay?' Matt suggested.

'Good idea,' Lauren acknowledged. 'But she's stronger than she looks and we're in this together.'

'Of course.' Matt nodded. 'And we have you leading us.'

'Yes, we do,' Lauren said, with a hint of a smile. 'Now let's get to work. We have a case to solve.'

TWENTY-FIVE

FRIDAY, 15 MARCH

Lauren walked briskly into the bustling office on Friday morning, ready to kickstart the day's briefing.

'Ma'am,' Jenna called out, her urgency evident, as she ran over towards her.

Lauren's brow furrowed, curious about what was so urgent. 'What is it?'

Jenna held out her phone, a text message displayed on the screen. 'It's from Deakins.'

My last appointment of the afternoon has cancelled. Would you like it?

'We can't do anything without permission from the DCI, so reply and say you'll let him know because you have to ask for time off work,' Lauren suggested, staring at the phone in her hand.

'Yes, ma'am,' Jenna said, taking back the mobile and sending a text.

The mobile pinged almost immediately, and Jenna opened the message and held it out for Lauren to read.

Okay. We could go out for a drink after if you'd like to?

Lauren's mind raced, analysing every word and possible

implication. She'd had a feeling that it was all going to kick off today, but she'd dismissed it as irrational. She'd been wrong. A mix of caution and excitement surged through her. This was what they wanted to happen, but now it had, they had to be so careful in how they allowed it to progress, and planning was paramount.

'Attention, everyone,' Lauren called out, her strong voice commanding the room's attention. 'Deakins has offered Jenna a further appointment this afternoon and has also asked her to go out for a drink with him afterwards.'

The team erupted into a chorus of exclamations and congratulations. The excitement palpable.

'That's great. And it's proof that he's the one who took the three women,' Billy exclaimed, a wide grin spreading across his face.

Lauren nodded, acknowledging Billy's observation. She couldn't help but feel a surge of optimism. It seemed like their careful investigation was finally leading them to Deakins. But whether or not the three women were still alive... The sobering thought brought her back to reality.

'Well, it's certainly pointing in that direction, but we must be careful in how we're going to play this. This is a man we suspect of abduction at the very least, and quite possibly murder. My view is that you turn down the appointment, Jenna, but accept the drink. That will give us more control over the situation. I don't want you alone in his consulting room at a time when there are no other patients likely to be around. Not to mention that you wouldn't be able to wear a wire while he was treating you because he'd see it.'

'What about in the pub?' Billy asked.

'That wouldn't work either. There'll be too much ambient noise in the pub and any commotion in Jenna's earpiece could tip Deakins off,' Lauren said.

The room fell into a hushed silence as the team absorbed

Lauren's words. They all knew that a single misstep could jeopardise their chances of apprehending Deakins and put Jenna's life at risk. The stakes were higher than ever.

'Sorry, ma'am. I didn't mean to make light of it,' Billy said.

'It's fine, Billy,' Lauren said with a dismissive flick of her hand. She understood his excitement, but it needed tempering or he'd become unfocused.

'Okay, ma'am. I'll arrange a place to meet him where we're in full view of everyone,' Jenna suggested, a touch of uncertainty in her voice.

'I'm sure we can work it out,' Lauren replied, her voice exuding a quiet confidence. 'We'll have officers strategically positioned inside the pub, discreetly keeping an eye on the situation. Matt and I will be stationed outside, maintaining surveillance without risking being recognised, because Deakins has already met us.' Her eyes scanned the room, ensuring she had everyone's attention. 'But we can't proceed without the approval of the DCI. I'll sort that out now, and then we'll reconvene to make the final arrangements.'

With a determined nod, Lauren retreated to her office, closing the door behind her. The muffled sounds of the bustling office were replaced by a tense silence. She approached her desk, her fingers hovering over the buttons on her phone, ready to act. Her mind raced with contingency plans, preparing for the possibility of the DCI being unavailable.

As if she'd had some sort of foresight, there was no answer from the DCI's phone; it simply went to voicemail. She wasn't prepared to leave a message because it needed sorting out straight away. She decided to call his executive assistant, in the hope that she could contact the DCI and ask him to call Lauren as a matter of urgency.

'Hello, Nancy here,' a voice answered on the other end.

'It's DI Pengelly. I'd like to contact DCI Mistry. It's

extremely urgent,' she said, wasting no time in getting to the point.

'I'm sorry, he's away from the office at an all-day meeting. He won't be back today and he's left specific instructions that he's not to be disturbed under any circumstances.'

'But this is important. I'm sure he won't mind being interrupted,' Lauren pushed, her tone conveying the weight of the situation.

'Sorry, I should have been clearer. It's not so much that he *can't* be contacted but that he doesn't wish to be. I have my instructions and can't go against them...' Her voice trailed off as if she was thinking that, because Lauren was beneath the DCI in rank, then tough. Would it be the same if it was Mistry's boss who wanted him? Lauren doubted it. But she didn't have time to dwell on that now.

'Okay. Thanks, Nancy. I'll contact Detective Superintendent Bligh,' she said, referring to Mistry's immediate superior.

Lauren ended the call and was about to phone the Super when she decided that a conversation in person would probably be more effective.

Taking a deep breath to gather herself, Lauren left her office and headed purposefully down the corridor, her mind racing with ideas of how she was going to word her request in order to gain permission for the operation to go ahead.

She knocked on the Super's door and waited for a response.

'Come in,' the woman answered in a clear voice.

Lauren released the breath that she'd been holding, in case the Super hadn't been there and she was left with nowhere else to go. She then walked into the room and was greeted by the smiling officer.

Detective Superintendent Bligh was in her late fifties and had worked for Devon and Cornwall Police for the majority of her career. Although Lauren hadn't interacted with her extensively, she'd always found the Super to be reasonable and collaborative.

'Ma'am, I need sign off on some undercover work that my team would like to undertake,' Lauren began, her voice carrying a sense of urgency. 'DCI Mistry isn't contactable today, and the operation is to take place this evening. One of my officers has been undercover, investigating an osteopath, Fergus Deakins, whom we suspect may be involved in the disappearance of the three women from St Ives. He's now contacted my officer and asked her to meet him for a drink. Members of my team will be inside, watching discreetly, while my sergeant and I will maintain surveillance from outside. But I do need your permission for this to go ahead.'

The Super listened attentively, her expression thoughtful. 'In your discussions with DCI Mistry, was anything decided regarding a follow-up from the initial visit to the osteopath by your officer?'

Lauren took a moment to gather her thoughts. 'We discussed that if there was any significant development I would obtain his permission before moving forward.'

The Super nodded, her eyes fixed on Lauren. 'And what are the risks for the officer involved?'

Lauren met the Super's gaze with unwavering determination. 'As with any operation, ma'am, there are always risks. However, we have measures in place to mitigate them. My team will be vigilant, ensuring the officer's safety while she's gathering vital information that we hope will lead to his arrest and the discovery of...' Lauren had been about to say *bodies of the missing women*, but they had no evidence that was the case yet.

The Super's eyes narrowed slightly as she pondered the situation. 'Have you considered the officer wearing a wire?'

Lauren nodded, understanding the rationale behind the Super's question, but needing to explain why it wouldn't work. 'It's not practical in a busy pub situation due to potential interference. However, we'll devise an alternative plan. We'll have a signal for my officer to give if she wants to inform us of anything or if she needs to exit the meeting. We'll use the Ladies restroom.'

The Super leant back in her chair, appearing deep in thought. 'I trust your judgement, Lauren,' she eventually said, with a firmness that mirrored her words. 'If you believe the operation could lead to discovering the truth behind these women's disappearances, with minimal risk to your team, then I will authorise it.'

'Thank you, ma'am,' Lauren said, gratitude and relief in her voice. 'We won't take this opportunity lightly.'

The Super's expression softened slightly. 'I want to be kept informed of how the operation unfolds. You can report directly to me, bypassing the usual channels.'

'Yes, ma'am. I'll provide regular updates,' Lauren affirmed, feeling a renewed sense of purpose.

With a subtle flick of her hand, the Super signalled the end of their conversation, prompting Lauren to rise from her seat and leave. A sense of energy coursed through her veins as she headed down the corridor, her mind focused on the task in hand. She was anxious to share the news with her team.

'Okay,' she began, her words cutting through the air the moment she stepped inside the office. 'I have permission from Detective Superintendent Bligh for us to go ahead with the operation.'

A murmur of approval rippled through the room, the team visibly relieved by the positive development.

'You went straight to her?' Billy asked, his curiosity evident.

'Yes, because the DCI wasn't available. But the decision-making process doesn't require your involvement,' Lauren said, a hint of sternness creeping into her voice.

Billy flushed, clearly realising that he'd overstepped the mark... yet again. 'No, ma'am,' he muttered.

'We've been discussing the operation in your absence, ma'am,' Jenna said. 'Like you suggested, we discussed me texting Deakins, saying no to the appointment because I can't leave work and then agree to meet him for a drink. I'll recommend the Coach House pub which is in Penzance town centre and easy for the rest of you to monitor.'

Lauren considered the suggestion, recognising its merit. 'Yes, that's a good idea, Jenna. Reply to him, now.'

Lauren watched as Jenna swiftly composed a text message and sent it off. The room fell into an expectant silence, tension building as they awaited Deakins' response.

'He might not reply immediately, if he's with a patient,' Jenna reminded them all.

There was a collective groan and then everyone turned back to what they'd been working on.

Lauren was about to return to her office when Jenna's phone pinged. The officer reached for the phone on her desk and slid to open the message.

'He's keen,' Billy said, his words hanging ominously in the air. 'Well, what did he say?'

'He said we should meet around five, but he'd rather go to the Black Horse,' Jenna relayed, her voice tinged with a hint of apprehension. 'He mentioned wanting to avoid chance encounters with any of his patients.'

'Where's this pub?' Matt asked, frowning.

'It's a little way out of town,' Jenna said.

'So, he wants to take you somewhere quiet and out of the way. What a load of crap about not wanting to bump into any of his clients,' Billy scoffed, his distrust apparent. 'He wants to make sure you're not seen together, full stop.'

'Maybe, but even though the pub isn't central, it often gets busy,' Clem said, sounding optimistic. 'It's a lovely place. Me and the wife often go. I think you'll be okay there, Jenna. Especially as it's a Friday night.'

'Yes, Clem's right,' Tamsin added. 'I've been before and it does get busy.'

'Okay,' Lauren said, finding comfort in the words of the team. 'Text back and say yes, Jenna. Then we'll sort everything out from here,' Lauren continued, injecting confidence into her voice. 'It will be fine. We'll be there with you every step of the way.'

The team nodded in agreement, a renewed sense of purpose filling the air. They were ready to move forward as a unified force, determined to solve the case.

TWENTY-SIX

FRIDAY, 15 MARCH

'Hi, Mum, it's me,' Matt said, glancing at Lauren's door to make sure she wasn't yet coming into the team office for the final briefing. 'I wanted to let you know that I'm going to be late home tonight. We've got an operation and I've no idea when it will be over.'

'Okay, love. Would you like to speak to Dani?' His mum's soothing voice helped calm his nerves. His stress levels inevitably rose when there was an operation, especially one like this, where an officer was going undercover. 'She's standing next to me.'

Matt couldn't help but smile at the image of Dani hovering close to his mum and no doubt wanting to answer the phone when it rang. His daughter had a thing for phones and one of her favourite games was for them to have pretend calls using the actual phones. It was easy because his parents mainly used a landline, neither of them liking their mobiles, complaining that they couldn't see the keys properly.

'Of course, put her on.'

There was a momentary shuffle in the background. 'Hello, Daddy, are you coming home soon?'

'Sorry, sweetheart, I can't. I've got to work late tonight.' Guilt coursed through him because he wasn't going to be there to tuck her in at bedtime. But it wasn't like he was regularly home late. That was one of the reasons he enjoyed working at Penzance so much.

'Will you be with Lauren?'

'Yes. We're working together.'

'Who's looking after Tia?' Dani asked, sounding concerned.

'Betty, Lauren's next-door neighbour.'

'Oh... That's good then.'

'I promise to check on you soon as I get home and give you a kiss goodnight. Be good for Grandma,' Matt said, knowing that he couldn't speak for much longer.

'Okay,' Dani said, sounding dejected. 'We're making cakes with lots of hundreds and thousands,' she added, sounding all cheerful again.

'That sounds lovely.' He chuckled, a mental picture of their kitchen being transformed into a hundreds-and-thousands warzone. 'Make sure to save me one. Don't eat them all.'

'Don't be silly, Daddy. We can't eat them all or we'll be sick. Won't we, Grandma?'

He laughed out loud as he heard his mum in the background agreeing with Dani.

'Well that's good. I'll look forward to eating mine later. I must go now. I'll see you in the morning. Love you.'

'Love you, too, Daddy.'

'Let me speak to Grandma before I go.'

'Hello, love.' The sound of his mum's voice echoed in his ear. 'Take care and don't get yourself into any trouble.'

'I'll try not to,' he promised, though he knew the nature of his work had a nasty habit of laughing in the face of such promises. 'Have dinner without me because I've no idea what time I'll be home. I'll grab something to eat later.'

With a sigh, he ended the call and glanced at his watch.

There was five minutes before the briefing, not enough time to do anything else but wait. Except... he noticed Lauren was already heading out of her office to join the team.

She glanced in his direction, her stern expression softening slightly as she gestured for him to join her at the whiteboard. He could almost see the gears turning in her head as she mentally prepared to face them all.

'Right, let's start,' Lauren commanded, her voice immediately causing a hush to fall. Despite her other foibles, planning and strategising an operation, making sure all bases were covered, was where she excelled. 'We need to ensure that everybody is crystal clear about their roles. Tamsin, you're up first. Your job is to stay here and act as our liaison. You can continue digging into Deakins' background. We need as much information about him as possible. That will hopefully tip the scales in our favour.'

Tamsin's face fell at the announcement, a shadow of disappointment flickering across her features. But Matt knew, as did the rest of the team, that her keen analytical skills were best utilised there.

'Yes, ma'am,' Tamsin said, her shoulders slumping slightly.

Lauren turned her attention to Jenna. 'Are you ready and prepared for this evening?'

'Yes, ma'am.'

'Should you learn anything crucial, excuse yourself and go to the Ladies bathroom. One of us will meet you there.'

'Well, it can only be you, ma'am, because you're the only other woman there,' Clem reminded them.

'Except I'll be outside with Matt because Deakins knows us,' Lauren said, frowning.

'Maybe Tamsin should be at the pub, too, instead of stuck here,' Billy suggested, his gaze darting towards Tamsin, an almost imperceptible nod passing between them.

Matt could see where this was heading. Billy was lobbying

for Tamsin, although she really was better in the office. Except, they needed her in the field.

'Okay, we'll swap you for Tamsin,' Lauren suggested.

Matt smiled to himself. He'd bet that wasn't what Billy had in mind.

'Actually, ma'am, I don't mind staying back here, and Tamsin and Billy can be in the pub as a couple. I can liaise with you and do some research into Deakins,' Clem said.

Matt nodded his approval. Clem might not be as proficient as Tamsin, but that was more than made up for by his encyclopaedic knowledge. He'd know where to look in digging up anything on Deakins.

'Okay, that will work. Are you okay with that, Tamsin?' Lauren asked.

That took Matt by surprise. Lauren didn't usually ask approval; she tended to make the decision and announce it as a fait accompli. Matt could tell from the surprised expressions on the others' faces that they, too, had noticed this.

'Yes, ma'am. I'm more than happy to be in the pub with Billy,' Tamsin said.

'Good. Sergeant Price and I will use my car. We'll park in a spot where we have a clear view of the pub entrance but are also hidden. It will be dusk when we arrive, and it'll get dark around six, which could complicate things a bit. Tamsin and Billy, you're to keep a subtle eye on Jenna and Deakins. We'll keep in contact via two-way radio and text. Any questions?'

'I know the pub quite well, ma'am, and I'm not sure that you can have a good view from outside. The car park has two entrances. The main one, and another one going into a side road,' Tamsin said.

'We'll have to play that one by ear, depending on where Deakins parks,' Lauren said. 'We'll make sure to be there early, at four forty-five, and position ourselves strategically. Jenna, aim to arrive five minutes late, which will hopefully be after

Deakins. Park in the car park and make sure it's close to the front entrance. We can then keep an eye on your car.'

Matt approved. The plan was good and there shouldn't be any trouble, providing everyone stuck to their designated roles. The only issue was the two entrances into the car park, but now they knew about it, they could make sure it was covered.

He glanced at the team. They were a good unit and worked well under Lauren, but he knew from experience that they had to expect the unexpected in any operation. But... they were as prepared as they could be.

TWENTY-SEVEN
FRIDAY, 15 MARCH

At exactly four forty-five, Lauren swung her car into position across the road, in a spot that gave them a view of the pub entrance. Her hands were gripped tightly around the steering wheel as her mind raced with details of the operation. Tamsin and Billy pulled up not long after, their nonchalant stroll into the pub belying the gravity of the task at hand.

'And now we wait,' Lauren stated, glancing at her watch and observing the regular tick of the second hand, which seemed to calm her pounding heart. 'We need to keep a lookout for him.'

Dutifully scanning the area, she shared a tense silence with Matt. His calming presence was reassuring in the uncertainty that faced them. In fact, she couldn't even remember what the team was like before he'd joined.

'How's Tia doing?' Matt asked, breaking the silence.

Lauren smiled, touched by his thoughtfulness. 'A lot better thank you. She's almost back to her old self but it's taken quite a while. Ben won't leave her alone. It's like he's watching over her and he's taking his responsibility very seriously.'

'I'm so pleased. I'll let Dani know. She's still asking me

every day.' Matt's voice was soft, in the way it only ever was when he was discussing his daughter.

'I'm sorry not to have asked you this before,' Lauren said, annoyed that she hadn't thought about it. 'Have there been any long-term repercussions from when she was kidnapped?'

'No, thank God,' Matt responded, relief in his voice. 'We talked it through with Dani after it happened, but she hasn't brought it up since, and so we haven't mentioned it either. We did take her to a counsellor and they told us some signs to look out for that would indicate she might've been affected.'

'What sort of signs?' Lauren asked, curious about how it could manifest itself in such a young child.

'Well, if she starts acting out the experience with her toys... maybe playing that someone is being taken away by a nasty woman. But, fingers crossed, so far she's been fine. When we saw the counsellor she was pleased with Dani's progress. In fact, the woman seemed more eager to chat with Dani due to her extensive vocabulary.' Matt's laugh, mellow and genuine, echoed in the confines of the car, bringing a momentary respite from the tension. 'She certainly didn't get that from me. Leigh was the clever one.'

Lauren couldn't help but smile at his humour. 'You're not exactly stupid yourself,' she acknowledged.

It was true. Matt was downplaying his intelligence. His insights had often proved invaluable.

Matt's attention suddenly shifted, the focus in his eyes homing in on something in the distance.

'There he is. I hope he didn't see us,' Matt murmured, a frown lining his forehead.

Following her sergeant's gaze, Lauren spotted Deakins' Mazda CX-5 turning into the car park and parking towards the rear out of their eyesight.

'Why would he? He doesn't know my car, and he won't be

expecting to see us parked here,' Lauren responded, attempting to ease Matt's concern.

'Yes, you're right. He doesn't know who Jenna really is.'

'I wish he'd parked so we could see him, though,' Lauren added before turning on the two-way radio. 'Suspect has entered the car park.' She kept her voice calm and matter-of-fact, knowing that if she showed any nerves to the rest of the team, it wouldn't bode well for their confidence in the operation.

'We're in position,' came Billy's voice, crackling through the speaker. 'Deakins has come in and gone to the bar.'

Lauren's heart pounded in her chest like a drummer playing a staccato rhythm, adrenaline coursing through her veins.

'Jenna should be here any minute now.' She scanned the surroundings, her eyes landing on a familiar car turning into the car park. 'Ah, here she is.'

They watched as Jenna drove her car into a suitable parking spot, visible from their vantage point. She exited the car and strolled towards the pub, an image of confidence. She'd changed from her usual work gear of trousers and shirt and was wearing a floral skirt that fell to her mid-calf, a pair of ankle boots, and a denim jacket. Her blond hair, which was normally tied up, was loose and hanging to her shoulders. Lauren felt a prickle of apprehension, sparked by the potential danger her officer faced.

'Jenna's met him at the bar, and he's ordering drinks,' Billy reported. 'It looks like she's having a lemonade or some sort of soft drink, and he has a half-pint of beer. They're talking. He's picked up the two drinks and they're now heading towards us, with Jenna in front, so I'll stop talking.'

'I hope Billy's careful,' Lauren murmured, more to herself than anything.

'He will be. I know he's a bit wayward, but he's not stupid,' Matt replied, sounding confident.

'Yes, you're right,' Lauren conceded, deciding she must trust in her team. She returned her gaze to the pub, her senses razor sharp, ready for whatever came next.

'It's me.' Billy's voice filtered through the static of the radio. 'It looks like they're heading into the garden.'

'Why would they go out there?' Lauren questioned, her brows knitting together in confusion.

'There are a few people out there already; they have one of those heaters so it's quite warm,' Billy explained. 'Right, I can just see them. They've gone to the far corner and I assume will be sitting at one of the tables there. Shit. Now they're out of sight. We'll move somewhere else.'

'Don't be obvious, Billy,' Lauren cautioned, her words stern but not unkind. 'It's important Deakins doesn't suspect anything.'

'No, ma'am.' Billy's tone was clipped, defensive almost. The radio fell silent for a moment, the absence of communication amplifying the tension in the car. 'Right, we're at the opposite end of the garden to them but can now see them. They seem to be deep in conversation. I'll sign out for the moment.'

As Billy fell quiet, Lauren felt a knot of anxiety in her stomach. Each second of silence felt heavy, the uncertainty amplifying her worry.

'Ma'am, Jenna's standing up and going back inside. Tamsin will follow. She must be going to the toilet,' Billy finally reported.

'Okay. Again, don't be obvious,' Lauren reiterated, her stern tone underlining the importance of discretion.

'No, ma'am,' Billy's voice crackled back, a hint of frustration colouring his words.

'Before you say anything, I heard the tone in his voice,' Lauren said, glancing at Matt.

'You must trust him, Lauren. I mean, ma'am,' Matt reassured, his words a gentle plea.

'I do. But you know how I work. I can't turn it on and off at will.' Lauren's words were a defence and an admission at the same time, her concern for the operation and the safety of her team overriding any personal sentiments.

'Ma'am, Tamsin's back.' Billy's voice came over the radio, sounding faintly relieved. 'Deakins told her that he lives in a small house and he also mentioned when he lived in Cardiff he had a much larger place. Jenna got to thinking that maybe he put his furniture in store somewhere and thought we could check.'

'A lock-up?' Matt said.

'Yeah,' Billy said.

A spark of excitement ignited within Lauren as the pieces of the puzzle started to slot into place.

'Excellent. Thanks, Billy. I'll get Clem onto it.' She swiftly pressed speed-dial for the office.

'CID, DC Roscoe speaking,' came the swift response.

'Clem, it's me, the DI. We think that Deakins might have a lock-up or storage unit somewhere. See if you can find out whether he does and, if so, where it is,' Lauren said, her words quick and decisive, echoing in the silent confines of the car.

'I'm on to it, ma'am,' Clem confirmed, his efficient tone providing a small comfort in the midst of the tension.

Suddenly, Billy's voice cut through the radio again. 'Ma'am, we've lost sight of them.'

What?

'What do you mean?' Lauren said, anxiety lacing her words.

'It's got really busy out here and I was chatting with Tamsin, looking like we were out for a drink together. I only turned my head for a moment and the next thing I knew, they were gone. I don't know how because they didn't go past us.'

'Is there another way through to the car park?' Lauren asked, her mind quickly scanning through potential escape routes.

'No, ma'am,' Billy replied, sounding as baffled as she felt.

'They should have come this way and then gone out through the back door and into the car park. Whichever of the two entrances they went through, they would have had to come this way.'

'Billy, search round there. They must be somewhere. They might have gone inside,' Lauren commanded, an urgent knot of worry twisting her stomach. They had to locate Jenna and Deakins before the situation escalated further. She drummed her fingers on the steering wheel impatiently. 'Come on,' she muttered.

'Shall we go inside, ma'am?' Matt asked, shifting in his seat to look at her. His face was a mask of cool composure, but his eyes were filled with quiet concern.

'No, in case they're still there,' Lauren replied, her gaze remaining fixed on the pub's entrance. Each second seemed to stretch out infinitely as she waited to hear from Billy, her body tense like a spring ready to leap into action.

'Ma'am, I think I found how they got out,' Billy's anxious voice burst through the radio. 'There's a little gate in the fence that goes around the garden. They must have gone through there and back to the car park.'

Lauren froze.

What the hell had happened?

Where were they?

How could they not have known about the gate?

'Get out to the car park, both of you. See if there's anything there. Matt, come on, let's go. We'll have a look round, too,' Lauren said, a sense of urgency coursing through her veins.

'Okay, ma'am.' Matt responded, the two of them jumping out of the car and making a beeline for the car park. Tamsin and Billy were already there, their expressions tense and alert.

'There's Jenna's car,' Lauren pointed out. 'But where's Deakins'?'

'It's not here, ma'am,' Tamsin replied, sounding panicked.

This couldn't be happening. Lauren thought they'd had everything under control, but Jenna had gone missing right under their noses.

'This isn't good, ma'am,' Billy said anxiously. 'No way would Jenna go off with Deakins without letting us know. And even then, she wouldn't go anywhere alone with him. Something's happened to her. I know it has.'

'I agree,' Lauren said, forcing back the panic. 'We'll go to Deakins' house to see if he's taken Jenna there.'

Billy and Tamsin ran back to the car they came in, and Lauren and Matt returned to hers.

As Lauren sped towards Deakins' house, the car was filled with an eerie silence, the only sound being the occasional static crackle of the radio.

How could she have let this happen?

What if Deakins harmed Jenna before they could get to her?

Lauren tried to force the thoughts to the back of her mind, but it was impossible. If anything happened to her officer, she'd never forgive herself. Never.

TWENTY-EIGHT

FRIDAY, 15 MARCH

Lauren gripped the steering wheel so tight her knuckles turned white with the force of it. The cold wave of realisation of what had happened washing over her.

Jenna was gone.

And it was all Lauren's fault.

Despite being within their sight, under their surveillance in the crowded pub, Deakins had outmanoeuvred them. The bitter taste of failure rose in her throat, making her catch her breath.

Would wiring Jenna have made any difference? She shook her head, dismissing the fleeting thought. She'd definitely made the right call about that. The pub had been teeming with people, and the sound of overlapping conversations would have scuppered any chance of isolating Jenna's voice. Their plan should have worked. Would have worked... If it wasn't for that damned gate in the fence.

They should have been aware of it. Should have visited the pub earlier in the day and taken the time to assess it more thoroughly. Each *should have* reverberated within her. And now Jenna was in danger.

'Ma'am.' Matt's voice broke through her thoughts, anchoring her back in the present.

Lauren glanced over at him. 'Sorry, what were you saying?'

'It's not your fault.' Matt's tone was steady, reassuring. 'We had eyes on Jenna. The fact that the pub got busy and there was an exit leading to the car park that we were unaware of isn't down to you.'

'Whose fault is it then?' she demanded. 'Because from where I'm sitting there's only one person to blame, and that's me. What if we're too late and Jenna's...' The words stuck in her throat.

Matt rested his hand on her arm. 'Lauren, stop,' he said calmly. 'It's not down to you. Even if we'd visited the pub earlier – and remember we didn't really have the time – even if we'd gone there, we could have easily missed that gate. It was covered with overgrown foliage. Deakins didn't find it by chance. He knew of its existence. We wouldn't have seen it.'

'I know you're trying to make me feel better, but you're not succeeding,' she said, turning quickly to look at him, before returning her eyes to the road ahead.

'That's not what I'm doing. I want you to see the situation as it truly is. We'll find Jenna. But you must be strong enough to lead the team and not get bogged down in blaming yourself.'

Was he questioning her leadership? The one thing that she prided herself on. She wasn't going to let this derail her. She had to pull herself together.

'You're right. But whatever you say, we shouldn't have let this happen. I know all undercover operations have an element of risk but that doesn't make this any easier.'

'Exactly. There's an element of risk that we all take and Jenna was fully aware of this. She volunteered to go, remember. And my leg is a perfect example, too. We weren't to know the woman I was meeting undercover had a gun. It was a risk that I took. But it paid off because she was caught and charged.'

'And how did your DCI Walker feel about it? Guilty, I'm sure.'

'That's beside the point, ma'am.'

Lauren sucked in a breath. 'Thank you, Matt. This isn't about me. I get it now. We need to focus one hundred per cent on finding Jenna.'

Lauren's heart hammered against her ribcage as she pulled up to the 1930s semi-detached redbrick property that Deakins rented. Moments later, Billy and Tamsin arrived.

In silence they jumped out of their cars and Lauren gestured for them to pull on their disposable gloves and follow her. She ran down the path, the gravel crunching beneath her feet, and knocked sharply on the door. The house was in darkness, but Deakins' car was parked in the drive. He must have taken Jenna there.

'I'll go round the back with Billy,' Matt announced, heading towards the side of the house, followed by the younger officer, before Lauren even had time to nod her assent.

She pressed her face against the cold windowpane, her eyes straining to see, but there was no movement, no hint of life. A chill ran down her spine. 'We'll have to break the front door down,' she said, her voice determined.

'Let's see if Sarge and Billy can get in through the back first, ma'am,' Tamsin suggested, her voice cautious and her eyes flitting between Lauren and the back of the house. 'It's a solid door. I don't think we have the strength between us to kick it in.'

'I can give it a good go,' Lauren fired back, determined to do something.

She took a step back, her shoulder squared and ready to ram the door. But before she could even launch herself, the door opened, revealing Matt's serious face.

'We got in through the back door. I found a key under the flowerpot. But the place seems deserted.'

'For God's sake, when will people stop doing that?' Lauren

muttered under her breath, her exasperation evident, but grateful, nevertheless, that she didn't have to make a charge at the door. She straightened up, turning her attention back to the task at hand. 'If the place is empty then he's taken Jenna somewhere else. We need to search the place to find out where, and also try to discover why his car is here. Matt and Tamsin, you take upstairs. Billy, you and I will take down. I'll start in the lounge; you check the rear of the house.'

'Okay, ma'am,' Billy said, already taking off down the hallway.

The team dispersed and Lauren hurried into the lounge. She scanned the room, her gaze landing on the table where there were stacks of magazines and papers. She ran over and started flicking through them. But there was nothing out of the ordinary. Nothing that would lead them to Jenna.

'There's a cellar door here in the kitchen, but it's locked. I'll break it down.' Billy's voice echoed from the back of the house, interrupting Lauren as she turned to search the rest of the room.

'Wait for us,' Lauren yelled, spinning on her heels at the urgency in his voice, rushing out of the lounge and heading to the kitchen.

At the same time, Matt and Tamsin clattered down the stairs, their faces etched with worry.

'Nothing up here,' Matt said.

'Nor in the lounge, so far,' Lauren said as they hurried into the kitchen to where Billy was standing. 'Okay, Billy. Now.'

With a powerful kick he forced the door open, the sound reverberating through the rest of the house. Following Billy's lead, Lauren carefully descended the stairs, her hand fumbling along the dark wall in search of a light switch which she found and pressed.

The light cut through the darkness. Revealing a bare room. Absent of Jenna.

Lauren's heart sank. The team began looking around.

'Look at this, ma'am,' Billy called out, holding up an old biscuit tin, its lid open.

'What is it?' Lauren asked, her voice sharp with apprehension.

He walked over to her so she could see inside the tin. It held a collection of objects. 'This driving licence belongs to Freya Kempston,' Billy said, holding it up. 'I'm not sure who these other items belong to,' he added, pointing at what looked like a lipstick and a key ring and other things. 'This must be his souvenir tin. We've got to find Deakins before he harms Jenna.'

His chilling words hovered in the air, casting an even heavier shadow over the room.

'Right, that all needs to come with us,' Lauren ordered, pulling out an evidence bag from her pocket and handing it to him. 'But where the hell has he taken Jenna?' Panic crept into her voice as they hastily climbed back up the stairs into the kitchen.

Her phone rang, the shrill sound echoing in the silence. 'Pengelly,' she answered, forcing herself to keep her voice steady despite the panic churning through her.

'Ma'am, it's Clem. Deakins owns a lock-up on the outskirts of St Ives. I've also discovered he's leased a white van. I'll text you the address and registration details.'

She let out a pent-up breath. Thank goodness. She nodded at the team, who were all staring at her, indicating that they had something to work on.

'Right, we're on our way. Send backup and forensics to start processing the house.' She ended the call, anticipation coursing through her. They were closing in on Deakins. He wasn't going to get away from them. But they had to act fast and find Jenna before he could harm her.

TWENTY-NINE
FRIDAY, 15 MARCH

Lauren brought the car to a screeching halt a little way up the road from the lock-up, its tyres leaving thick trails of smoke in the air. As Matt took a moment to steady his breathing, he noticed a stark white van in the distance.

'Look, ma'am,' he said, pointing at it.

'Okay. Let's speak to Tamsin and Billy,' Lauren said, her words instantly followed by her opening the car door and jumping out of the vehicle.

Without missing a beat, Matt followed suit, and they raced over to their colleagues, whose grim faces were reflected in the dim lights from the streetlamps.

'How are we going to play this, ma'am?' Billy asked.

'Deakins' van is over there, so we have to assume that he's here with Jenna,' Lauren said calmly.

'Do you think the other women are here, too?' Tamsin asked.

'I hope so,' Lauren said. 'I really hope so.'

'But will they be alive?' Billy asked, echoing Matt's thoughts.

'We have to hope for the best,' Lauren said.

'Shall we wait for backup?' Matt glanced at his watch.

'We've no idea how long they'll be, and we need to act fast before anything happens to Jenna. So, no. I don't think we can. But we can't take any chances. He might have a weapon.' Lauren's voice cut through the thick tension, and they exchanged glances with each other.

'Okay, ma'am,' Matt said. Lauren was right. They couldn't delay any longer.

He surveyed the surroundings before his eyes finally settled on the gunmetal-grey roller door of the lock-up with a side door adjacent to it. A shiver of apprehension ran down his spine as he focused on their desperate rescue mission. He glanced across at Lauren, who was staring in the same direction.

'It appears the only two entrances to the lock-up are those doors,' Lauren said as they assessed their options. 'Our approach must be swift and silent.' Her command echoed in the eerie stillness.

'Shall I check around the back to ensure there's no escape route?' Billy asked anxiously, breaking the silence that had fallen over them.

'Good idea, Billy. Get a sense of the layout and call me with an update.' Her words hung heavy in the air as they watched Billy disappear around the back of the row of lock-ups. The one belonging to Deakins was positioned second from the left.

'Ma'am, there's an open window at the back. Someone could potentially climb out of it, but there's no door. Shall I stand guard here in case he tries to escape?' Billy's voice crackled over the radio, adding another layer of intensity to their nerve-racking operation.

'Yes, stay there, Billy, just in case. The rest of us will make our move from this side,' Lauren said.

'Ma'am, shall we move in single file?' Matt asked, his mind racing with worst-case scenarios.

'Yes,' Lauren affirmed, her gaze unwavering as it met Matt's.

'You lead the way. We'll follow and fan out once inside. Let's hope the door isn't locked. In his haste, Deakins may have overlooked that detail.' There was a hint of optimism in her voice that Matt was pleased to latch on to.

Their boots crunched on the gravel as they crept towards the reinforced side door, a formidable barrier between them and Jenna. Matt reached out, his hand closing around the cold metal of the handle. His eyes met Lauren's as he gave a slight nod. It was unlocked.

He turned the handle slowly and painstakingly eased the door open, wincing as the hinge squeaked. Matt froze, the sound echoing ominously in his ears. A few heart-stopping seconds passed, then, as if time had begun to flow again, he stepped into the lock-up, the others behind him.

They found themselves in an area stacked with heaps of haphazardly piled furniture and other miscellaneous items. An ominous maze that could easily hide a captive.

As his eyes adjusted to the dim light, Matt's heart lurched. Barely visible amidst the surrounding chaos was Jenna. She was strapped to a chair, her posture slumped and her head lolling slightly. But the most chilling sight was Deakins. He was standing before Jenna, resting one hand on his hip while shaking an accusing finger at her with the other. She appeared semi-conscious, her eyes half-open in a dazed expression.

Matt turned towards Lauren, her eyes flashing a silent communication. She held up three fingers, then two, then one. Her lips mouthing the countdown. As soon as her clenched fist signalled zero, they surged forward, a united front charging at Deakins.

'Stay where you are! You're under arrest!' Lauren's voice rang out.

Deakins spun around, a look of terror washing over his face. He lunged for Jenna in a futile attempt to use her as a shield, but she shifted enough to send a powerful headbutt to his face.

A shrill squeal of pain erupted from the man as Jenna's unexpected retaliation hit its mark.

In a flash, Matt was on Deakins, his movements swift and calculated as he wrestled the kidnapper to the ground. Lauren snapped the cuffs around Deakins' wrists, the metallic click resounding like a gavel sentencing him.

Rushing to Jenna's side, Lauren crouched down beside the captive woman. 'Are you okay?' she asked, her voice soft yet laced with worry.

Jenna nodded slowly. 'Yes,' she muttered, her voice slurred and barely above a whisper. 'Drugs.'

In the distance, the wail of sirens grew louder, and soon the lock-up was flooded with uniformed officers. The moment was a whirlwind of activity, yet amidst it all, Matt couldn't help but breathe a sigh of relief. They had found Jenna. They had stopped Deakins. But where were the other women?

He turned to the man who was sitting motionless on the floor.

'Where are they?' he demanded.

'Fuck off,' Deakins said, his lips turned up in a sneer.

'Fergus Deakins, I'm arresting you on suspicion of the murder of Freya Kempston, Yvonne Hughes and Hannah Gifford, and the attempted murder of Jenna Moyle,' Matt declared, his voice steel-clad with resolve. He forcefully hoisted Deakins to his feet, the man barely putting up a fight against his grip. 'You do not have to say anything, but it may harm your defence if you do not mention something which you later rely on in court. Anything you do say may be given in evidence. Do you understand?'

Deakins' response was to spit on the floor, his eyes burning with defiance. 'I want a solicitor.'

Lauren, her expression unreadable, turned to a uniformed officer who had just arrived at the scene. 'Take him away.'

As Deakins was marched out, Tamsin approached Lauren,

her voice steady despite the chaos. 'I've called for an ambulance, ma'am. It should be here soon.'

Out of the corner of his eye, Matt saw that Billy had made his way to Jenna, a pair of pliers in his hand, and was cutting her bonds.

As the ties fell away, Billy pulled Jenna into a comforting embrace. 'Don't worry, Jen, it's over now,' he said softly.

Shortly after, the wail of a siren announced the arrival of the ambulance. Jenna was promptly whisked away, her body frail but her spirit resilient.

Lauren turned to Tamsin. 'Do you want to go with? You can let her husband know on the way.'

Tamsin nodded, her response firm. 'Yes, ma'am.'

'Don't ask her any questions, just be there with her while we sort things out here. Matt and I will come to the hospital to see how she is later.'

Once Jenna had been taken care of, Matt turned his attention back to the eerie lock-up.

'Ma'am, Sarge,' Billy called out. 'Look at this.'

They headed over to where Billy was standing next to a tin bath by the workbench. It was filled with a clear substance. Next to it was a barrel with a skull and crossbones on the outside.

A chill ran down Matt's spine as he realised its purpose.

'If that barrel has acid in it... And the bath's full of a liquid. Oh my God, ma'am. I think he's been putting his victims in the bath... and destroying them that way.' Bile shot up into his mouth and he swallowed it back down as he turned his head away from the grotesque scene. 'Is this what happened to the other women?'

'What the hell...' Billy exclaimed from where he was now standing beside a large chest of drawers.

'What is it, Billy?' Lauren asked.

'You have to come and look, ma'am... It's...' His voice fell away as Matt and Lauren hurried over.

They all peered into the open drawer. Staring them in the face was a transparent bag filled with bones, labelled: *Freya Kempston*.

With a shaky hand, Lauren pointed at the next drawer. 'Open it, Billy.'

The subsequent drawers revealed more bones, more labels: *Yvonne Hughes, Hannah Gifford*. Each name a haunting echo of lives cut short by Deakins.

'What a monster,' Billy muttered. 'There's another bag here, but with no name on it.'

'It might be his wife,' Matt suggested.

'Billy, call forensics. Get them down here straight away. You wait for them while we go to the hospital. We'll met you back at the station.'

As they filed out of the lock-up in silence, the chilling reality of their discovery hung heavily over them. The search was over, but the fight to nail Deakins was just beginning.

THIRTY
FRIDAY, 15 MARCH

'How is she?' Matt's question echoed in the sterile silence of the hospital room as he and Lauren entered. Tamsin was sitting vigil by the bed where Jenna lay, looking pale and fragile in a hospital gown and covered with a pale blue blanket.

'I'm fine.' Jenna's voice, though frail, had a determined edge to it that brought a smile to Lauren's face.

'That's debatable,' Tamsin said, glancing at Lauren and Matt, a mix of concern and relief in her eyes. 'She's still a bit out of it.'

Lauren's gaze shifted to Jenna, then returned to Tamsin. 'What have the doctors said?'

Tamsin took a moment before responding. 'Based on the symptoms, they think Deakins gave her GHB. She was sleepy, weak, a bit forgetful and her breathing was quite slow when we got here. Apparently, those are textbook symptoms. The effects are meant to last between three to six hours.'

Jenna tried to sit up a little. 'Well, it's probably been about two hours and I'm feeling much better. So stop pussyfooting around me,' she said, her voice more resolute than before.

Matt cast a glance at Tamsin. 'Have you told Ken?' he asked, referring to Jenna's husband.

Tamsin nodded, her voice subdued. 'He's been out of town all day but he's on his way back and will come straight to the hospital.'

'I told you, it's not necessary. All you're going to do is worry him,' Jenna said.

'Look, Jenna,' Matt said calmly, 'of course we had to tell Ken. What would you have done if the situation was reversed and it was Tamsin lying there?'

Jenna gave a loud sigh. 'Okay. Yeah. I understand. I didn't mean to take it out on you, Tamsin.'

'No problem,' Tamsin said, shrugging and giving a shy smile. 'I'm just glad that you're okay.'

'Do you feel up to talking about it yet, Jenna?' Lauren asked, her voice slightly hesitant. 'Before we go back to interview Deakins?'

Jenna nodded, her gaze hardening. 'Yes, I can tell you what I remember. He bought the drinks and suggested that we sit outside. He made sure that I was leading the way and I think that's when he put something into my drink. Either then or when I went to the toilet to meet with Tamsin.'

'The arsewipe,' Tamsin muttered under her breath, her words laced with anger and bitterness.

Lauren turned towards the young officer, her expression stern. 'Yes, we know that, but let Jenna carry on,' she said, her voice commanding, but not sounding angry.

'Sorry, ma'am,' Tamsin said, her cheeks turning pink.

Lauren looked again at Jenna. 'I think it's more likely that he slipped something into your drink before you went to meet Tamsin. He wasn't to know you'd be leaving the table, so he couldn't risk waiting.'

'Yes. That's right,' Jenna agreed, a tremor in her voice as she drew in a shaky breath.

'Are you okay?' Lauren asked. 'We can do this later, if you'd rather.'

Jenna shook her head. 'I'm fine. Honestly.' She paused as if gathering her thoughts. 'We sat in the corner and I could see Tamsin and Billy initially, but it quickly got busy and then they were out of sight. When I met Tamsin in the Ladies, I'd only had one sip of my drink, so it can't have had any effect. But then I went back and had a little more to drink. It was after that when things went weird...' Her words fell away, as if she was reliving the experience. 'It was about twenty minutes after seeing Tamsin that I started feeling tired. At the time, I didn't realise what was happening. Then I vaguely remember him taking me by the arm and leading me through a gate hidden in the shrubbery that led into the car park.'

'But if you chose the table, because of going out there first, how did he manage to get you to sit at the one by the gate?' Matt asked, confusion etched across his face.

'Although I led the way, he suggested where we should sit. Quite a few of the tables were taken; I thought we were lucky that there was one going free,' Jenna continued, her voice growing weaker with each word. 'I remember him pushing me into the front seat of his car. I was almost passed out by then. I think we stopped at a house, which must have been his. And then somehow he put me into a van that was parked on the street. I'm not sure how he managed that. He took me to the lock-up... where you found me.'

'Was he talking to you the whole time during the journey?' Lauren asked, her voice soft, acutely aware of the emotional toll this conversation was taking on her officer.

'I remember him telling me that he hated women who cheat on their partners. That they deserve to die. He kept repeating that over and over... that's why it's in my head.'

Jenna's recollection of Deakins' words sent shivers down Lauren's spine.

An onslaught of 'what ifs' charged through Lauren's mind. The most critical one being: what if they'd arrived at the lock-up too late and all that remained of Jenna were her bones?

A wave of nausea surged through Lauren, causing her to clamp her mouth shut as her stomach threatened to empty itself. She lunged for the foot of the bed, her grip the only thing preventing her knees from buckling under the sheer shock of the possibilities.

'When we found you, you were tied up in the chair. Do you remember him doing that to you?' Matt asked, bringing Lauren's thoughts back to the present.

'Yes...' Jenna's voice was a whisper. 'He was talking to me all the time. Well, *at* me really. I felt... I felt like I wasn't even there. He was rambling like a mad man.'

Lauren tensed. She knew she had to ask the question, but didn't want to bring it all back to Jenna. 'Did he tell you what he was going to do?'

'I think he was going to... he was muttering something about the bath... And kept pointing at it. It was full of liquid. Water, I think, but it might not have been... he was shouting at me. And then you came in and overpowered him. He was planning to kill me, wasn't he?'

'Yes. I believe so.' Lauren swallowed, her guilt rising. 'We're so sorry to have lost sight of you at the pub.'

Jenna dismissed her apology with a weak wave of her hand. 'It wasn't your fault. I knew the risks when I agreed to do this. We weren't to know that he was going to drug me. He had no idea that you were there. I'm sure of it.'

'Once you're better, we'll take a proper statement from you,' Matt said, his voice gentle. 'In the meantime, you take it easy, rest. Okay?' He gave a smile and Jenna smiled back.

'Yes, Sarge.' She paused a moment. 'And thanks for saving me.'

'I'm only sorry that it came to this,' Lauren said. 'But, you're welcome. Do as Matt suggests. Rest. Tamsin, you stay with Jenna until Ken gets here. Then you can go home and we'll see you in the morning.'

'Yes, ma'am,' Tamsin said, tears filling her eyes.

Was there something else going on that Lauren had missed?

'Matt, stay with Jenna; I'd like a quick word with Tamsin outside.'

'Okay.'

Lauren nodded towards the door and Tamsin followed her into the corridor. The fluorescent lights of the hospital corridor seemed harsh and unreal after the subdued lighting in the room.

'What's wrong?' Lauren asked getting straight to the point.

'Nothing, ma'am,' Tamsin replied, avoiding eye contact.

'I think there is. Tell me.'

Tamsin let out a long sigh. 'I can't help thinking that none of this would have happened if I'd found Deakins' lock-up when searching into his background.'

Now Lauren understood.

'It's not your fault. You worked hard researching into him. Time wasn't on our side. Whenever we look back on an investigation there's always something we wish we'd done better.'

'I suppose so, ma'am.'

'I know so. Now go back into Jenna's room and send Matt out. I'll see you in the morning.'

Lauren waited for Matt to join her.

'Is everything okay, ma'am?' he asked.

'Yes, it's fine. Tamsin felt guilty about having not discovered the lock-up in her investigation into Deakins. But she wasn't to blame.' She waved her hand dismissively as they set off towards the entrance. 'Anyway, we need a plan for his interview.' She kept her voice low, not wanting anyone to overhear. The hospital was busy, patients being wheeled in the corridors, visitors appearing worried and harassed.

Matt nodded, his expression grave. 'We must be careful.

Deakins is cunning, and I suspect he knows how to play the system.'

'Yes,' Lauren agreed, her mind racing. 'We'll approach it from different angles, probe into his psyche, find out what makes him tick. We need to understand his motive, his process... the motivation behind what he did. Although, from what he told Jenna, we most likely know.' She paused, the image of Jenna, pale and traumatised on the hospital bed, still vivid in her mind. 'He tried to murder Jenna because she pretended to cheat on her partner... and... he rationalised his actions, made himself the judge, jury and... executioner of these women who, in his warped mind, deserved to die.'

They walked in silence for a few minutes, each lost in their own thoughts. The enormity of Deakins' actions hanging over them like a dark cloud.

'Did you notice how he didn't show any remorse when we caught him and read him his rights? It's as if he truly believes he was justified,' Matt said, breaking the silence.

Lauren nodded. 'Yes. And that's what makes him even more dangerous. It's not just about power or control for him... it's about righteousness, a sick, twisted righteousness.'

She stopped and turned to Matt, determination in her eyes. 'We need to expose him, Matt. Make him face the magnitude of his crimes. He should realise that these women were victims of his warped mind. We're not just doing this for Jenna, but for Freya, Yvonne and Hannah, too.'

'I agree, ma'am. And even if he never realises the truth, we'll make sure that he'll never be in the position to do anything like that again.'

THIRTY-ONE
FRIDAY, 15 MARCH

Lauren strode into the interview room, her heart pounding in time with her steps. Matt was beside her, matching her stride for stride, a supportive presence. Before them, a steely-faced Fergus Deakins sat waiting, his solicitor beside him.

The room was small and stark. A table, four chairs, and a recording device. The air was heavy with tension, the atmosphere oppressive.

Matt pressed the record button as they sat opposite Deakins. 'Interview, Friday, fifteenth March. Those present: Detective Inspector Pengelly, Detective Sergeant Price, and...' He nodded towards the men opposite.

'Clive Fleming, solicitor,' the man replied, his voice crisp and professional.

'Fergus Damon Deakins,' the accused added, his voice echoing in the quiet room. His eyes bored into Lauren's, challenging her. She met his gaze head-on. No way was he going to get the better of her.

'Mr Deakins, you are under arrest for the murders of Freya Kempston, Yvonne Hughes and Hannah Gifford,' Lauren said, her voice cold. 'There may be others, but for now, we're starting with these three. Perhaps you can tell us what happened. Let's start with Freya Kempston.'

'No comment,' Deakins said, his response immediate and expected.

Lauren pressed on. 'Okay. Let's talk about Yvonne Hughes, then.'

'No comment.'

Frustration simmered beneath her calm exterior, but Lauren kept her cool. She had seen this tactic before, and it wasn't going to faze her.

'You're not making life very easy, Mr Deakins,' she said, maintaining eye contact. 'Why don't you tell us what happened? If there are any mitigating circumstances, we can present them to the Crown Prosecution Service and then the judge. It might help in your sentencing.'

'No comment.' His response was robotic and empty.

A chill crawled down Lauren's spine. This wasn't the first time she'd dealt with a serial killer, and no doubt wouldn't be the last. But the way Deakins stared back at her, his expression unchanging, his eyes void of any human warmth, filled her with a sense of unease.

He was a monster. But she wasn't about to back down. This was a battle of wills, and she was determined to win.

Leaning forward slightly, she broke the silence that had fallen over the room. 'Okay, if you're refusing to answer my questions, then I'll tell you what I think has happened. This all stems from your wife. You were a crap husband and she cheated on you. You failed her in every way and she had to find someone else to give her what she needed... Am I right?' Lauren's eyes locked with Deakins' and she witnessed the anger and torment he was feeling. But she didn't wait for an answer. Didn't want to let up. He was at breaking point... she could sense it. 'And then you decided to take out your rage and humiliation on women who had supposedly cheated on their partners. But the real issue was you. Wasn't it? It wasn't their fault. If you'd have been a decent husband, then why would your wife have strayed?'

The reaction was immediate. Deakins' eyes flared with anger. 'Shut the fuck up. What the hell do you know about my wife and my life? She was a cheating bitch and she got what she deserved. And so did that wanker she ran off with.'

A perverse sense of satisfaction coursed through Lauren. She took a quick glance at Matt, who was on the edge of his seat, realising, too, that Deakins was unravelling. Now was the time to get him.

'So, you're admitting to killing your wife and her boyfriend?' she pounced, seizing the moment.

Deakins' solicitor muttered something to him, placing a restraining hand on his arm. But Deakins shook it off.

'You can't prove anything,' he snarled, his body rigid.

Lauren's lips curled into a grim smile. 'Maybe not at the moment, but we certainly will. Our forensics team is examining your lock-up as we speak. If there's anything there, we'll find it. We've already found bags of bones labelled with Freya, Yvonne and Hannah's names. There was another unnamed bag. Is that your wife?'

'You tell me.' The corner of his mouth turned up into a sneer, his arrogance almost palpable. He leant back in his chair, the icy demeanour back in place.

Irritation washed over Lauren. They were so close, yet there was still something missing.

Curiosity etched on his face, Matt leant forward. 'What did you do to the bodies to reduce them to bones so quickly? Did you immerse them in acid and simply wait for them to decompose?'

The faintest glimmer of amusement sparkled in Deakins' eyes. 'It's far more complex than that. Not something that a copper like you would understand.'

'Why don't you enlighten us *mere coppers*,' Matt goaded.

'How did you ensure that the bones remained intact so you could keep them? I'd have thought they would have dissolved with the body. You must have an in-depth understanding of the process to execute it so meticulously.'

'Obviously,' Deakins retorted, a perverse pride glinting in his eyes. 'Do you assume I studied for years without gaining any knowledge of bones?'

A heavy silence hung in the room. 'Then tell us. How did you do it?' Matt finally asked.

Deakins paused, looking between Lauren and Matt, a slow smile spreading across his face. The solicitor gave a sigh, folded his arms across his chest and sat back in his chair. He seemed happy to let his client incriminate himself even further.

'It's a precise process. You don't simply immerse the bodies in sulphuric acid and expect to be left with perfect skeletal remains. You have to mix the acid with water in an exact ratio. The flesh disintegrates within twelve hours.'

'Why were you so focused on preserving these women's bones, rather than just disposing of them?' Lauren asked, her eyes narrowing.

He shrugged. 'Because I wanted to.'

Lauren felt a shiver run down her spine as she continued, 'You kept them as... mementos?'

A chilling nod. 'Yes, I suppose I did.'

'And there are others, aren't there?' Lauren said, assuming the worst.

'That's for you to discover,' Deakins replied, smirking.

Lauren's fists clenched in her lap as she forced back the urge to slap the expression off the monster's face.

'Why did you kill Freya, Yvonne and Hannah in such quick succession? Three in a week. And almost four, if you'd have succeeded with Jenna. Why so many?' Lauren asked.

His smile disappeared, replaced by a solemn look. 'Because

it's the anniversary week of when I found out about my wife's infidelity. Two years since my world turned upside down.'

A piece of the puzzle clicked into place. 'But your wife disappeared only a year ago, following the divorce. Why did the legal separation take so long?'

His hands clenched. 'I discovered her cheating, but our marriage didn't end straight away. It was only after the divorce was finalised that I... I...' His voice trailed off, leaving a chilling silence.

'That's when you killed your wife and the man she ran off with,' Matt said, picking up where Deakins left off, his tone cold and analytical.

Deakins only offered a satisfied grin. 'Allegedly,' he countered.

Silence fell over the room, the tension so thick it was almost possible to reach out and touch it. As she studied Deakins, Lauren felt a pit forming in her stomach. There was something more, something they hadn't yet uncovered.

Lauren's phone pinged and she glanced down at a text sent by Clem.

Forensics have said the unnamed bag of bones belongs to a male. No more bones found at the lock-up.

Damn. Where on earth was his wife, then?

'Mr Deakins, I've been informed that the unnamed bones at your lock-up belong to a male. Is that the man your wife ran off with?'

'No comment.'

'I'll take that as a yes. So, where's your wife? What have you done with her?'

Deakins shrugged. 'You tell me. Except you won't be able to.'

She was getting nowhere fast.

'Interview over,' she said. 'You'll be taken to the custody suite and formally charged.'

'Yeah, whatever,' Deakins said with a shrug of disdain, a chilling tone to his voice.

The moment Deakins was escorted away, Lauren turned to Matt. 'We must find his wife's remains. Her family need to know what happened to her.'

'We haven't yet searched his consulting room. There might be a clue there,' Matt suggested.

'Thank you,' Lauren said to the woman who owned the health centre and had met them there to unlock the door and let them inside.

'Shall I come downstairs with you?'

'No, it's fine. We know the way. There's no need to wait. This may be a crime scene and, if so, forensics will be here to go through it.'

'Everywhere or just downstairs in Fergus' rooms?'

'I'm not sure yet,' Lauren said. 'Here's my card. Give me a call later and I'll let you know what's happening.'

'Okay. I can't believe that Fergus has been involved in anything criminal. It's just not like him.'

'Well, we don't know for sure, yet. This is part of an ongoing investigation,' Lauren said, not prepared to give the woman any clues about what they were doing there.

The woman left and Lauren and Matt went downstairs into the waiting room and through to the consulting room. They both slipped on disposable gloves.

'Shall I take the filing cabinet and you take the desk?' Matt asked.

'Sure,' Lauren said. 'I'll see if I can get into his computer. He might have something incriminating on there. If it's not locked.'

'Okay,' Matt said, heading across the room.

Lauren moved to the desk, sat on the chair and clicked on

the mouse. The screen came to life, but it was password-protected. Giving a disgruntled sigh, she pulled open the middle drawer of the desk. Under some papers she found a photo of a younger Deakins on what looked like his wedding day, with his arm around the bride. His wife.

'Look at this. He keeps a photo of his wedding day in his drawer.'

Matt walked over and stared at it. 'That's weird. Maybe...' Matt's voice trailed off and he looked away from Lauren.

'What is it?'

'I think I know where his wife is,' Matt said, his voice hardly above a whisper, as if the mere mention of it could change where it was situated. 'We've already seen her.'

Lauren frowned, confused. 'What?'

'It's here, in full view,' Matt said, pointing to the corner of the room. 'That's not a model. It's real.'

An icy shiver slid down Lauren's spine as it hit her with the force of a sledgehammer. The full-sized set of bones that Deakins proudly kept on display. That he used to explain to his patients what was wrong with them.

'Oh my God... That's so gross. To have his trophy... in the open. In plain sight of everyone. He's one sick bastard, that's for sure. I'd never have worked it out. How did you?' she asked, curiosity lacing her voice.

Matt shrugged, a hint of satisfaction in his eyes. 'It was his confidence. His absolute certainty that we'd never locate his wife's remains. They had to be somewhere other than in his lock-up. And then it hit me while we were here. But obviously we don't know for sure, yet.'

'We don't, but I'd be surprised if you were wrong. Brilliant insight, Matt. Truly brilliant. We'd better contact forensics and get back to the office.'

THIRTY-TWO

MONDAY, 18 MARCH

A sense of satisfaction washed over Lauren as she ended the call and straight away walked into the main office to tell the team. 'Attention, everyone. The pathologist has confirmed that the skeleton in Deakins' office is indeed his wife. You nailed it, Matt.' She smiled in his direction, at the same time as there were cheers from everyone in the room.

'How do they know?' Billy asked, once the noise had died down.

'Dental records,' Lauren explained.

'What about the other remains?' Billy asked, his expression grim.

'They belonged to the man Deakins' wife was seeing. Additionally, they found several more bags of bones in a suitcase in the lock-up which have yet to be identified.'

'Could a set be his daughter?' Billy asked.

'No,' Tamsin said. 'There's no record of him fathering a child.'

'For now, let's focus on the fact that we can charge him with five murders and the abduction of Jenna,' Lauren said.

The sound of the door opening interrupted her and Jenna

stepped in, her expression a mixture of determination and apprehension. Every member of the team seemed to hold their breath, a testament to the resilience of their fellow officer who had faced such unimaginable horror.

'Well, speak of angels and they flap their wings,' Clem called out, breaking the silence with a light-hearted quip. He jumped up from his seat, ran over to Jenna and enveloped her in a huge hug. 'How are you holding up?'

'I'm okay. Honestly,' Jenna said, breaking away from his clutches and stepping to the side so everyone could see her. 'I wanted to check in, see how things were progressing.' Jenna's voice was steady, her resolve evident.

'Deakins is being charged with five murders and your abduction, Jenna. There are some unidentified remains we still have to work on,' Lauren said, watching her officer for signs of tension but she seemed to accept the news without any unease.

'He's our very first serial killer,' Billy piped up, sounding almost proud of the fact. 'I hope this isn't because you've joined us, Sarge. We know where you came from, and you had more killers in a year there than Cornwall's probably had in the last fifty.'

'Nothing to do with me,' Matt replied, laughing, holding his hands up defensively. 'You're not thinking of returning to work already, are you, Jenna? You should be taking the week off.'

Jenna shrugged, a small smile playing on her lips. 'I feel fine and didn't want to stay cooped up at home. I wanted to come and see you all. Are we celebrating tonight now the case is over?'

Clem, still standing close to Jenna, raised an eyebrow. 'Sure, we can manage a drink, but are you sure you should be drinking?'

'I can have a soft drink,' Jenna responded, her tone light.

'Well, it is almost five.' Clem turned to Lauren. 'What do you say, ma'am? Can we all go out for a drink with Jenna?'

'Why not,' Lauren replied, her voice warm. 'The paperwork can wait until tomorrow. Go and celebrate. You all deserve it.'

Billy turned towards Lauren. 'Are you going to join us, ma'am?'

Lauren caught the genuine invitation in his voice. This was the first time she'd been included sincerely. She fought to keep her surprise in check.

'Another time, perhaps. I need to get back to my dogs. My neighbour has been looking after them this week, because one of them recently had an operation. She has plans tonight so I want to go home as soon as possible.'

She watched as her team members prepared to leave, a newfound bond of camaraderie formed through the shared horror and subsequent victory. Her heart swelled with a sense of pride for them, for their resilience, their commitment to justice. She'd have to keep an eye on Jenna and ensure that she had counselling after such an ordeal.

As she watched them leave, she knew that they were stronger than they had ever been, ready to face whatever challenges awaited them in the future.

A LETTER FROM THE AUTHOR

Dear reader,

Huge thanks for reading *The Hidden Graves of St Ives* – I hope you liked the most recent instalment of Lauren and Matt's story. If you want to join other readers in hearing all about my new releases and bonus content, you can sign up here:

www.stormpublishing.co/sally-rigby

If you enjoyed this book and could spare a few moments to leave a review that would be hugely appreciated. Even a short review can make all the difference in encouraging a reader to discover my books for the first time. Thank you so much!

I chose to write about a serial-killing osteopath because I thought it was really interesting to show someone who's supposed to help people actually doing something terrible. This story makes people think twice about who they can really trust. It also gave me a chance to explore what makes a person turn bad and do awful things.

Thanks again for being part of this amazing journey with me and I hope you'll stay in touch – I have so many more stories and ideas to entertain you with!

Sally

f facebook.com/Sally-Rigby-131414630527848

ACKNOWLEDGEMENTS

First and foremost, I want to express thanks to my editor, Kathryn Taussig, for her keen eye and brilliant insights. This novel wouldn't be what it is without her guidance and vision.

I'd also like to thank the entire team at Storm, from the cover designers to the marketing professionals and editorial staff. Their collective efforts have made this dream a reality.

A special shoutout to my advanced reader team, whose early feedback, enthusiasm, and constructive critiques were instrumental in shaping this book.

Thanks, too, to Adrian for his invaluable help in getting the technical stuff right and helping with the twist at the end.

Last, but certainly not least, I owe an immense debt of gratitude to my family and friends for their constant encouragement, emotional support, and unwavering belief in me.

Printed in Great Britain
by Amazon

43526513R00148